W9-ARN-588

WITHDRAWN

THE WILDWATER
WALKING CLUB

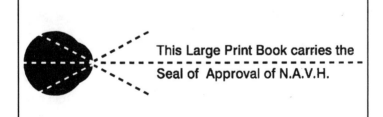

This Large Print Book carries the
Seal of Approval of N.A.V.H.

THE WILDWATER WALKING CLUB

CLAIRE COOK

THORNDIKE PRESS

A part of Gale, Cengage Learning

GALE
CENGAGE Learning

Detroit • New York • San Francisco • New Haven, Conn • Waterville, Maine • London

GALE
CENGAGE Learning

Thorndike Press® Large Print Core.
The text of this Large Print edition is unabridged.
Other aspects of the book may vary from the original edition.
Set in 16 pt. Plantin.
Printed on permanent paper.

LIBRARY OF CONGRESS CATALOGING-IN-PUBLICATION DATA

Cook, Claire, 1955–
    The wildwater walking club / by Claire Cook.
        p. cm. — (Thorndike Press large print core)
    ISBN-13: 978-1-4104-1739-8 (alk. paper)
    ISBN-10: 1-4104-1739-5 (alk. paper)
    1. Neighbors—Fiction. 2. Middle-aged women—Fiction. 3.
Female friendship—Fiction. 4. Suburban life—Fiction. 5.
Domestic fiction. 6. Large type books. I. Title.
PS3553.O55317W56 2009b
813'.54—dc22   2009013138

Published in 2009 by arrangement with Voice, an imprint of Hyperion,
a division of Buena Vista Books, Inc.

Printed in the United States of America
1 2 3 4 5 6 7 13 12 11 10 09

To women walking everywhere

ACKNOWLEDGMENTS

When this book landed in her lap, Brenda Copeland told me she felt like she'd won the lottery. It turned out I was the lucky one — an editor couldn't be smarter, funnier, kinder, or more enthusiastic than the thoroughly amazing Brenda.

A huge thanks to Ellen Archer and Barbara Jones for their brilliance and vision in knowing that women want to hear real women's voices and read their stories, and for believing in me and what I can do. I'm so proud to be a Voice author.

Many thanks to Jessica Wiener for her creativity and marketing savvy, to Sally McCartin for being a dream publicist, to Laura Klynstra for a truly fabulous cover, and to Betsy Spigelman for her very cool cards. The entire Hyperion and Voice team is simply the best, and I send my heartfelt and alphabetical thanks to Anna Campbell, Marie Coolman, Rachel Durfee, Kate Griffin,

Maha Khalil, Claire McKean, Lindsay Mergens, Jo Anne Metsch, Shelley Perron, Mike Rotondo, Sarah Rucker, Shubhani Sarkar, Mindy Stockfield, and Katherine Tasheff.

Lisa Bankoff always knows just what to say and do, and I'm extraordinarily grateful to have her as my agent and my friend. It's been a thrill to watch the wonderful Tina Wexler spread her wings and fly to her own office at ICM, and a huge thanks to Elizabeth Perrella, who jumped in to fill Tina's seat without missing a beat. A big thank you to ICM's Josie Freedman for handling my film rights, and to Karolina Sutton, Elizabeth Iveson, and Helen Manders at Curtis Brown Group Ltd. for foreign rights representation.

How great to find out firsthand that the HarperCollins sales force is as fantastic as I'd heard. Thanks so much to Gabriel Barillas, Kristin Bowers, Rachel Brenner, Ralph D'Arienzo, Anne Hollinshead DeCourcey, Ian Doherty, Karen Gudmundson, Mark Gustafson, Jim Hankey, Diane Jackson, Mark Landau, Carl Lennertz, Judy Madonia, Kay Makanju, Kate McCune, Michael Morris, Olga Nolan and the telephone sales team, Jeff Rogart, Rhonda Rose, Kerry Rosen, Dale Schmidt, Cathy Schornstein, Jennifer Sheridan, Robin Smith, Pete Soper,

Virginia Stanley, Eric Svenson, Mary Beth Thomas, Bruce Unck, Donna Waitkus, Seira Wilson, John Zeck, and Jeanette Zwart.

When you have seven brothers and sisters, there's an expert in the family for pretty much every subject. Thanks to Mary and Jim for stepping up on this particular novel, not that either of them have ever considered a buyout or needed career counseling. Thanks to Mary Carroll for additional insider info. Many thanks to Ken Harvey for an insightful read whenever I needed one. A huge thanks to all the wonderful women I've walked with over the years.

Thanks to all the friendly people I met in and around Sequim and Seattle, even the guard at the Dungeness National Wildlife Refuge who told everyone, "Claire Cook is out there doing research for her next novel." Sometimes when it feels like everyone is staring at you, they really are.

Heartfelt thanks to all the fabulous booksellers, librarians, book clubs, members of the media, and readers who have spread the word about my books. Your support means so much, and I'm truly grateful to each and every one of you for making this book possible.

Much love and many thanks to Kaden and Garet for helping me keep my characters on track, and to Jake, first, final, and forever reader.

Walk on By (Revisited)

When you see me walking down the
    beach,
I pick up the pace to stay out of your reach.
Walk on by, baby, walk on by.

Men believe
That you'll cry all their tears.
But I'm relieved.
And each time I see you,
You break down and cry.
Don't stop, I'm walkin' on by.
Who needs it, I'm walkin' on by.
Cry, baby, walk on by, baby.

A woman's heart can be broken and blue.
But when it comes to her mind,
A girl knows what she's gotta do.
Walk on by, just walk on by.

Day 1:
132 Steps

On the day I became redundant, I began to walk. Okay, not right away. First I lay in bed and savored the sound of the alarm not going off. I'd been hearing that stupid beep at the same ridiculous time pretty much every weekday morning for the entire eighteen years I'd worked at Balancing Act Shoes.

I stretched decadently and let out a loud, self-indulgent sigh. I pictured the zillion-count Egyptian cotton sheets I'd finally get around to buying. I'd pull them up to my chin to create a cozy cocoon, then wiggle down into the feather bed I'd buy, too, a big, fluffy one made with feathers from wildly exotic free-range birds.

I'd once had a pair of peacock earrings that came with a note saying, "Since peacocks lose their feathers naturally, no peacocks were harmed in the making of these earrings." I'd always meant to look that up to see if it was a marketing ploy or if it was actually true. If so, then maybe I could find a peacock feather comforter. Though I suppose what would be the point of using peacock feathers in a comforter if you couldn't see them? Perhaps I could invent a see-through comforter that let the iridescent blues and greens shimmer through. Though I guess first I'd need to come up with a zillion-count see-through Egyptian cotton.

I closed my eyes. I flipped over onto my back and opened them again. I stared up at a serious crack, which I liked to think of as the Mason-Dixon Line of my ceiling. My seventh-grade history teacher would be proud she'd made that one stick.

I rolled over, then back again. I kicked off my ordinary covers. On the first morning I could finally sleep in, I seemed to be more awake than I'd been at this hour in decades. Go figure.

After a long, leisurely shower, a bowl of cereal, and an online check of the news and weather, I called Michael on his cell at 8:45 A.M. It rang twice, then cut off abruptly without going to voice mail.

So I sent him an e-mail. "Call me when you can," it said.

A nanosecond later my e-mail bounced back. "Returned Mail: Permanent Fatal Errors," it said.

I dialed his office number. At least that voice mail picked up. "Hi, it's me," I said. "I seem to be having technical difficulties reaching you. But the good news is I have all the time in the world now. Anyway, call me when you get this." I laughed what I hoped was the perfect laugh, light and sexy. "Unless, of course, you're trying to get rid of me."

By 11 A.M., I'd watched enough morning TV to last me a lifetime, and I still hadn't heard back from him. I tried to remember if we had specific plans for that night. Michael worked for the buyout company, Olympus, so we'd had to keep things on the down low. I mean, it wasn't that big a deal. I was leaving anyway, and he'd be right behind me, so it was just a matter of time.

After the initial army of auditors had stopped acting like nothing was going on, when everybody with half a brain knew something was obviously up at Balancing Act, Michael had been one of the first Olympus managers to come aboard. He was handsome, but not too, and exactly my age, which gave us an immediate bond in an industry that more and more was comprised of iPod-wearing recent college grads. Some of them had become friends, at least work friends, but they were still essentially children.

Michael and I had commonality, both current and past. I was a Senior Manager of Brand Identity for Balancing Act. He was a Senior Brand Communications Manager for Olympus. Potato, potahto. The athletic shoe industry is market-driven rather than product-driven, which means, basically, that even though we don't actually need a two-hundred-dollar pair of sneakers, we can be convinced that we do. Fads can be created, predicted, or at least quickly reacted to, and in a nutshell, that's how Michael and I both spent our days.

But even more important, we'd both danced to Van Morrison's "Moondance," gotten high to the Eagles' "Witchy Woman," made love to "Sweet Baby James" back when James Taylor had hair. Maybe not with each other, but still, we had the generational connection of parallel experiences, coupled with your basic boomer's urge to do something new, fast, while there was still time.

One of the first things he said to me was, "It's business, baby."

We were sitting in the employee cafeteria, and I felt a little jolt when he called me *baby*. He had rich chocolate eyes and a full head of shiny brown hair without a strand of gray, which meant he probably dyed it, but who was I to talk.

"Of course, it's business," I said. I gave my own recently camouflaged hair a little flip and added, "Baby."

He laughed. He had gorgeous white teeth, probably veneers, but so what.

"What's your off-the-record recommendation?" I asked.

He leaned forward over the button-shaped table that separated us, and the arms of his suit jacket gripped his biceps. I caught the sharp, spicy smell of his cologne. Some kind of citrus and maybe a hint of sandalwood, but also something retro. Patchouli?

"The first deal," he said, "is always the best."

"So grab the VRIF and run?" I asked, partly to show off my new vocabulary. Balancing Act employees, even senior managers like me, didn't find out we'd become the latest Olympus acquisition until the day it went public. Since then, the buzz had been that the way to go was to take your package during the VRIF or Voluntary Reductions in Force phase. Olympus was all about looking for redundancies and establishing synergies, code for getting rid of the departments that overlapped.

Right now, the packages were pretty

generous. I could coast along for eighteen months at full base salary, plus medical and dental. They were even throwing in outplacement services to help me figure out what to do with the rest of my life. The only thing missing was a grief counselor. And maybe a good masseuse. By the time we got to the Involuntary Reductions in Force phase, aka the IRIF, who knew what I'd be looking at.

Michael glanced over his shoulder, then back into my eyes. "Here's the thing, Noreen. Or do you prefer Nora?"

"Nora," I said, even though no one had ever called me that until this very moment. I'd been called Nor, Norry, Reeny, Beany, NoreanyBeany, even StringBeany, though I had to admit that one was a few years and pounds ago. Mostly it was just plain Noreen. Michael's *baby* reeled me in, but I swallowed his *Nora* hook, line, and sinker.

I forced myself to focus. "Wall Street," he was saying, "will expect some performance from the synergy created by combining companies. The way to get performance is to streamline numbers, to create efficiencies. Human resources, finance, operations, marketing — lots of overlap. Ergo . . ."

I raised an eyebrow. "Ergo?" I teased.

He raised his eyebrow to match mine, and

even though it would be another two weeks before we ended up in bed together, I think we both knew right then it was only a matter of time.

I leaned my elbows on the table. "So, what?" I said. "I leave so you can have my job?"

"Off the record," he said, "I'll probably be right behind you. I mean, take *my* job, please. You'd be doing me a favor. I'm just waiting till they offer the VRIF package to the Olympus employees they've brought in."

"Seriously?" I said. "You really think you'll take it? And do what?"

He laced his fingers together behind his head and arched back in his chair. "Let's see. First off, I think I'd light a bonfire and burn up all my suits and ties. Then I'd chill for a while. Maybe buy a van, find me a good woman, drive cross-country." He smiled. "Then look around for a partner, someone to start a small business with."

At eleven-thirty, I called Michael's cell again. The second ring cut off midway, once more without going to voice mail. I waited, then pushed Redial. This time it cut off almost as soon as it started ringing. I sent another e-mail. It bounced back with the same fatal message. I called his office number, but when that voice mail picked

19

up, I just hung up.

I was seriously creeped out by now. I thought about calling someone else at work to see if maybe there was a logical explanation, like everybody in the whole building was having both cell service and mail server problems, but I couldn't seem to make myself do it.

I thought some more, then threw on a pair of slimming black pants and a coral V-neck top over a lightly padded, modified push-up bra pitched as a cutting-edge scientific undergarment breakthrough in subtle enhancement. A little figure-flattering never hurt, even if it was hyperbole, and if nothing else, the coral worked well with my pale skin and dark hair. The last time I'd worn it, Michael had said I looked hot. Smoking hot, come to think of it, though that was probably an overstatement, too.

The midday drive into Boston was a lot shorter without the commuter congestion. Who knew that unemployment would be the best way to beat the traffic? Still, I had plenty of time to get a plan. I'd simply pretend I'd left one of my favorite sweaters behind and wanted to grab it before someone ran off with it. And I was in the neighborhood anyway because I was meeting a friend for lunch. And I just thought I'd poke

20

my head in and say *Hi, Michael.* And he'd say he was just thinking about me, trying to remember if we had plans for dinner. I'd tilt my head and tell him if he was lucky, maybe I'd even consider cooking for him. And he'd smile and make a crack about maybe it would be safer to get takeout.

The main lot was packed, but eventually I found a parking spot. I reached into my glove compartment for the lanyard that held my employee badge, slipped it over my head, and made for the front entrance.

When the revolving door spilled me out into the lobby, I held up my badge for the uniformed guard.

He waved his handheld scanner over the laminated bar code like a wand.

I headed for the elevators, the way I had a million times before.

"Ma'am?" he said.

I turned. He held up his scanner. I held out my badge again.

This time I watched. When the laser light hit the bar code, it flashed red instead of the customary green.

We looked at each other. This was the grouchy guard, the one who never said a word and always looked like he wished he were anywhere but here. I found myself wishing I'd tried a little harder to befriend him.

I laughed. "Well, I guess it didn't take them long to get over me." I gave my hair a toss. "Lucky me, I took a buyout. I just need a minute to run up and grab something I forgot." He didn't say anything, so I added, "A sweater. A cardigan. Black, with some nice seaming around the buttons. I'll be back before you even start to miss me."

"Sorry, ma'am, I can't let you do that. Orders."

I blew out a gust of air. "Just call up," I said. "Sixth floor." I held out my card again so he could read my name.

He ran his finger down a list on a clipboard. "Sorry, ma'am. You're on the No Admittance List."

"You're not serious," I said, though it was pretty obvious that he was.

I waited. He looked up again. I met his eyes and couldn't find even a trace of sympathy in them, so I tried to look extra pathetic, which by that point I didn't really even have to fake.

"Maybe you can call somebody and ask them to bring it down," he said finally. "On your cell phone," he added.

"Unbelievable," I said. I stomped across the lobby so I could have some privacy.

Since I hadn't really left a sweater behind, I decided to just cut to the chase and call Michael's cell. Half a ring and it went dead.

There is always that exact moment when the last shreds of denial slip away and your reality check bounces. I closed my eyes. Eventually, I opened them again. I called his office number. "You piece of shit," I whispered to his voice mail.

I stood there for a minute, scratching my scalp with both hands. Hard, as if I might somehow dig my way to a good idea. When that didn't happen, I walked out, without even a glance at the guard. I kept my head up high as I walked across the parking lot, in case someone was watching from one of the windows. I found my car and climbed back into it.

Just as I was getting ready to pull out onto the access road, I caught the purple-and-white-striped Balancing Act Employee Store awning out of the corner of my eye. I banged a right and pulled into a parking space right in front of it.

I stopped at the first circular display I came to and grabbed a pair of our, I mean *their*, newest shoe, the Walk On By, in a size 8 1/2. It was strictly a women's model, positioned as the shoe every woman needed to walk herself away from the things that were holding her back and toward the next exciting phase of her life. *Shed the Outgrown. Embrace Your Next Horizon. Walk On By.*

Even though I'd been part of the team to fabricate this hook out of thin air, I still wanted to believe in the possibility. I handed the box to the woman at the register. I held up my badge. I held my breath.

Her scanner flashed green, and she rattled off a price that was a full 50 percent off retail.

"Wait," I said. I ran back to the display, grabbing all the Walk On Bys in my size. Then I sprinted around the room, scooping up whatever I could find in an 8 1/2. Dream Walker. (*You'll Swear You're Walking on Clouds.*) Step Litely. (*Do These Sneakers Make Me Look Thin?*) Feng Shuoe. (*New Sneakers for a New Age.*) I didn't stop until I'd built a tower of shoe boxes on the counter.

"Take a buyout?" the woman asked as she rang me up.

I nodded.

I gave her my credit card, and she handed me a bright purple pedometer. "On the house," she said. "It's the least Balancing Act can do for you."

24

"Thanks," I said. I hooked it onto my waistband, and that's when I started to walk.

DAY 2:
54 STEPS

Ugh.

DAY 3:
28 STEPS

So this is rock bottom.

DAY 4:
17 STEPS

No, this is.

Day 5:
11,464 STEPS

I'd finally peeled off the stained T-shirt and baggy sweatpants I'd been wearing for days, taken a shower, and zapped a frozen breakfast burrito. Up until then, all I'd managed to do was sleep, devour several pints of Ben & Jerry's Chunky Monkey, go to the bathroom, and reset my pedometer daily. It was a pretty fancy pedometer, with seven days' worth of record-keeping built in. So far, my four-day total was 231 steps, or .1 miles, which didn't seem much more promising than the rest of my stupid life.

Since I didn't think I could sink much lower into the depths of despair, I'd taken stock after I toweled off. First I stepped on the scale, something I'd been avoiding since my last checkup. Yikes. It was as if a small person, or at least a small animal, had jumped up on there with me. I slid my heels back to the edge of the scale and leaned back as far as I could. I lost two pounds, but I knew it was only a sleight of scale.

I forced myself to walk naked into my bedroom and stand in front of the full-length mirror on the inside of my closet door. Whoa. I closed my eyes and shut the closet door fast.

How did it start, this downward spiral? At what point did I lose myself to sixty-hour work weeks, slovenly behavior, and really crappy taste in men? It wasn't the kind of thing that happened all at once. It crept up gradually: deadline upon deadline, one takeout meal at a time. Factor in a dating pool shrunk not just by the demographics of age, but also by lack of contact with the world outside Balancing Act.

And then one day, I awoke to find myself not only jobless, but old and fat, or at least oldish and fattish. And worst of all I was alone, seriously alone, and now I had nothing but time to notice it.

I still hadn't heard a word from Michael. Part of me, the embarrassingly self-destructive part, kept thinking he'd call any moment. Maybe he'd meant to nudge me into taking the buyout, and then he had really fallen for me, but he didn't have the guts to leave his own job, and now he was too humiliated to talk to me. He should know me better than that. Or maybe he just had the flu, had been out of work, wasn't checking e-mail or phone messages, and forgot to pay his cell phone bill, so his cell was temporarily out of commission, and even the message saying this number was temporarily out of service wasn't working.

I shook my head. I wondered if there was a man on the face of the earth who'd ever spent half this much time overanalyzing a woman's poor behavior. In one of the oldest tricks in the book, some guy had pretended to be interested in me to get me to do what he wanted, and we'd had sex a couple times along the way. No big deal. I'd been used and abused — end of story.

For lack of a better idea, I wandered out into my backyard. In the four years I'd lived here, I could probably count the number of times I'd been in my own backyard on the fingers of both hands. A local landscape service mowed once a week in the summer and also did spring and fall cleanups. My contribution was to write the checks and to buy a hanging plant for the front porch, and then watch it die a slow death either from under- or over-watering, or possibly some lethal combination of both.

One ambitious spring I'd bought a whole tray of hot pink impatiens. I kept meaning to buy big terra-cotta pots and potting soil

31

and whatever else I might need, but I never did manage to transplant them from their flats. By August they'd shot up tall in their tiny square plastic prisons, lost most of their leaves, and turned a kind of gangrene yellow. Somehow they still managed to bloom — big, defiant pinker-than-pink pinwheel-faced flowers sprouted from the top of almost every spindly plant.

How many times was it that Michael and I'd slept together? Dozens? More? Not that it mattered, not that it was just about the sex. The sex was good, but the stroll down memory lane might have been even better. I remembered reading that on the *Dick Van Dyke Show* in the '60s, Rob and Laura Petrie had to keep one foot on the floor if they even sat on the same bed. When Michael and I were together, I think we each kept one foot in the '70s.

We joked about streaking around my suburban neighborhood, something neither of us had had the guts to do in college. I'd thrown out my albums years ago, but Michael still had some of the same vinyl records I'd played to death: Joni Mitchell's *Court and Spark,* Todd Rundgren's *Something/Anything?,* Cat Stevens's *Tea for the Tillerman.* He even had something to play them on: a brand-new old-looking Mission Stack-O-Matic combination record, radio, and CD player. In bed or out, it all happened to the rhythm of the past for Michael and me.

It was funny. I hadn't loved high school and had been only incrementally happier in college, but the older I got, the more I enjoyed trading memories with people who'd been unhappy at the same time I was.

"You should have seen my hair," Michael would say. "A tragedy of epic proportions. It was so wavy I had to wash it before I went to bed and sleep with one of my sister's nylon stockings pulled down over my head so I could get that surfer dude look."

"That reminds me of my first garter belt," I'd say. "The hooks in the back somehow malfunctioned, and the whole thing fell to the ground between classes. I think it was seventh grade, maybe eighth."

Michael rolled the sheet down and kissed my right breast. "So what did you do?" he asked.

"I slipped behind a door and kicked off my shoes — I'm remembering penny loafers, but maybe they were Mary Janes. Anyway, I stepped out of the stockings, put my shoes back on, and kept walking." I nuzzled his neck, where he was ticklish, and he laughed. "It was between classes and the halls were packed, so I'm not sure anyone even noticed."

"Wow," he said. "I'd like to have been the kid who found that garter belt. I would have sneaked it into my room and slept with it for years."

"Oh, please," I said. "I bet you had all sorts of girls throwing their garter belts at you."

"Maybe a few," he said.

I wondered if Michael would have given me the time of day in high school. Not that he was exactly giving me the time of day now. I bent down and broke off a beautiful sky blue and canary yellow flower that I was pretty sure was an iris. Mysterious things were growing all over my backyard, flourishing despite my neglect. Too bad my life hadn't fared as well.

My house was the smallest of five houses built on the grounds of a former estate, when the owners had decided to sell off some of their property. As the Realtor had explained it to me, if you imagined a pie, the original house still owned half, and the five newer houses each had a pie-shaped slice of the other half. I had the middle slice.

The name of the street, Wildwater Way, was more puzzling, since I hadn't noticed any appreciable wildness or water in the immediate vicinity. "No worries," the Realtor had said cheerily. "If coastal erosion keeps up, you'll be waterfront before you know it."

The beach hadn't gotten any closer since I'd moved in, but I did notice that if the tide and wind were just right, I could sometimes smell the ocean.

In hindsight, I probably should have stayed closer to the city, but I'd built up some good equity in my town house and wanted to move up to a single-family and thought it was a good investment. Marshbury, Massachusetts, was a pretty little beach community with property values that only went up. It was the perfect white-picket-fence kind of suburb, and I guess I thought if I bought the house, the life could somehow follow. Even at my age.

My neighbor to the right was out in her yard. She had her back to me, and she was hanging up a load of white laundry. When I'd moved in, she'd left me a basket of cookies and a note that said, *Welcome to Wildwater Way.* I'd finally gotten around to putting a thank-you note in her mailbox a week or so later as I was racing off to work. In the years since, we'd wave when we passed on the road or were both heading out to our driveways at the same time.

Her laundry, mostly sheets and towels, looked clean and crisp and oddly beautiful. It was whipping around in the wind, trying to dance its way free of the clothespins that were holding it down. I suddenly really wanted a clothesline of my own, though I hadn't the foggiest idea how to arrange one. Maybe there was a service I could call.

I wandered over to our property line, marked by a waist-high fence on her side. "Hi," I said. "I was wondering about your clothesline."

When she turned around, I could see that she'd been crying.

"Oh," I said.

She wiped her eyes with the back of her hands, then shook her head. "Listen," she said. "I don't care what the Marshbury Town Council says. I'm a card-carrying member of Project Air Dry, and we're going to take this all the way to the Supreme Court if we have to. I have the right to dry my clothes any damn way I want to."

"But . . . ," I said.

She picked up her laundry basket and stomped away.

"Nice talking to you," I whispered.

I made a vase for the iris from an empty bottle of Sam Adams Boston Ale that Michael had left behind. I placed it on my kitchen windowsill and really hated the way that it looked like a shrine to lost love. Or at least potential love.

I checked unsuccessfully for phone messages of any kind, then moved on to my pedometer: 121 steps so far today. I'd been reading up online about walking, and I knew 10,000 steps a day was recommended for maximum fitness and weight loss. My entire total so far for the week was 352. Woo-hoo.

I slathered on some sunscreen. I drank a glass of water. I went to the bathroom. All those shoes I'd charged were still in the trunk of my car, so I threw some socks on my couch and headed out barefoot to get a pair. I almost decided to back my car into the garage and unload them all. Maybe I could make a little fitness area in one corner. Somewhere to stretch. Or sit and read motivational fitness books. And I definitely needed a place to store all my sneakers. I'd go shopping for some shelves. I could always walk later, when the sun wasn't so bright.

I forced myself to take out exactly one box of sneakers and carry them into the house. I sat on the couch, put on my socks and shoes, and tied the laces. I took a deep breath and made myself walk out my front door.

I don't know why I felt so conspicuous. After all, I'd been walking since I was eleven months old. But I'd let myself get so ridiculously out of shape, and I could feel my T-shirt sticking to every extra ounce. The exercise pants I was wearing were so outdated that they had zippers from the knee to the ankle on the outside of both legs, and the waistband was so tight it was creating a serious muffin top. Probably pumpkin. Maybe even pumpkin cream cheese.

I was also a little bit worried that things might be even worse than I thought. What if I walked and walked, and suddenly I was too out of shape to make it back home? I should have thought to bring my cell phone, just in case I needed to call a cab for a rescue. If I could even get a cab out here in the boondocks. To be on the safe side, maybe I'd just keep walking Wildwater Way. Though that clothesline nut neighbor of mine would probably step right over me if she found me sprawled out on the street. I was lucky she hadn't tried to poison me with those cookies she'd dropped off when I moved in.

I walked down to the end of Wildwater, around the cul-de-sac, and back to the beginning. It was a nice enough street, but by about the tenth lap, I was over it. I was feeling great, swinging my arms and going for a nice, natural stride. I'd forgotten how much I used to love to move. I'd played field hockey and softball in high school, did some rowing in college, was an okay tennis player, as long as it was doubles and I had a good partner. I loved to swim.

Part of the reason I'd been drawn to working at Balancing Act all those years ago was that I'd thought one of the perks would be staying in shape. State-of-the-art fitness center, indoor basketball court, outdoor fitness trail and playing fields. The first couple of years I'd signed up for an aerobics class and even shown up for it a few times, and I played on one of the company softball teams for a couple seasons. But once I climbed my way up to management, most of my available time seemed to be consumed by a never-ending series of meetings. In all those years, why hadn't anybody thought of circling those shiny company treadmills around a conference table?

I reached the beginning of my street again, turned right, and started heading toward the beach. It was an absolutely stunning June day — sunshine, blue skies, just the right amount of breeze to cool things off.

My new sneakers were a perfect fit, and I felt like I could walk forever. Maybe everything really did happen for a reason, and if Michael hadn't given me the final push, I'd still be sitting on my ever-widening butt at Balancing Act, trying to decide whether or not I had the guts to take a buyout.

Who really cared if I ever saw him again? But, boyohboy, when I did see him, I was going to be in such good shape he'd be kicking himself that he let me get away.

DAY 6:
24 STEPS

Ouch.

Day 7:
5010 steps

I was sprawled out on the couch, remote in hand. I'd started with *Decorator's Challenge*, then segued to *Curb Appeal*. Now I was finishing my virtual make over with *Pimp Your Patio*. I'd learned a lot, but I had to admit that my house looked exactly the same.

My calves were still so tight they felt like they had tennis balls embedded under the skin. When the phone rang, I limped my way out to the kitchen.

"Hi, Mom," I said. I hadn't even realized it was Sunday until I saw my mother's name on my caller ID.

"Well, at least you still recognize my voice."

For the first couple of years after my father died, my sister and brothers and I had passed my mother back and forth like a fruitcake. Now she was relatively happily ensconced in a senior condo community in

Florida. She made the telephone rounds once a week, letting each of her children know how much better the others were doing. My goal, as I saw it, was to get through an entire conversation without giving her any ammunition.

"Of course I do, Mom. How's the weather down there?"

"Who knows with all this air-conditioning? Your sister's husband got another raise, a big one."

"That's great, Mom."

"Little Jimmy's kids all have jobs for the summer. Good ones. Kids these days need to work more. All of you worked every summer."

"That's great, Mom."

"Kevin's wife is pregnant again. Twins run in her family, so you never know."

"That's great, Mom."

I hobbled a few steps around my kitchen while I waited. I was out of siblings, so I knew it was my turn next.

"How's that fellow of yours? Don, isn't it? Not that I should remember his name, since I haven't met him. Any talk of plans yet?"

My mother was still back on the guy before Michael. I was glad I hadn't bothered to update her. I hadn't told her I'd taken a buyout either. *Poor Noreen,* I imagined her saying to my brothers and sister, *now she doesn't have a husband or a job.*

I decided my best bet was redirection. "So," I said, "what's new at your end?"

"Oh, you know. Same old, same old. Eat, sleep, go to water aerobics. I think I'll head up for a visit one of these days soon. I figure it's the only way I'll ever meet that boyfriend of yours. Or you two could come here. I do have a guest room, you know."

"Sure," I said. "Sounds great. Listen, I have to go now, Mom. I've got another call coming in."

"Nice to be busy," my mother said.

"Love you," I said.

I actually did have another call coming in, but my mother was such an expert in the guilt department that I felt like I'd been lying anyway.

"Where were you Wednesday night?"

"Wednesday night?" I said. I lifted up one foot and tried to circle my ankle around, just to see if I could loosen things up a little. "Oh, hi, Carol."

"We missed you. I thought you were going to make an effort. You're not depressed, are you? They say it's one of the first stages of redundancy. Katie Johnson was practically suicidal her first few weeks."

I switched legs and circled my other ankle.

44

Carol was the unofficial social organizer at Balancing Act, our very own, I mean *their* very own *I'm Julie, your cruise director* from *The Love Boat*. Carol dressed better, but she was just as perky and knew everybody and everything. She filled in all the gaps for the rest of us over drinks to celebrate "over the hump day" at O'Malley's pub every Wednesday night after work.

"Sorry," I said. "I've just been having so much fun I completely forgot." Cautiously, I stood on my tiptoes, holding on to the wall for balance. Now I knew how Barbie felt, with her ankles locked and her feet permanently frozen in the point position.

I lowered my heels slowly down to the floor, then went back up on my toes again. My calves were still tight, but my legs were becoming bendable after all.

"Really? What kind of fun?"

"Oh, you know." I tried taking a few more steps around my kitchen. It hurt, but I could almost imagine walking normally again.

"Well, Trish and Cathy and Dan and Sue were there, and most of Marketing. Mary is thinking about taking a buyout, too. And I think Sherry is seeing someone, but we couldn't get her to dish any details." Carol took a deep breath. "So, what kind of fun?"

45

It wouldn't be a bad idea to have something to look forward to. I really did like some of the people I worked with, and maybe a night at O'Malley's would be easier than actually calling the coworkers I'd promised to stay in touch with. And, if I were totally honest, part of the draw was that it might also lead to some Michael news.

"Oh, all kinds of fun," I said, with what I hoped was a convincing laugh. "I'll fill you in this Wednesday."

I put on my sneakers and walked carefully out to my car. What was I thinking, buying all these sneakers? I'd be lucky to live long enough to wear half of them, especially if I kept up this walking stuff. Who knew it was such an extreme sport?

I was trying to decide whether to bring the first four boxes all the way into the house or just pile them in the garage, when a pretty teenage girl ran out of the house next door. "I hate you," she yelled.

Crazy Clothesline Person held the front door open. "Get back in here this instant, young lady," she yelled.

The girl jumped into a green minivan and took off.

A door slammed. My nutty neighbor

started walking across her front yard in my direction.

I pretended I didn't see her. The side door of my garage was the closest, so I turned and took a few quick steps toward it. My calves screamed in protest.

"Ouch," I said.

"Are you all right?" my neighbor asked.

Are you? seemed the obvious answer, but probably not the best thing to say to a potential psychopath. "Fine," I said. I shuffled a few steps closer to the garage door, tilting my head in an attempt to see around the boxes.

"Did I actually call her 'young lady'?"

"Hmm," I said noncommittally.

A box dropped off the top of the pile and landed on my toes. "Shit," I said.

My neighbor picked it up. "Here, let me take one of those for you," she said. She reached out and grabbed another box off the pile. She was about my age, with blondish highlighted hair pulled back in a tight ponytail. Right now her pale blue eyes looked more sad than crazy.

"Can I talk to you for a minute?" she asked.

I shrugged and took another step toward my garage.

"Listen," she said. "I'm really sorry I

47

snapped at you. I should have heard you out. Are you planning to sell or something? I'll take the clothesline down temporarily if you think it will hurt your property value. Or if you're staying, but you're planning to have a cookout or something. I just hate like hell that some elitist town ordinance is telling me I can't have a clothesline on my property. But I'm not an unreasonable person."

I wondered what the teenage daughter would say to that one. "All I wanted to know," I said, "was if you'd be willing to give me a clothesline referral. You know, the name of someone who installs them locally."

She scrunched up her forehead. "Is this a trick?"

I shook my head.

"You really don't know how to put up a clothesline?"

I shook my head again.

"Seriously?"

"Stop," I said. "You're giving me a clothesline complex."

"Sorry." She smiled. "I'll put one up for you. As long as you don't mind being my cell mate if someone drops a dime on us."

"It'd be the most excitement I've had in ages. Hey, what size shoe do you wear?"

"I can't believe you're an eight and a half," I said. We'd taken a right at the end of Wild-water Way, and once more I was heading in the direction of the beach. Maybe people who lived in beach communities were automatically pulled toward the water whenever they left their homes.

"Well," my neighbor, who'd reintroduced herself as Tess Tabares, said, "actually, I used to be a seven and a half, but my feet stretched out a half size with each kid."

"Really?" I said. "I wish I'd known that. It would have been a great shoe concept." My calves were still a little tender, but I seemed to be walking normally again, now that they'd warmed up.

Tess matched her steps to mine. "What? You mean you would have invented a shoe that stretched during pregnancy?"

I laughed. "No. We probably would have come up with a new model in a choice of pink or blue, and pitched the fact that new mothers can't possibly fit into their old walking shoes."

"Oh, please," Tess said. "You just cram your toes in until the shoes wear out. Once you have kids, it's all about them."

49

Since I didn't have any expertise in that area, I kept my mouth shut.

"It's a pregnancy hormone thing. Relaxin. Loosens up your tendons and ligaments, and your feet stretch out along with the rest of your body, especially if you have a high arch. And they never come back, but then again, not much else comes back either, at least after the second pregnancy. Have any kids?"

I shook my head.

"Smart move. Well, anyway, thanks. Best barter I've done in a while. I'll have your clothesline up by the end of the week."

"No rush," I said.

"I've got plenty of time. I'm a teacher. Third grade. Usually I tutor over the summer, but I took this one off to spend time with my youngest before she heads off to college."

I nodded. We looked both ways and stepped down into a crosswalk. Maybe it was the fact that our feet were the same size, but we'd already fallen into a nice walking rhythm.

"So, you want someone to walk with every morning, let me know. My daughter's not speaking to me, my son took a job in New York, and all the good tutoring jobs are gone at this point."

"Great," I said. "I mean, great about the walking part. What time of day are you thinking?"

"Whatever. The earlier the better, I guess. Although I was actually planning to gain weight this summer."

I turned to look at her, but she was staring straight ahead. Maybe it was a joke, but I wasn't sure enough to laugh.

"Yeah, so, my husband and I went on a cruise for our anniversary. His idea. Anyway, we're eating for like the eighth time that day, and I said, 'If this keeps up, I'll weigh four hundred pounds by the end of this cruise.' And he says, get this, 'Then I guess you'll be going home alone.'"

Tess started swinging her arms hard and picked up her pace. I tried to keep up, even though my calves weren't too crazy about the idea. "Do you believe that?" she said. "With the gut he has on him? I will never, ever forgive him for saying that to me. I mean, whatever happened to for better and for worse, you know?"

"I think you look great," I said.

"Right," she said. "Anyway, my plan was that I was going to eat all summer just to drive him crazy. Once, when the kids were younger, maybe fourteen and ten, he made a crack about the house turning into a

51

pigsty. So, I cut a little hole in a full vacuum cleaner bag, and every afternoon before he came home, I sprinkled some dirt around the house, a little more each day, just to see how long it would take before one of them actually cleaned it up."

"What happened?"

"Not a thing. Nobody ever noticed. Eventually I couldn't take it anymore, so I broke down and put in a new bag and vacuumed it all up."

We were going up a hill, and she was sucking in little gasps of air every few words. "Shit," she said. "I'm in even worse shape than I thought. How far do you usually walk?"

I pulled out my pedometer and pushed the memory button. "Well, it varies. Two days ago, I walked five point two miles" — I switched from mile mode to step mode — "and yesterday, twenty-four steps."

Tess leaned back against a tree and slid down to the sidewalk. "I say we start somewhere right about in the middle, and work our way up from there."

I put my hands on the tree trunk and tried a careful calf stretch. "Sounds like a plan," I said.

DAY 8:
6333 STEPS

Tess was sitting cross-legged in my driveway when I came out at 8 A.M. She jumped up when she saw me, and we fell into step beside each other. She liked to be on the outside of the sidewalk, I noticed. Fine with me.

"Left okay?" she asked when we got to the end of Wildwater Way. "Or do you want to go right again?"

"Left is okay."

We walked in silence. It was another beautiful day, with flowers popping up all over the place. I wished I knew what they were. When I was working, I was too busy to notice the things I didn't know, but now my ignorance seemed vast. I didn't have kids, I couldn't identify plants, I didn't have a clue about clotheslines. I didn't even know whether to try to start a conversation or keep my mouth shut. I'd have to take another look at the outplacement resources that had come with my package. Maybe there was a workshop I could take. Assimilating in Suburbia?

"So, why does your daughter hate you?" I finally asked.

Tess started swinging her arms like crazy. "I don't want to talk about it," she said.

So much for starting a conversation. Maybe this walking-with-the-next-door-neighbor thing wasn't such a great idea. I wondered how I'd get out of it if it really got bad. She'd certainly seemed a lot nicer yesterday.

The neighborhood was waking up. People were driving off to work. One man was watering his garden. Some little kids were out running around their yard already. Someone had painted their shutters a bright yellowy green, and it gave a fun contemporary touch to their weathered natural shingles. Maybe I should look into painting my house. How hard could it be?

"Sorry," Tess said. "It's tough enough trying to live through it, without having to talk about it, too." We walked past two guys unloading long pieces of wood from a truck. "So, what made you decide to take a buyout?"

"I don't want to talk about it," I said.

54

Tess burst out laughing. "Touché," she said.

High Street, the street we were walking on, meandered inexplicably, the way old roads do in New England, until we were parallel to our newer, perfectly laid-out street. A weathered wooden sign next to a dirt driveway read LAVENDER.

"Have you ever been up there?" Tess asked.

"No. It's the original estate that used to own our street, right? I've always wondered if it would be rude to walk up and check it out."

"It's still a working lavender farm. I'm sure they want you to walk right up — that's the point. I haven't been up there since the new owners bought it, but they used to have some nice stuff for sale. I brought my class on a field trip here once. One of the kids started a rumor about pony rides, and when that didn't pan out, it was kind of a bust."

We were already walking up the dirt road. It was narrow and twisty and threaded its way through what even I could identify as a forest of pine trees. The bed of pine needles under our feet felt great after the hard sidewalk, and it was quiet and shady and almost magical. I wondered if Wildwater Way had been this wildly beautiful before

55

they put in the houses and lawns.

Something ran in front of us. I screamed as it ran off. "What was that?" I asked.

Tess gave me a look. "A rabbit. Wow, you *are* a city mouse."

At the top of the hill, the trees gave way, and we were standing in the middle of a big, sunny clearing. There was a main house, with some trucks out front, and a couple of smaller buildings.

"Breathe," Tess said.

I did. How do you describe the scent of lavender? Like a spa? Strong and heavy? Sweet and spicy? Soothing. Exotic and yet familiar, too, maybe a not-too-distant cousin of fresh-cut hay or new-mown grass. Earthy and pungent and sexy, definitely sexy. I remembered once reading about a study where men rated pumpkin and lavender as the most arousing scents. The smell of lavender wrapped around me like a pair of strong male arms until I was completely enveloped in it. I was pretty sure I could even taste it.

"Great Aunt Millie," Tess said.

"Where?" I said.

Tess laughed. "No, Aunt Millie's long gone. But she was my Yardley English Lavender aunt. She positively reeked of the stuff. We had to walk up three flights of creaky wooden stairs to get to her apartment. I can still remember the smell of the hallway, all old and dry and airless, and then the second she opened the door — *bam!* — it was like being attacked by a cloud of lavender."

I followed Tess into the smallest outbuilding, a rickety old dark wood shack with a sign that matched the one out by the road. Dried bouquets hung upside down from the beams that crisscrossed the ceilings, and every available surface was covered with something involving lavender. Lavender books, postcards, prints, stationery. Lavender oil, soap, candles, scone mix, jelly, even lavender chocolate. My stomach growled.

"If heaven exists," I said, "this is definitely what it smells like."

There was an old wooden box with a slot in it sitting on a counter, along with a sign that said PLEASE PAY HERE. I unzipped the pocket of my exercise pants and pulled out a crumpled five-dollar bill. Years after I started bringing my cell phone everywhere, I'd finally stopped carrying change for a phone call. But I still rarely left the house without emergency money. "Just in case," my father used to say as he slipped me a few bills every time I ran off to meet my friends.

When I picked up an oversize tea bag made of unbleached muslin, my calves practically mooed in anticipation.

Aches Away Lavender Tea Soak

1 cup lavender
1/2 cup chamomile
1/4 cup sage
1/4 cup rosemary
6 crushed bay leaves

Mix all ingredients. Fill a metal tea ball or muslin or organza bag. Hang on the tap or float under warm running water in tub. Climb in and soak liberally to relax muscles, increase circulation, soften body, and re-energize soul.

"Okay, time's up," Tess said. "You can come back later. We're supposed to be walking, not shopping."

I pushed my money through the slot in the box and stuffed the little bag into my pocket. I jogged a few steps to catch up with Tess.

As we got closer to the main house, we could see a redheaded woman about our age sitting on the porch steps and lacing up

58

a pair of battered, formerly pink high-top sneakers she must have been wearing since the late '80s. I watched her Velcro them tight around her ankles. Yup, they were definitely Reebok Freestyles.

"What a gorgeous place," Tess yelled. "You're so lucky to live here."

"Some days," the pink-footed redheaded woman yelled back. "Hey, you don't want some company, do you?"

"Cool," Tess whispered under her breath. "A lavender connection."

We made our way to the porch and introduced ourselves. I took another look at the dilapidated Freestyles. "What size shoe do you wear?" I asked. "I think we need to get those things to a shoe museum fast."

I'd spent some time over the weekend reading up on the outplacement services that had come with my buyout package. Balancing Act had contracted with a company called Fresh Horizons, whose services were available for ninety days from my redundancy date.

The Fresh Horizons brochure was a lot like a catering menu. Pick one from Column A, two from Column B, and one from Column C. Or pick one from Column A, one from Column B, and two from Column

C. Or pick two from Column A and call it a day. But instead of choosing between Apple Brie Crostini and Scallop Ceviche in Cucumber Cups, I had to decide between twelve hours of private career coaching, a boxed set of Fresh Horizons career-coaching DVDs and five hours of private coaching, or three months of unlimited small-group meetings and a first edition copy of the Fresh Horizons job search and résumé writing manual.

Just thinking about it gave me a headache. I was nowhere near ready to deal with any of this. I mean, talk to me when my eighteen months of salary and benefits were about to run out. But I knew that as soon as my ninety days were over and my outplacement services had dried up, I'd be sorry I hadn't at least given it a try.

There was a little coupon tucked into the brochure that was good for one free-trial small-group meeting. I figured I'd start there, see how it went. If I decided I wanted to opt for all private sessions, maybe I could make an appointment with a career coach while I was there.

I found the Small-Group Meeting Schedule. It didn't say anything about signing up in advance, so I wondered how they could guarantee the small part. I suppose it didn't really matter. None of us had anything to do, so the more the merrier. There were even meetings in the South office, which meant I wouldn't have to drive all the way into Boston. The South meetings were on Monday and Friday afternoons. Did they schedule them that way to give some semblance of structure to a work week that no longer existed?

I wasn't sure what the appropriate dress was, but I didn't want to be mistaken for a loser who couldn't get a job — as opposed to someone who'd *chosen* to take a buyout — so I took a second, après-walking shower and put on a crisp, white blouse and a taupe summer-weight suit. I blow-dried my hair, something I hadn't been doing a lot of lately, put on some makeup, and added an overpriced steel and black watch I thought of as my power watch, plus some silver hoop earrings.

When I got to Fresh Horizons South it didn't look too promising. It was actually a room in what was once an elementary school and was now mostly occupied by the South Shore Senior Center. "Geez," I said out loud, when I realized where I'd landed. "You've got to be kidding." I mean, I didn't even have an AARP card yet.

I didn't think it could possibly be good

for my post-redundancy self-esteem, but I was already here, so I figured I should at least check it out. I made my way down the center hallway, with its rows of ancient, dented, kiddie-size lockers. I wondered if any of the seniors had actually gone to elementary school here. Talk about déjà vu.

A handful of people were already sitting in folding metal chairs in a semicircle when I walked into the Fresh Horizons room. Fortunately, the chairs were adult size.

A scruffy but cute guy about my age patted the chair next to him. "Welcome to never-again land, honey," he said. He hadn't shaved in a while, but maybe that was a statement of style as opposed to a red flag for sloth. I headed in his direction.

Another guy, at least as disheveled, but possibly even better looking, patted a chair next to him. I hesitated.

"Fickle," the first guy said. "My first wife was like that. Never really knew what she wanted."

I took a step in the direction of the other guy. "Have some dignity, man," he said. "Enough with the never-again garbage." He looked up at me and smiled. "Welcome to Boomer Club. Squint and you can almost imagine it's 1973, and we're all back in detention hall."

A woman with dark hair that hadn't been brushed in a while smiled, too. One thing for sure, Boomer Club would never be mistaken for Groomer Club. "Sad, but true," the woman said. "It's like we're stuck in a bad sequel to *The Breakfast Club.*"

I sat down on the end chair next to the woman and closest to the door. "Wait till you get a load of the coach," she whispered. "You won't know whether you want to mother him or sleep with him."

As if on cue, an adorable cherub of a guy walked in. He was in his late twenties or early thirties, with curly blond hair and little wire-rimmed glasses. He was wearing chinos and an untucked white dress shirt with a navy blue tie, and he was carrying a briefcase and a tripod. "Aww," I whispered to the woman next to me.

"Told you," she whispered back. Maybe once things got going, we could start passing notes to each other.

Our career coach cleared his throat and placed his briefcase on one of the chairs. He set up his tripod. He opened his briefcase, pulled out a small video camera, and attached it to the tripod. I automatically started running my fingers through my hair. The brochure could have at least warned us that we were supposed to be camera ready.

The coach shut his eyes and let out three quick puffs of air. He opened his eyes again, tilted his chin up, and threw his shoulders back. "Welcome," he said. "Welcome to all of you, and make that welcome back if you've been here before. My name is Brock, and I'll be your Fresh Horizons certified small-group career coach for the next ninety minutes."

Nobody said anything.

"Okay," Brock said. "Our job here today is to get to know one another, and ourselves, a little better."

One guy groaned, and most of the rest of us slouched down in our chairs.

Brock adjusted the camera and pushed a button. "Okay," he said, "let's start with you." He nodded at me.

"Me?" I said. "You know, I think I'd prefer just to watch."

"My second wife was like that," one of the cute, messy guys said.

Brock crossed his arms over his chest. He looked about twelve. I wondered if his tie really tied or if it was a clip-on. "Look right at the camera," he said, "and pretend it's not even there."

I looked at the door and tried to calculate my chances for escape.

"Just be yourself," Brock said.

I froze. I hated that expression. I mean, if I even remotely knew who I was, would I be here?

Brock cleared his throat. "You can start by telling us your name, and a little bit about yourself."

"Oh, boy," I said. "Okay, my name is Noreen." I shook my head. "Nora Kelly."

Everybody was looking at me. I felt like an idiot. I cleared my throat. "Okay," I said. "I just took a buyout. For the last eighteen years I've been employed by Balancing Act Shoes, most recently as Senior Manager of Brand Identity, a position I'd held since May of —"

"Okay, fine," Brock said. "Tell us about you."

"I reported to —"

Brock put up one hand. "No, tell us about you."

"I was responsible for —"

"No, no, no." Brock clapped his hands once for each word, which made him look like a toddler having a tantrum. "You're regurgitating your résumé. Tell us about *you*. Who you are. What you hate. What you love. What you're good at. What you hope you never have to do again for the rest of your life. Tell us the story of Noreen Nora Kelly."

"I'm really sorry," I said. "But I'm afraid

65

I'm going to have to get back to you on that."

Brock nodded. "Okay, think about it. Who wants to go next?"

Some of the others were almost as bad as I was, but a few people really got into it. One woman just wouldn't shut up about all the things she was never, ever going to do again, everything from going to meetings to wearing mascara to singing "Happy Birthday" to people she didn't even like. It was actually nice to be around people, and the ninety minutes flew by.

Brock left us with a final nugget. "And, remember," he said, "when you're in transition, structure is key. Put yourself on a schedule and adhere to it. Without a routine, it's a slippery slope. Too much freedom and before you know it you've lost control of your day and turned into a slug. So when that structure isn't imposed from without, you have to take the time to build it carefully and irrevocably into your day . . . the Fresh Horizons way."

"I thought he was going to start tap-dancing and break into a song at the end there," I said to the woman with the messy hair as we walked out together. "But I have to admit that baby coach wasn't half bad."

A guy stepped up to my other side. Every

time he swung his arm, he flashed a little bit of skin through a hole in the armpit of his T-shirt. It was kind of sexy in a lowbrow way. "Yeah," he said. "That slug image was magic. Almost enough to make me find myself by next week." He half-turned and raised his voice. "So, what is it this week, kids, Wii bowling or PlayStation Rock Band?"

DAY 9:
6511 STEPS

"Structure is key," I said. "And I don't think it would hurt for us to set some goals, either." Rosie Stockton, who owned the lavender farm, had cut through the woods to my backyard, and Tess came out as soon as she saw us.

"Yeah, yeah," Tess said as we walked across my side yard to Wildwater Way. "I still can't believe your name is Rosemary and you own a lavender farm."

"They're related, you know," Rosie said. Her red hair was short and curly, and she was tiny, maybe five two, if that, so unfortunately she didn't wear an 8 1/2. "Sage and thyme are related to lavender, too. And lavenders belong to the genus *Lavandula* of the family Lamiaceae, which is the mint family."

"So, can I have mint in my garden, too?" I asked. The plan was that I'd try to exchange a pair of the sneakers for a size 6 1/2 for

Rosie, and in return she'd plant a starter lavender garden for me. Tess would get a bar of lavender chocolate for brokering the deal.

"Mint is really invasive," Rosie said. I noticed that we were falling into a pattern already. Only two of us could fit on the sidewalk at the same time, so we'd walk three abreast in the middle of the road, whenever we could get away with it. When we had to move back to the sidewalk, we'd take solo turns up in front of the other two. "It'll take over your whole garden. I can bring you some from my garden, but the best thing to do is plant it in a pot to keep it contained."

"I thought I planted mint one year," Tess said, "but it turned out to be catnip. Every cat in town started coming to our yard to get high. Like I didn't have enough problems with two teenagers in the house."

"Whatever you think," I said. "I'll try to exchange the sneakers tomorrow. I'm meeting some old friends from work."

"Catnip is a kind of mint," Rosie said. "It's also great for getting rid of mosquitoes."

"Maybe," Tess said, "the mosquitoes are just too busy laughing at the cats to bite anybody."

69

We'd reached North Beach already. We walked single file through a narrow opening in the seawall, and then spread out again to walk the beach. It was getting close to high tide, so only one of us could fit on the hard-packed sand, and the other two had to walk on the loose, dry sand at the top of the beach.

Last night I'd gone on the Internet to research walking and found out what anybody who'd ever tried it knew: walking on the sand requires more effort than walking on a solid surface. Because your foot moves around more, the tendons and muscles of your legs have to work more than twice as hard. Supposedly walking on the sand used up to 50 percent more calories than hard surface walking, too.

Whatever the benefits, the best reason to walk the beach was that it was so amazingly beautiful. Especially early in the morning like this when the walkers owned the sand. In another hour or so, it would become an obstacle course of chairs and towels, pails and shovels, and throngs of sunscreen-slathered, bathing suit–clad people in all shapes and sizes.

Out of the blue, Rosie started to sing "Walk On By," maybe in honor of the shoes I'd promised her. Tess joined in. Then I did.

Actually, we didn't really remember the words, so we just kept making them up as we went along.

We kept going until a couple of guys walking their dog got close enough to hear us, and then we started to giggle.

"That was fun," Rosie said. "I always wanted to be in a girl group. I was devastated when I didn't even make my high school chorus."

"I had this great fantasy I'd become a rock star," Tess said, "and run a private school for the band's kids on the side. Not much job security though."

I didn't say anything, mostly because I couldn't seem to remember anything I'd ever wanted to be. Maybe being made redundant had wiped clean a portion of my brain; with my luck, it was the part that had been flourishing while I neglected it. Or maybe I couldn't think about what I'd always wanted to be because then I'd actually have to start thinking about what I wanted to do next.

I could feel a little cloud of anxiety starting to rise through the center of my chest, so I changed the subject. "Okay," I said. "Getting back to structure. I was thinking maybe we could commit to walking at the same time every day. . . ."

"Isn't that what we're doing?" Rosie said.

"Well, yeah," I said. "But what if there were a prize at the end? You know, a certain number of hours walked or pounds lost by a certain time."

"Not another diet," Tess said. "I am so over diets. You starve yourself, lose ten pounds, enjoy it for a week, then gain back twenty-two. I rebel against the whole concept. And I'm never going to have plastic surgery either, so don't even bring that up. Somebody has to look old, you know?"

"No offense," Rosie said. "But I have to say I agree."

"Fine," I said. I bent down to pick up a piece of sea glass and let the other two walk ahead.

Tess turned around. "Don't pout," she said. "It's not becoming."

I stood up. "I'm not pouting. I just wanted something to look forward to."

Tess and Rosie stopped walking. I threw the sea glass, and it disappeared into the water.

"I could use something to look forward to," Rosie said.

"At school," Tess said, "the P.E. teachers give us these big maps for our classroom wall. The kids keep track of their mileage with these little tokens they earn and wear on their sneaker laces, and we plot the classroom mileage totals and pretend to travel across the country. Math skills, geography skills, history tie-ins, plus it really gets them moving."

"That's a great idea," I said. "Okay, what if we say that whatever mileage the three of us can accumulate in one month, we get to go somewhere that's the same distance away for real."

We started walking again. "What do the tokens look like?" Rosie asked.

"Young," Tess said. "Okay, here's the problem. Say we each walk five miles a day, seven days a week." Her voice clicked into teacher mode. "Thirty-five miles times three would be. . . ."

I closed my eyes to do the math.

"A hundred and five," Rosie said.

Tess nodded. "Good job. And times four weeks . . ."

"Four hundred and twenty," I said as fast as I could. Not to be competitive, but I completely blew Rosie out of the water on that one.

"Great," Tess said. "Which would probably get us to, where, East Wesipisipp? I think if we're going to do this, we need to up the ante."

"Is there really an East Wesipisipp?" I

asked. Maybe I would have had better luck there than in Marshbury.

"Of course, there is," Tess said. "It has the biggest population of golden retrievers per square acre in the state."

"And don't forget that tennis tournament," Rosie said. "The Wesipisipp Cup."

"Good one," Tess said.

"Thanks," Rosie said. "You, too."

We reached the far end of the beach and started crossing the parking lot to get back out to the road. Just the thought of upping the ante had caused us to pick up speed.

"Moving on," Rosie said. "What if we made it six months?" Every so often Rosie had to take a little hop and a skip to keep up with our longer legs.

"I don't know," Tess said. "I'm not sure delayed gratification is the way to go. I'd kind of like to get out of here as soon as possible. Plus, summer's the best time for me to go away."

"Maybe," I said, "we can count other things, like strength training, or even gardening. Come up with a formula to convert them to miles."

"As long as we don't count calories," Tess said. "I'm fine with eating healthy, but I'm not keeping a food diary, and I am so not giving up wine."

"We could recruit people to donate miles to us," Rosie said.

"What? 'Help send these poor women to camp'?" Tess stopped walking and put her hands on her hips. "You know, that might just work. My whole family would probably donate."

Day 10:
7144 STEPS

As soon as I reached the parking lot, I
started thinking about Michael again. It was
like I could feel his presence once I broke
through the Balancing Act force field. Even
though close to a thousand employees
worked — in Balancing Act lingo — "on
campus," I had such a strong feeling I was
going to run into him at some point, as if
fate wouldn't be able to resist crashing us
together again.

I wasn't even sure I believed in fate, but
just in case, I'd dressed extra carefully. I
was wearing a subdued but flirty periwinkle
and white sundress in a contemporary floral
print, a complete departure from my usual
professional casual work attire, which con-
sisted mostly of pants and jackets in neutral
solids.

It actually felt good to wear a dress for a
change, and when I'd looked in the mirror
before I left the house, I'd thought I looked

pretty good for a redundant woman of a certain age without a certain someone/ certain job/ounce of certainty in her life. The periwinkle brought out the mossy green in my eyes, and my chin-length brown hair was still at that good place between touch-ups when the graying roots hadn't even started to emerge yet. The dress had a V-neck and a touch of ruching that gave me the illusion of a long, lean silhouette. My upper arms weren't great, but I didn't think there was any serious wiggling going on yet.

I pulled into the exact same spot in front of the Balancing Act Employee Store I'd parked in last time. I'd flipped through my buyout papers last night and couldn't find anything about the expiration of my employee discount, so I'd have to take my chances. Balancing Act employees had two open weeks before Christmas and one in August when they were allowed to buy for family and friends, but the rest of the year, we were only supposed to buy shoes in our own size. With luck, my feet looked smaller in sandals.

As soon as I entered the store, I walked quickly over to the Walk On By display. I scooped up a box labeled 6 1/2 with my free hand and headed right for the register.

"Hi," I said to the same woman who'd

waited on me last time. "I can't believe this, but I just took a buyout, so I came in here and bought a whole bunch of shoes, you know, while I still could, and well, I guess I wasn't paying much attention, because one pair wasn't even my size." I curled my toes. "Six and a half," I said. "Small feet."

I held up both boxes, then put the 8 1/2 on the counter. The woman gave me a look that said, essentially, *whatever.*

I cradled the 6 1/2 box in my arms. If she didn't care, then I certainly wasn't going to keep feeling like a criminal. "Hey," I said, "remember that purple pedometer you gave me last time? You don't happen to have two more of those you can sell me, do you?"

She reached under the counter and handed me two purple pedometers. "On the house," she said. "It's the least Balancing Act can do for you."

I thought she could use some new material, but Balancing Act wasn't my problem anymore, so *whatever.* I thanked her and walked back out to my car with Rosie's shoes. It had all gone so easily, it was almost a bit of a letdown. I wished I hadn't overexplained myself like that in the beginning. It left me feeling slightly sullied, as if another shower today wouldn't be such a bad idea. It just wasn't the kind of thing I would normally do.

I mean, what was the big deal? Worst case scenario, I could have kept the shoes and bought Rosie a pair at retail. I wouldn't even have had to tell her. She'd still have gotten her shoes, and I'd still have ended up with a lavender garden. None of the fun of the barter would have been lost, and I was getting a paycheck, so it's not like I was destitute or anything, at least not yet.

I clicked my car door open and put one hand on my door handle. One row of cars away and off to my right, a man in a suit was walking with his back toward me. He was tall, with dark hair, and I knew that walk. At least I thought I did.

I walked quickly, closing the distance between us. I'd almost caught up to him when it hit me. What the hell was I going to say to Michael? Not only that, but it would look like I was following him, mostly because, well, technically, I *was* following him.

I had to take control of the situation. I wondered if there was a way I could create a disturbance, turn around, and walk the other way. That way he'd be following me, which would put me in the power seat.

I looked down at the shoe box I was carrying. I held it behind my back, then lobbed it away from me. When I turned around,

Rosie's shoe box was sprawled on the pavement, one shoe in and one shoe out. The top had turned into a Frisbee and was just coming in for a landing on the hood of a shiny silver sports car.

I twisted my head just enough to assess the situation behind me. The guy had turned around, too, but instead of Michael, it was a perfect stranger who was glaring at me. I didn't have to know him to tell he was not a happy camper.

I gave him a little smile.

He scowled at me for a long moment, then looked in the direction of the shiny car. "There better not be one single scratch," he said.

"Ohmigod," I said. "I'm sorry. I'm really sorry. But it's only cardboard, and I'm sure. . . ."

"You better have good insurance," he said.

"Oh, I do," I said. "I have great insurance, and I even know a terrific auto body shop, if you need a referral. Once, a few years ago . . ."

I took a step back as he stormed past me. He picked the box top off his hood with two fingers and flicked it onto the pavement. I scrambled for it and tucked it under my arm. I started rifling in my purse for my license while he ran his finger slowly over the hood of his car. I assumed he was feeling for scratches, but it looked like he was trying to read something in Braille.

His silver baby must have turned out to be scratch free, because he gave me one more mean look and started walking away.

"Sorry," I said to his back.

"That's an understatement," he said, without turning around.

By the time I got to O'Malley's, I really needed a drink. Carol had staked out the head of our usual table and was flanked by several Wednesday regulars. I ran my eyes quickly around the table. I hadn't realized I was holding my breath until I started breathing again when I didn't see Michael.

"Well," Carol said perkily. "If it isn't Reeny, Reeny, Redundancy Queeny."

"Hi, everybody," I said. I sat down, leaving an empty chair on one side, just in case Michael showed up. Not that he would. Not that I cared.

A waiter was just delivering drinks, so I ordered a glass of wine.

"So what's it like to be a free woman?" somebody asked.

"Great," I said. "I'm loving it."

"You look good," Beth from Accounting said.

"Thanks."

"I didn't know you wore dresses," Lena from Marketing said.

My wine came and I took a big gulp. The conversation had already moved on. They were talking about a big interdepartmental meeting they'd just had, and I suddenly felt like I'd been away for a century instead of a week and a half.

"You're awfully quiet, Noreen," somebody said eventually. "Tell us what you've been up to."

I took another sip of wine and put the glass down on the table. "Well," I said. "It turns out I've got some nice neighbors. We've started walking together. We're even thinking —"

"Must be nice," Josh from Customer Relations said. "Hey, did you hear what happened in IT yesterday?"

Their conversation floated in one of my ears and right on out the other. It was as if I couldn't even process the words I was hearing. I hadn't been myself since I'd set foot on Balancing Act property.

But if I wasn't myself, then who was I? The old Noreen certainly wouldn't have behaved like that in the Balancing Act store. The first rule of negotiation, in this case a simple, if slightly illegal, shoe exchange, is not to volunteer too much information.

82

Bring the shoes up to the register, give the salesperson a confident, nonadversarial smile, and tell her matter-of-factly that you're making an equal exchange.

And that guy in the parking lot. I mean, come on. When you're dealing with an asshole, you keep your mouth shut. You make him do all the talking. You don't start hemorrhaging apologies all over the place. And what the hell was I doing, hallucinating Michael and throwing a box of sneakers across the parking lot like a lovesick teenager?

It had taken me a long time to learn to thrive at Balancing Act. I'd spent the first few years under the control of a really tough supervisor. I kept thinking I could please her if I worked just a little bit harder, came up with an even more brilliant idea, flattered her some more. But the more I tried to please her, the more she withheld her approval, and somehow it always ended up feeling like it was my fault.

She completely controlled me. She said jump; I asked how high. I didn't make a single decision without wondering what she would think of it. Just the thought of my quarterly employee evaluation was enough to send me into a full-blown anxiety attack.

And then one day, in the midst of some

snowballing departmental crisis, she really let me have it. We were sitting in her office, and there were no witnesses. She took off her reading glasses and placed them in front of her on the desk. She launched into an angry tirade about how she'd created me, how I'd be nothing without her. She belittled my past efforts, ridiculed the project I was working on, minimized everything I'd be likely to bring to the table in the future.

The odd thing was that as she ranted, I suddenly got it. She was a bully, plain and simple. Because she'd never shoved me into a locker, or held me upside down by my ankles and shaken the change out of my pockets, I just hadn't been able to see it until then. It was a huge epiphany for me, maybe one of the biggest of my life. In that instant, I stopped trying to please her, and she lost all power over me.

I think she knew it, too. Bullies need people to control, and when they can't play the game with you, they find another victim.

I continued to do my work, but I stopped worrying about whether or not she liked it. Eventually an opportunity presented itself in another department, run by a more nurturing, less abusive boss. I grabbed it and never looked back. In the years since, I'd run into other bullies, and I'd gotten pretty good at defusing them.

My behavior today felt like major backsliding. Was it possible I'd lost my edge in less than two weeks? Maybe without a job, all your skills just withered up because you no longer had a place to practice them. I looked around the table again, and I felt a total disconnect. It was like I was sitting with perfect strangers, and not only did I not recognize any of them, but I didn't even recognize myself. Maybe without a job, I didn't have a self.

One of the women, Sherry, was pushing her chair back from the table and saying something about having to get going because she was meeting someone for dinner. She stood up, placed some bills on the table, and looked over at me.

"Nice to see you again, Noreen," she said. "Call me if you want to hang out sometime."

I liked Sherry. She was about my age and had started working at Balancing Act maybe a year or two after I did. We sometimes shared a table in the cafeteria at lunch, and we'd gone to the movies and shopping together a few times over the years. She was a nice person, with a dry wit, and I'd always enjoyed her company.

"Thanks," I said. "I will."

The minute Sherry was out the door, Carol leaned forward. "I know who she's mee-ting," she actually sang.

"Who?" somebody asked.

"Wouldn't you like to kno-ow?" Carol was still singing. She was in her glory.

"I heard from a friend of mine in her department that she's thinking about taking a buyout while the VRIF is still on the table," somebody said.

"Come on, who?" somebody else said.

"Come on, Carol," somebody else said. "Play fair. You brought it up, so now you *have* to tell us."

Carol leaned back in her chair like it was a throne. We all waited. She tilted forward again, placed one elbow on the table, and rested her chin on the palm of her hand.

"Michael Carleton," she stage-whispered. "You know, Michael-don't-call-me-Mike from Olympus. They've been sneaking around practically since the takeover."

Day 11:
462 Steps

I stared up at the crack in my ceiling, then turned my head just long enough to watch 8:00 A.M. come and go in slime green on my alarm clock. My entire body ached, as if a Mack truck had driven through my bedroom in the middle of the night and flattened me into my mattress.

I barely remembered the drive home from O'Malley's. While everybody talked about Sherry and Michael, I'd just sat there, feeling numb right down to my toes. I'd forced myself to wait until they'd moved on to another subject. Then I told everyone I had to get up early the next day, said my goodbyes, and got the hell out of there.

I should have been relieved they'd never caught on to Michael and me. I should have been worried about Sherry, too, and whether Michael was going to manipulate her into taking a VRIF she didn't really know if she wanted. Maybe it was even in his Olympus job description: *Eliminate overpaid female senior employees by seducing them and then nudging them out to pasture before they know what hit them.*

I could have been quietly making plans to warn Sherry myself. Or I could have brought a rumor to the table for the group to feed on for dessert. Said something cryptic about Sherry not being the first, that I'd heard Michael was Olympus's secret weapon, that somebody really should do something about him. They would have swarmed like vultures, with Carol stepping up immediately to spearhead the Save Sherry/Kill Michael project.

But I didn't. As they picked up their forks and dug into the juicy gossip on the table before us, I just sat there like a lump and never said a word. Because the embarrassing truth was that the only thing that pierced the numbness was a blinding flash of jealousy. I couldn't believe Michael liked Sherry better than me.

My doorbell rang at 8:07 A.M. I ignored it, rolled over, pulled the covers up over my head.

At 8:10 A.M., it rang again.

"Shit," I said out loud. I kicked off the covers, yanked the hem of my T-shirt down until I was relatively decent, and stumbled

88

to my front door. I opened the door a crack but kept the chain lock fastened.

Rosie and Tess smiled up at me from my doorstep.

"Not feeling well," I said. I orchestrated a pathetic cough and started to shut the door again.

Tess grabbed the door handle from the other side. "Fever?" she asked.

I had the feeling that if I said yes, she'd whip a thermometer out of her back pocket just to be sure.

I shook my head.

"Any sign of infection?" she asked. "You know, swelling on one side of your neck or green mucus or anything?"

I shook my head again.

Tess smiled. "Okay, you're good to go. Throw your shoes on — whatever it is, the endorphins will help." She looked at her watch. "You've got three minutes."

My eyes teared up. "I just can't do it," I said. And then I slammed the door.

I spent most of the day in bed. I didn't want to think. I wanted to bury myself in sleep, remain unconscious, oblivious, pain-free. And it worked pretty well, at least for a while.

At 3:22 P.M., I had to pee so badly I

finally got up. I took a shower, because it was such a great place to cry. The water washed my tears away almost as soon as they appeared, which somehow gave the whole thing an element of control, as if shower crying was slightly less tragic than stand-alone sobs would have been.

I was eating a bowl of cereal when the doorbell rang. "Geez," I said out loud. "Not again." I took another quick bite, then dumped the rest of my cereal down the garbage disposal.

Tess and Rosie were standing on my doorstep like they'd been there all day.

"Haven't we done this once already?" I asked.

Tess pulled a piece of white rope out from the round beige pulley she was holding. "Don't make me use this on you," she said.

I smiled. Behind them I could see a wheelbarrow filled with a bunch of small plants and three shovels. I pushed my door open. "Come on in," I said. "I just have to put some shoes on."

I probably should have looked for an old pair of sneakers, but it's not like I didn't have backups. I sat on the couch to tie my Walk On Bys.

"Have a seat," I said. "Thanks," I added. Not to get goopy, but I couldn't believe they'd cared enough to come back.

Tess and Rosie stayed by the door. "No problem," Tess said. "I wasn't sure if it was serious enough to bring wine."

"Or chocolate," Rosie said. "I could run home for some."

"Wine over chocolate," Tess said. "Any day."

"Not me," Rosie said. "I'm a total chocoholic in a crisis."

"Okay, we need a tie breaker," Tess said. "Come on, Noreen, wine wins hands down, doesn't it?"

"Tough call," I said. "If you two hadn't shown up, I'd probably be dipping chocolate *in* my wine right about now."

I stood up. "Thanks," I said again.

Tess opened my front door. A flash of white cut in front of me and made a beeline for my kitchen. Three smaller blurs of brown were right behind it.

I screamed. "Are those chickens?"

"Rod Stewart!" Rosie yelled. "Sorry," she said to me in a quieter voice. "Do you have a box of cereal handy?"

I pointed to my kitchen. My hand was trembling, I noticed, and I could feel my heart pounding in my chest.

Rosie came out of my kitchen, shaking the box of Special K I'd left on my counter.

The creatures followed her like the Pied Piper across my living room and out the front door. "I'll just run them home," she yelled. "I'll be back in a second."

Tess was checking out my living room. "Great window treatments," she said.

"Were those chickens?" I asked again.

"Yup," Tess said. "The brown ones were hens, but I think Rod Stewart's probably a rooster."

"Why is he called Rod Stewart?"

Tess shrugged. "You think he looks more like Barry Manilow?"

I followed Tess out to my backyard. A ladder I'd never seen before was tilted up against the back of my house. Maybe it was all that sleeping, or maybe it was the chickens, but I was feeling a little bit like Alice after she'd fallen through the rabbit hole. Not that I would have recognized a rabbit hole if I fell through it.

"We're going to go with a retractable," Tess was saying. "That way you can get it out of the way fast if you have to. We've got sixty feet of clothesline to work with, so I think we'll put the mounting bracket right outside your kitchen window, and the hook on that tree over there. The line will run north to south, which will give your clothes maximum sunlight, so it's the perfect setup.

Electric dryers account for ten percent of home energy use. It's crazy. That *is* your kitchen window, isn't it?"

I nodded. "Thanks for doing this. I really appreciate it."

"A deal for me," Tess said. "It only cost nineteen ninety-five, plus tax."

"Don't forget labor," I said.

"Speaking of which," Tess said. She adjusted the angle of the ladder. "Hold this for me, okay? Unless you want to go up."

"No thanks," I said.

I was so focused on holding the ladder tight I didn't see Rosie come back with the wheelbarrow. Behind me, a shovel hit the ground with a thud.

I jumped.

"Whoa," Tess said. "I'd like to live through this clothesline installation."

Rosie put her hands next to mine on the ladder to help me hold it steady. We tilted our heads up to watch Tess juggle a screwdriver, some screws, and a mounting bracket above us.

"Sorry about that," Rosie said. "I don't think they liked their manure leaving the yard without them. But now that they know where you keep your cereal, just be careful when you leave your door open. You know, when you're bringing in groceries, that sort of thing."

"Are you serious?"

Rosie shrugged. "They'll do anything for breakfast cereal. If it happens again, just shake a box, and they'll follow you anywhere."

Like I didn't have enough to worry about without adding fear of chicken invasions to the list. Maybe I'd just put my house on the market.

"Do they have a brand preference?" It seemed like something I should know.

"Well, Rod's not too fussy, but the hens prefer Kashi Good Friends, though they just did a number on your Special K, so maybe it's a new favorite. By the way, the hens kind of stick together, so we call them the Supremes."

"Oh, that's perfect," I said. "They're so cute." I wasn't sure I believed that, but I thought I'd try it on for size.

"Sometimes they're cute," Rosie said. "As long as nobody messes with them. They had a bad rooster before Rod, and they ganged up on him and killed him."

"What did he do?" I whispered. I was back in my house-on-the-market zone again.

Rosie shifted her hands on the ladder. "Besides fertilizing the eggs, a rooster's job is to scout for danger, to keep the hens safe from predators, even to lay his own life on the line to protect them if he has to. The last rooster just didn't really give a shit about them. And hens don't take disloyalty lightly."

"Wow," I said. "That's so impressive."

"Yeah," Rosie said. "You can learn a lot from chickens."

Tess started making her way down the ladder, pulling a lengthening white cord with her.

"Okay," she said. "Now we just attach a screw hook to the tree, loop this doohickey at the end of the clothesline over the hook, and you'll be officially breaking the law. If you need to get it down in a hurry, just unhook it from the tree, and it will retract automatically. You'll have to reach out from your kitchen window to feed the line down to someone on the ground, or borrow my ladder, to set it up again, but there's really no way around that."

As soon as the clothesline was attached to the tree, we carried the ladder back to Tess's house and moved on to the garden.

Rosie pushed my box of Special K out of the way and picked up a shovel. "So," she said. "I'm envisioning an informal lavender patch. I brought starter plants in three varieties — Grosso, Hidcote, and Munstead —

to give you a good mix of color, form, and height. You can add to it once we see which kinds do best in your yard, and also which ones you like the most. Sound okay to you?"

"Sure, whatever you think," I said.

Tess picked up a shovel, so I did, too. We started turning over the soil in an area in front of some bushes that Rosie said would give the plants winter protection from the wind as well as good southern exposure. I'd never once thought of my house in terms of direction, and suddenly I had both a clothesline and a garden facing south.

Rosie stopped digging and leaned on her shovel. "The trick to taking care of lavender is not to overlove it."

"The trick to taking care of anything is not to overlove it," Tess said.

I had a sudden urge to write that down.

"So true," Rosie said. "Anyway, lavender doesn't like a rich soil, so we're going to go really easy on the chicken manure. Drainage is key, which means we'll build up the bed and add sand, plus throw in some time-released lime to make the soil more alkaline."

"How do you know so much?" I asked.

"How do you know so much about shoes?" Rosie asked.

I dug my shovel in, and it barely made a

dent in the packed soil. "Occupational hazard, I guess."

Rosie jumped on her shovel with both feet. "Well, mine is more an accident of birth. You grow up on a lavender farm, you learn more than you ever want to."

"Wait," Tess said. "I don't get it. I thought you were the new owner."

"I am. Well, I guess I'm the new old owner. My mother died, my father couldn't keep up with things, so I was the dutiful daughter who stepped up. And dragged my family kicking and screaming with me."

I wondered what I would have done if my mother had wanted me to move in after my father died. I wondered what it meant that she hadn't.

Rosie stopped shoveling long enough to push some red curls out of her face. "It's the last place I would have pictured myself at this point in my life, but what could I do?"

Tess and I nodded sympathetically.

"My husband is a contractor, and I do his landscape design, plus my own jobs, and the kids didn't have to switch schools, so it was all doable, but . . ."

"But that doesn't make it easy," Tess said.

Rosie dug the shovel in again. "My parents were inseparable, and even when my mother started slipping into dementia, it was all about lavender for her. She stopped cleaning the house, and one day when my husband and I brought the kids to visit, we found she'd painted everything purple so the dirt wouldn't show. The walls and the refrigerator, inside and out. Even the toilet seat. The paint wasn't quite dry on that, and we all had purple rings around our butts for the next two weeks."

"Oh, your poor father," Tess said. "How's he doing now?"

The garden was taking on a nice shape, kind of like a paisley at the edge of my yard. Tess started pulling clumps of grass and weeds out and shaking the dirt off them.

"He's doing okay," Rosie said. "We moved him downstairs to the family room and put in a bathroom just for him. We had a family party to celebrate, and he spent the whole time giving bathroom tours."

"Well, that's good," Tess said.

Rosie nodded. "It's tough though. We had to think ahead. So we had them put a grab bar next to the toilet. We told him it's a towel rack, so he wouldn't get upset. They put in a thirty-six-inch doorway, big enough for a wheelchair, and he said, *What in tarnation is that barn door for?* So my husband said it was because they were out of small doors."

"Good thinking," I said.

Rosie leaned on the handle of her shovel again. "We put in a double shower, too. We told him it's in case he has company." She smiled. "I think he liked that one."

After Tess and Rosie left, for the first time in a long time, I picked up the phone and called my mother, instead of waiting for her to call me on Sunday.

DAY 12:
10,001 STEPS

Rosie and Tess were standing in my driveway when I pushed my front door open.

"Wait," I said. I unlocked my car with a click and grabbed the shoes I'd exchanged for Rosie, plus the two purple pedometers. I'd completely forgotten about them yesterday.

"Genius," Tess said. "Pedometers are all a little bit different, so this way we'll be on the same page with our mileage. Let me run back to my house and grab my reading glasses so I can set it. Unless one of you still has decent eyes?"

Rosie and I shook our heads. The thing I minded the most about getting older was that I no longer had twenty-twenty vision. It had hit me like a ton of bricks one night right after I turned forty. I was sitting in a restaurant with a date, and suddenly I couldn't quite read the menu. *What's good?* I remembered asking the waiter.

100

Rosie was holding her pedometer in one hand, stretching her arm as far away from her as it would go and squinting.

"Do you want me to go inside and grab some reading glasses for you?" I asked.

"No, I think I've got it," she said. She pushed a button and hooked the pedometer onto the waistband of her shorts. "I'll just do the step mode for now and figure out the mile mode later." She sat down on my driveway and began taking off her old sneakers. "Boyohboy, could I use some new sneakers."

I opened the shoe box, handed one sneaker to Rosie, and started lacing up the other one for her.

"Great, they're just like yours and Tess's," Rosie said. "We'll look like triplets. Oh, this feels amazing."

"State-of-the-art technology scientifically activates your posture," I said. "Excellent flexibility plus a good measure of stability makes for a stellar heel-to-toe transition. Double-patented gel pad in heel, as well as a triple-patented air-cushioned arch support."

"Wow," Rosie said.

"The Walk On By," I finished, "the shoe every woman needs to walk herself away from the things that are holding her back and toward the next exciting phase of her life."

I took a bow and handed Rosie the shoe I'd finished lacing.

"Thanks. I know it's spin, but I still like it. Did you make it up yourself?"

"Some of it, I think," I said. "It's hard to even remember anymore."

Tess's screen door slammed. We heard it click as she opened it again. "Well, try getting home at a decent hour and you'd be awake by now!" she yelled. She slammed the door again and jogged over to us.

"Your husband?" Rosie asked.

"Funny," Tess said. "Okay, where the hell did I put my glasses?"

I pointed. They were hooked on the front of her T-shirt.

"Thanks," she said. She tucked the rolled-up chart she was carrying under her arm and put on a pair of black reading glasses edged in pink. "Ohmigod, I just remembered," she said. "At the last primary, my husband and I both forgot our reading glasses when we went in to vote. I kept thinking we could be voting for anybody."

There was a beat of silence, and then Rosie said, "How can they clone sheep and not have an operation to do away with reading glasses?"

I breathed a little sigh of relief. For a minute there, I'd thought we were going to talk politics. There's nothing worse than thinking you have so much in common with someone, and suddenly she opens her mouth and you find out she's on the board of directors of a religious cult, or still smokes cigarettes, or vomits after every meal. I didn't care what Tess and Rosie believed in, politically, spiritually, or nutritionally. I wanted to like them. I wanted to walk.

"There's some new kind of lens implant," Tess said. "But I'm going to wait till they work out the kinks first." She unrolled the chart. "Okay, this is one of the mileage maps we use at school. Continental United States, with a decent map scale. There are also a couple of Web sites we can use to track mileage online, but I think we should hang this up somewhere for visual impact — and motivation."

I pointed to my garage. "Plenty of room," I said. "I only have one car, so we can take over half of it and make it Command Central. Or we can use a room in the house if you'd rather."

"No, the garage is perfect." Tess looked up. Her glasses made her look like some kind of tropical bird. "Okay, let's synchronize our pedometers, set the ground rules, and start today."

A thought came over me with such force that I was surprised my head didn't light up like a bulb. "Oh, oh," I said. "I think I've got the perfect idea to get our mileage up where we need it to be so we can go someplace good."

"Great," Tess said. "But come on, I'd kind of like to walk today."

"Here, give me that," I said. I took the map and tucked it inside my garage door.

Tess held up her pedometer. "Ready," she said. "One, two, three, and push." We all pushed the reset buttons on our purple pedometers at the exact same instant.

I waited till we were out on Wildwater Way before I sprang it on them. "Okay," I said. "Get this. We're allowed to use our frequent flier miles."

"What do you mean?" Rosie asked.

"What I mean," I said, "is that we can add our frequent flier miles to the miles we actually walk to bring up the total miles we can travel."

Rosie and Tess stopped walking. "That's brilliant," Tess said. "Absolutely brilliant. I've racked up tons of frequent flier miles with my airline credit card. It's such a pain in the neck to use them, I never get around to it."

"I have a bunch stockpiled, too," Rosie said. "We can go anywhere we want to go."

I hadn't felt this good in ages. I turned right at the corner and started race-walking ahead of them.

"Hurry up," I said. "The sky's the limit."

I was late getting to the Fresh Horizons South small-group meeting. After we'd finished walking, I'd jumped in the shower, put on a nice pair of jeans and a crisp white blouse, and spent some time doing my hair and makeup before I lost those skills, too. I wanted to look more casual than I had at the last meeting, but I also wanted to look good in case one of the more-shabby-than-chic guys started to grow on me. You never know.

I couldn't resist hanging up my wet towels on my new clothesline before I left. Later, I'd wash a load of laundry, maybe the first one I'd looked forward to in my entire life. Tess had been kind enough to throw in a little basket of wooden clothespins that hooked right over the line.

After clothesline duty, I headed over to check on my lavender patch. I ran back into the house and grabbed a coffee cup and used the outdoor spigot to fill it with water. I gave the plants, each neatly labeled by Rosie with a little metal sign that poked into the ground, just a touch of water down by their roots. I made sure I didn't get water on their foliage, because Rosie said it might cause mold.

Her further instructions had been to keep them damp for the first few days while they adjusted to their new home, but after that, to let them dry out completely between waterings. They liked lots of sunshine but didn't need much in terms of food or water. It sounded like a great way to live.

So far my favorite lavender was Grosso. When I stroked its foliage to release its fragrance the way Rosie had shown me, it didn't have quite the sweet smell of the shorter, feistier Munstead. Grosso's scent was stronger, with almost a hint of camphor. I liked its long, brave, pointy stems and the way the whole plant stretched gracefully and unapologetically, not afraid to take its full space in the world.

I parked my car in front of the former elementary school and half-ran, half-skipped down the hallway between the rows of kiddie-size lockers. Since we'd decided all our extra pedometer mileage would count, too, maybe I'd stay after the meeting and do some laps around the school. It was incredible how just having a reason to put one foot in front of the other had lifted my mood. I could almost imagine that someday I'd have a full life again.

"Time management is one of the first things to slide," Brock, the cute little career coach, was saying as I tiptoed into the room.

"Case in point," one of the guys said. Everybody looked up at me, and he patted the chair next to him.

"Wardrobe's next to go," another guy said. Unless all his T-shirts were gray and had holes in the armpits, he was wearing the same one as last time. "One week you're in a suit, and the next thing you know . . ." He looked me up and down, then shook his head.

It felt amazingly like being in high school. The cute, or at least the scruffily cute, guys were finally talking to me, and I couldn't think of a thing to say. I grabbed an empty chair at one end of the semicircle and sat down.

I must have been really late, since Brock had the video camera set up already. I tried to take up as little space as possible on my chair, so he wouldn't call on me.

He looked right at me. "We'll start with you."

"But . . . ," I said.

"Come on, what's your story, morning glory?" one of the guys said.

Brock gave his hands a little clap. "That's it. Exactly. Tell us your story, Gloria."

The class started to snicker. It was kind of hard to know where to go from there. Should I start by giving my real name, and if so, should I go for Nora, or just resign myself to Noreen? Or maybe we only had to start with an introduction the first time we embarrassed ourselves in front of the camera.

"Come on, we don't have all day here," a woman with blond hair and graying roots a mile long said. "Oh wait, we do."

Everybody cracked up. I waited, hoping they'd forget about me and go on to someone else.

"Laugh if you will," Brock said. "But your ability to tell the world who you are is the first step to figuring out what you want your life to be."

He pushed a button on the video camera. He lifted one hand over his head and brought it down like the clapper on a movie set. "Go," he said.

"Me?" I said.

"Good try," one of the guys said.

I looked at the camera and tried to smile.

"Okay, I'm Noreen Kelly, but I think I'd like to be Nora. I have absolutely no idea who I am since I stopped working, or how I got to be my age knowing as little about the world outside the office as I do, but I'd really like to think there's still hope for me."

"Cut," Brock said.

"Sorry," I said. "Did I do it wrong?"

Brock was too busy attaching the camera to a monitor with a cord to answer.

"If you're going to play that or anything, would it be okay if I left the room?" I asked.

Brock pushed a button on the monitor, and suddenly there I was, looking like a Looney Tunes character who wanted to run but couldn't, since her knees had turned to jelly and she'd just found out her feet were nailed to the floor. For a long moment nothing happened, then one side of my mouth turned up in a sickly smile.

"Oh, God," I said. I buried my face in my hands and peeked out between my fingers.

On the screen, I started flapping my hands around like an idiot and talking really fast. I seemed to be saying something about *havingabsolutelynoideawholam.*

It was so bad, nobody even made a crack. We all just sat there in silence while Brock disconnected the cable from the camera.

"So," Brock said. "Tell us what you're

thinking."

I scrunched my eyes closed. "Who the hell was that?"

"Exactly," Brock said. "So think about it for next time and we'll try again. In the meantime, if you don't have a video camera at home, you might try putting your one-page story in writing. A first step on the way to creating a life script, if you will."

I faded in and out while the rest of the class took their turns, but I saw enough to know I was definitely the worst.

As soon as the session was over, I made a beeline for the door.

"Yo, Gloria," a male voice said behind me.

I kept walking.

An arm came around my shoulder, and I tried to shrug it off. It stuck, so I stopped walking and ducked out from under it.

"Hey, nice move," another male voice said. "Maybe you should consider a career in the martial arts."

There was an unemployed guy in front of me and an unemployed guy behind me, so I wasn't quite sure which way to turn. I decided to hold my ground. I crossed my arms over my chest and just stood there.

The woman with the messy hair I'd sat next to last time walked up beside me. "Don't worry," she said, "what they're lack-

110

ing in maturity they make up for in age."

"Okay, truce, Janie," one of the guys said. He turned to me. He had dark hair and stubble and deep-set dark eyes, and up close he smelled really good. "She's just upset because she wanted to go out with me, and I said I didn't want a casual fling — I was saving myself for someone special. By the way, my name is Mark."

"Ignore him," the other guy said. He held out his hand. He had cat green eyes and lighter hair and stubble, and he smelled pretty damn good, too. "I don't think we've officially met. My name is Rick."

"But he's thinking about changing it to Dick," the other guy said.

I let go and started walking away again. Fast.

Janie caught up to me first. She matched her stride to mine. "Don't let them get to you," she said. "Call yourself whatever you want. It's actually a great time to make a name change."

"Thanks," I said.

"Hey, where are you going?" one of the guys yelled behind us. "We need two more players for a Wii doubles tennis match. We played singles last week and it was way too strenuous."

Janie and I walked out to the parking lot

together, completely ignoring the scruffy guys.

When I pulled into my driveway, Tess's daughter was sitting cross-legged at the edge of her lawn. I stopped my car down by the road and got out.

"Hi," I said. "I'm Noreen. I don't think we've ever met."

"Hannah," she said. Even sullen, she was pretty. She had blond hair and pale blue eyes, plus that long-limbed, effortless teenage beauty you only appreciate decades later when you look back at it in old photos.

"Aren't you getting eaten alive out here? I mean, do you want to come in or something?"

"Can't. I'm not allowed to leave the property."

I sat down next to her and crossed my legs, too. "How come?"

"I stayed out a little late, like that's a big deal." She rolled her eyes. "Grounded."

"How long?"

"The rest of my life?"

I laughed. "Don't worry. I know your mother. She'll cave before you're thirty."

"Ha." Hannah sighed. "It's so unfair. It's my last summer before college. I'm *supposed* to go out."

"Do you want me to talk to her?" popped out of my mouth.

"You'd do that?"

"Sure," I said. "Why not?"

"Sweet," Hannah said.

Day 13:
13,555 STEPS

Tess rolled an old red wagon filled with handheld weights over to my garage. We taped up the strength-training poster that had come with them on the wall next to our mileage map.

"Are you sure nobody at your house is using them?" I asked.

"Oh, please," Tess said. "Do you want the treadmill and rowing machine, too? Talk about overpriced clothes hangers. I've also got a butt buster, a tummy toner, and a thigh thing, and somewhere up in the attic I still even have one of those vibrating exercise belts, plus one of those wooden roller machines you sit on to break up the cellulite. Maybe you could dust them all off and open up a garage gym."

"Thanks," I said, "but I think this is probably plenty. By the way, I met Hannah yesterday. She's adorable. Wow, it really brings it all back, doesn't it? Remember that

114

last summer before you went away to college, how important it was to spend every minute going out with your old friends, before you all went your separate ways?"

Tess put her hands on her hips. "Don't tell me she got to you already. I thought you were smarter than that."

"Morning," Rosie said. "Hey, I've got some extra exercise mats I could bring over." She held up a handful of tangled pale purple shoelaces. "This is all I brought today."

"Aww," I said. "Lavender laces. Where did you find them?"

"My mother must have dyed them," Rosie said. "I was going through the junk drawer yesterday, and there they were." She wiggled a shoelace free and handed it to me.

Tess was already on the floor, unlacing her sneakers.

As soon as we'd replaced our laces, we headed for the street.

"Nobody'll miss us, that's for sure," Tess said. "Maybe we should have calling cards made. You know, The Lavender Ladies."

"Or The Lavender Lace Ladies," Rosie said. "It sounds like a Victorian sewing circle."

"Can't wait to pass those cards around," I said. "I'm sure they'll do wonders for my social life."

Rosie stepped up ahead of us on the side-walk.

"If we have to have a name," I said, "I think we should be The Wildwater Way Women. It sounds more adventurous."

"Or even The Wildwater Walking Club," Tess said. "It's still adventurous, but it's got a nice official ring to it."

Rosie turned around. "I don't know. Doesn't that sound to you like we should be walking *on* the water?"

"Not necessarily," Tess said. "And I don't think it would hurt to occasionally consider the possibility."

"Okay," Rosie said. "Done."

"And done," I said.

I raised both hands over my head. "How do we walk?" I yelled.

"Fast?" Rosie said.

"No," I said. "The Wildwater Way!"

"Cute," Tess said. "Okay, how do we do everything?"

"The Wildwater Way!" Rosie and I yelled. A car drove by and beeped. We all waved.

"Okay," I said. "Moving on. I looked up my frequent flier miles last night. I have tons, too, and I'm happy to share. I always meant to use them, but I could never find any flights that worked. Plus I hardly ever took my vacation time."

"Do you have a boyfriend?" Tess asked.

"Not anymore," I said.

"What happened?" Rosie asked.

I shrugged. "Who knows."

"I'd like to be single again on a part-time basis," Tess said. "Nothing personal against my husband, at least most of the time. I'd just like to divide my time between being married and single, you know, like maybe have two houses and each be in the same one sometimes and in different ones the rest of the time."

"I get that," Rosie said. "Then when you saw each other, you'd actually see each other."

"Yeah," Tess said. "The scheduling might get complicated though. And by the time you paid the bills on two houses, it's not like you'd have any money left for dates."

I didn't have any hard data on it, but it seemed to me that married women always pretended to be more bored in their marriages than they actually were in front of their single friends, and in return, single women acted a little bit happier about being single than they were really feeling. I mean, all things being equal, who wouldn't prefer having somebody to be occasionally bored with? Not that things were ever equal.

I caught myself before I sighed out loud.

"So what I was thinking," I said, "was that we should go to Provence and see the lavender fields."

Rosie dropped back beside me. "Wow, give her a few lavender plants, and she turns into an addict."

"I think it would be such a fabulous trip," I said. "You should see the photos. Rolling hills cloaked in lavender, charming little villages, mountains of great food and wine. And you can even take cooking classes on some of the tours. My mouth was watering looking at the food pictures. The lavender chicken kabobs looked amazing. I wonder how they make them."

"It's so easy," Rosie said. "You just add some culinary quality lavender buds to an oil-and-vinegar-based marinade. The Munstead I gave you is perfect — it's a nice, sweet lavender, and it's never been treated with pesticides. Just remember — a little lavender goes a long way. Too much and it starts to taste like perfume. So sample as you go."

"Thanks," I said. "So, what about Provence?"

"Provence would be incredible," Rosie said. "I've always wanted to go."

Tess moved up in front of us on the

sidewalk but half-turned her head so we could hear her. "Can't do Europe," she said. "My passport expired. It'll take too long to get a new one, unless I pay a king's ransom for expedited service. And I won't do that, just on principle. It's such a racket."

We took a right at the end of Wildwater Way and turned toward the beach. We walked for a while in silence. It was kind of dank and dreary out, more like April than July, but I didn't mind. I'd stopped at the grocery store last night and picked up some fresh fruits and vegetables. I even pushed my carriage around the parking lot a few times before I got back in my car to rack up some more mileage. Then I'd spent my entire Friday night contentedly surfing the Internet, first checking my frequent flier miles and then looking for lavender-y places to go.

We stepped off the curb and took a left from the main drag onto the quiet little side street that was our shortcut to the beach. Tess waited for us to catch up, and we started walking three abreast on the road. We automatically synchronized the swing of our arms and the length of our strides, all except for Rosie's occasional extra hop, which was almost like a hiccup.

"You know where I'd like to go?" Tess

said. "Okay, don't make fun of me for saying this, but since I'm not tutoring this summer, I was thinking I'd like to do some kind of community service."

"You're such a do-gooder," Rosie said. "Not that that's a bad thing."

"Yeah, I know," Tess said. "I have a hard time doing things that are just for me. At the end of the school year, when I've got a fistful of teacher gift certificates in my hot little hands, I can't even spend them on myself. I always buy things for other people with them — my kids, my husband, my friends whose birthdays are coming up."

"Mine's August twenty-fourth," Rosie said.

"When did you get to be such a smart-ass?" Tess asked.

"It just takes me a while to warm up," Rosie said.

I waited for a place to jump back into the conversation. They had this easy way of talking to each other that made me feel like a third wheel, and I wasn't sure if it was them or me. Maybe they had more in common with each other than with me, maybe I was just boring, or maybe I was imagining the whole thing.

Tess finally looked over at me, possibly to make sure I was still there.

"So where do you want to go?" I asked.

"Africa would be great," she said, "except then I still have my passport issue. But we could find a literacy outreach program in this country. Or maybe go to Appalachia or somewhere and help build a house."

Nobody said anything. We walked side by side through the beach parking lot, then switched to single file to fit through the narrow opening in the seawall. The beach was fairly empty because of the weather, and each day we had a little bit more sand to walk on at this hour. I'd never really stopped to think about high tide happening later each day.

"Gee," Tess said. "Don't all jump at once."

"Well," Rosie said. "It's just that it doesn't sound like much of a vacation, that's all. I hope this doesn't sound selfish, but I was kind of thinking more like a spa or something."

"You have to admit," Tess said, "that does sound pretty selfish."

"Fine," Rosie said. "You crack the whip so my two kids get through their summer reading lists, cook for my family, and finish de-purpling my house, and I'll catch the next plane to Appalachia."

I wondered if they'd notice if I just tiptoed away.

"Fine," Tess said. "It was just a thought."

"I know," I said in my cheeriest voice. "Why don't we all Google some places we'd like to go, lavender-related and otherwise, and tomorrow while we walk, we each get to lobby for our top pick."

"Whatever," Tess said.

Rosie just shrugged.

What a difference a day makes. Or in this case a night. After sailing through Friday evening in a sea of contentment, the tide turned, and Saturday night left me feeling lost and lonely.

After we'd finished walking, I'd gone out to my garden to behead some stalks of Munstead. "You won't feel a thing," I whispered as I bent over one of my plants. I couldn't believe I'd said it out loud. I looked over my shoulder to make sure no one was out in Tess's yard. I pinched quickly. "Sorry," I mouthed.

I had to drive to the store for the rest of the ingredients. Hannah pulled into her driveway just as I was pulling out of mine.

I rolled down my window. "You got out," I said. Maybe she'd think I'd helped make it happen.

She shrugged as she drove by. "Work," she said.

As soon as I got back, I heated up the little Weber minigrill on my deck. I set a single place mat at my dining room table and lit some candles. I roasted some garlic while the chicken marinated in lavender-laced virgin olive oil and balsamic vinegar. I threaded the chicken and garlic, plus some cherry tomatoes, onto bamboo skewers, then breathed deeply as they sizzled on the grill. I microwaved a single pouch of rice.

I ate slowly, savoring the woody, almost rosemarylike flavor of the chicken. I remembered everything I'd ever read about enjoying a solo meal. Stay in the moment. Remember you're worth pampering. Chew each bite ten times. But I couldn't stop thinking this was a meal to be shared, and eating it alone was such a waste.

I took a solitary walk after my solitary dinner, adding another 302 steps to my mileage for the day. I wandered around my backyard, sad and restless, until the mosquitoes chased me inside. I pictured Tess and Rosie at home with their families, probably sitting around the dining room table, laughing and joking and having tender, fascinating conversations with their husbands and kids.

How I'd missed the husband and kid boat was a complete mystery to me. Men had been drawn to me in sufficient numbers over the years, so I knew I wasn't completely repulsive or anything. I knew how to date. I even knew how to live together. But then somehow I didn't know what to do next. Eventually, things just went flat, and the guy moved on. Or things went flat, and I'd think, hey, I'm not going to be one of those women who settle, and I'd move on. And then six months later, I'd look back and think, was that it? Was that *the guy?* Should I have tried harder to make it work? I mean, what was so fatally wrong with him?

Saturday night stretched on forever. I moved over to my couch, turned on the TV, and flipped through the channels. I picked up my cell phone from the coffee table. I looked at Michael's number on my speed dial.

"Don't do it," I said out loud.

I flipped through my cell phone address book, hoping to find an alternative. Maybe I'd find an ice cream place that delivered, and order up calories instead of humiliation. Or phone my mother again, though she'd probably have a stroke if she got two unexpected calls from me in one week.

I had to have known it wasn't a good idea, but I did it anyway. I saw Sherry's name and pushed Call.

She answered on the second ring. "No-reen?" she said. "Are you okay?"

"Yeah," I said. "Why wouldn't I be?"

"Um," she said. "Because it's ten o'clock on a Saturday night?"

"Oh, God," I said. "Is it? I totally lost track of time. I was just calling to see if you wanted to go out for a drink or something."

"Come on, I'm on the phone," Sherry said. "Michael, stop it."

I tried to hang up, but I was frozen.

"Sorry," Sherry said. "Listen, I can't right now."

"Oh," I said. "I didn't mean now. I've got a really busy day tomorrow. I'm meeting someone and, well . . . I just meant some-time. So, great." I let out a laugh that sounded fake even to me. "Why don't you call me next week, and we'll both take out our calendars?"

"Sure," Sherry said. "How about . . ."

"Perfect," I said. And then I hung up.

I stared up at my pitch-black ceiling for a very long time before I finally fell asleep. Not only had I made a thoroughly undigni-fied call to Sherry at the most ridiculous hour possible, but Michael was right there with her, and by now he knew about it. No wonder I was still single and sitting at home by myself on a Saturday night like a lonely

hearts club cliché. How could I get to be
my age and still be such a fool?

Day 14:
10,987 steps

By morning I was relatively okay again. I got up early, stuffed a load of dirty clothes into the washing machine, poured a cup of coffee, and moseyed out to check on my garden. It was amazing how little moseying I'd had time to do when I was working. Maybe now it was an art I could cultivate, along with my lavender.

My phone call last night was no big deal. Sherry might not even remember it this morning. She probably hadn't even bothered to tell Michael who'd called. Clearly, they'd had more pressing things on the agenda.

I took a sip of my coffee. So what. It's not like Michael was exactly a catch. Sherry was probably doing me a favor. But, wait, I'd completely forgotten that I should be worried about her. It seemed like too much. I mean, I could get over Michael or I could worry about Sherry, but it really wasn't fair that I should have to do both.

So then why had I called her instead of staying away? Oh, who cared. At least I hadn't called *him.*

I heard some rustling, then Rosie stepped into my backyard, carrying three folded exercise mats. The path I'd never even noticed was becoming more clearly defined now, with trampled growth leading the way from my yard into the woods. It made me feel connected to the rest of the world.

Rosie held up the mats. "If we're going to walk and do strength training, we might as well add some stretches for flexibility. I keep buying mats and forgetting where I put them, so now I have three I don't use. What a day, huh? Nice to see the sun again. I couldn't wait to get out of the house, and it's only seven fifty-nine."

"How's your dad?" I asked. I took one last gulp and put my coffee cup on my back deck, and we started walking to my garage.

"He's okay, thanks for asking. They're all okay. It's just a lot. I'm late on three landscape plans and . . . Never mind. Let's walk."

Tess was just cutting across her yard. "Brilliant idea," she yelled.

We tucked Rosie's mats inside my garage door and headed out to the street. The beach walk was becoming our regular route, so we took a right at the end of Wildwater Way without even consulting one another. I moved up ahead on the sidewalk to let Tess and Rosie walk side by side.

"Can I go first?" Tess asked. "I've got the perfect idea."

"Sure," Rosie said. "Go ahead."

It took me a moment to realize what Tess was talking about, since I'd completely forgotten to come up with more suggestions for spending our mileage.

"Okay," Tess said. "So my daughter Hannah's class adopted a third-grade classroom in New Orleans after Katrina. You know, they're supposed to be mentors, though I'm not sure my darling daughter could mentor her way out of a paper bag these days. Anyway, Hannah's class e-mails the third-graders and sends them little presents, and they also hold a yearly book and computer drive for them."

"That's great," I said.

"Yeah," Tess said. "Those New Orleans kids have gone through so much. It's been a real eye-opener for my spoiled daughter and her classmates."

"I bet," Rosie said.

"Anyway," Tess said. "I've e-mailed the New Orleans teacher a few times, you know, since we both teach third grade, and sent her some extra things. I was thinking we could visit the school, bring some journals for next year's students. Nice journals, maybe even diaries with locks, and maybe some glitter pens. The kids love those. I hear lots of those schools still have no supplies. Not that teachers up here don't spend way too much of their own money, but still, it's got to be really tough in New Orleans."

"Didn't we have this conversation yesterday?" Rosie said.

"No," Tess said. "That was a completely different conversation."

"I give to everybody else all day long," Rosie said. "If I'm going to take a trip, I want it to be one hundred percent selfish. Besides, I think Noreen has her heart set on going somewhere with lavender. New Orleans doesn't really have the right climate. Too humid."

"Hey, don't throw me under the bus," I said. "I'm open."

"I'm not sure I can go anywhere anyway," Rosie said as she stepped up beside me. I dropped back next to Tess. It took us just a few paces to synchronize our steps again.

"It's just . . . ," Rosie finally said. "I'm lucky I can find the time to get out and walk every day. It's such a busy season for me. I could do a day trip maybe, but that's about it. Cape Cod Lavender Farm is great, and it's right in Harwich. They've developed a new variety of lavender I've been dying to see. It's a Hidcote called Harwich Blue, very dark, and it should be in bloom now. I'd like to buy plants to use in some installations anyway."

Tess looked over at me and rolled her eyes. "Are you kidding?" she said. "You want to squander our hard-earned miles on a trip to Cape Cod? I mean, we could probably walk there for real in a day or two. And I'm not supposed to be a do-gooder, but it's okay for you to drag us along on a work-related lavender-buying trip?"

We turned onto our side street shortcut, and Tess and I stepped up on either side of Rosie. "Geez," Rosie said. "Tell me what you really mean, Tess."

Tess put her arm around Rosie. "Sorry," she said. "It just doesn't sound like enough of a trip to me, that's all."

I don't know exactly how it happened, but I opened my mouth and somehow I started channeling my Fresh Horizons certified small-group career coach, Brock. I turned to Tess first. "You might consider thinking it through again," I said, "and taking some time to consider how that choice reflects who you want Tess to be as you move forward into the next chapter of your life. It's important to give to others, but you also have to learn to nurture yourself."

Then I turned to Rosie. "And if anybody needs a vacation, you do. So, take it. The work will still be there when you get back." I shook my head. "Boyohboy, when I think back on all the fun I missed out on because of work."

Rosie and Tess were both staring at me. "Whoa," Tess said. "When did you get to be so smart?"

I was standing in my kitchen, drinking a big glass of water and wondering if it was too early to go to bed, when my phone rang. I jumped. Water dribbled down my chin and onto my T-shirt. I wiped my mouth with my T-shirt, since it was wet anyway, and checked out my stomach as I walked over to my phone. I'd been doing crunches every morning when I woke up and again after dinner. It might have been my imagination, but I thought my abs were possibly looking a little bit tighter already.

I was also using Tess's weights to do one set of eight to twelve repetitions for each of my major muscle groups every other day, plus daily stretches on one of Rosie's mats every day after we finished walking. Some days Tess and Rosie joined me, and some days they didn't. The buddy system was nice, but I was fine either way.

My mother's number stared out from my caller ID. "Hi, Mom," I said. "Happy Sunday."

"I don't know what's so happy about it," my mother said. "Just wait, every day's the same once you retire."

"How's the weather down there, Mom?" I asked.

"Who knows with all this air-conditioning," my mother said. "Your sister and her family rented a house on Nantucket for the whole month of July. That doesn't come cheap."

"That's great," I said.

"Little Jimmy's kids haven't missed a day of work yet. They get themselves up and make breakfast on their own, too."

"That's great, Mom."

"Kevin's wife had her first checkup. No sign of twins yet, but she passed everything else with flying colors."

"Great." I gritted my teeth and got ready for my turn.

"So," my mother said. "Any wedding bells yet?"

"Not yet."

"Well, your sister's flying me up for a visit tomorrow. I don't know why I can't go when they're at their regular house. At least I know my way around the guest room. You could come visit them on Nantucket, too, while I'm there. And bring that boyfriend of yours. At least I'd finally get to meet him."

"Sure, Mom," I said. "As long as I can get the time off work. We've been crazy busy lately."

After I hung up with my mother, I made a mug of tea and sat down at my computer. I Googled *lavender.* Even ruling out Provence and anywhere else we needed a passport to get to, I found a bunch of great possibilities for our trip. I read article after article, making a list as I went and rating each choice on a scale of one to five.

I traded my empty tea mug for a bottle of water. A couple hours later, I looked down at my list. Only one was rated five. I took some notes, saved a Web site to my favorites, and prepared my pitch for Tess and Rosie. I couldn't wait to tell them about it.

Before I went to bed, I found a handkerchief I'd bought years ago, when my sister had dragged me along antiquing with her. It was made of thin white cotton, delicately threadbare, and it had an elaborate *N* embroidered in one corner, which was why it had caught my eye in the first place. I'd taken it home, washed it, tucked it into a drawer, and forgotten all about it.

I folded it in half and stitched the long side and one of the two shorter sides closed. I made careful stitches — maybe not Victorian sewing-circle stitches, but they weren't bad.

I had a mushy habit of saving the rose petals from bouquets I'd received over the years, so I raided the ceramic bowl I kept them in and added some lavender from my garden. I also pinched some leaves off the potted mint plant on my deck, and took a minute to breathe as the scents mingled with the cool night air. I mixed them all together and added drops from a little bottle of lavender oil Rosie had given me. I had to substitute an ancient bottle of peppermint extract for the peppermint oil, but at least it still had its smell.

I filled my dream pillow and stitched up the remaining side. Then I crawled into bed, placed it over my eyes, and waited for my dreams to begin.

Lavender Dream Pillow

1/2 cup lavender buds
1/2 cup rose petals
1/3 cup crushed mint leaves
3 drops peppermint oil
6 drops lavender essential oil

Mix all ingredients and fill 6-by-12-inch rectangular pillow. Place over your eyes to encourage a restful, rejuvenating sleep, and to make all your dreams come true.

Day 15:
13,001 steps

"Okay," Rosie said. "Well, there's Sleepy Bee Lavender in Connecticut and Daybreak Farm in Ohio, plus Peaceful Valley Lavender Farm in Pennsylvania."

Tess blew out a puff of air. "When exactly did this turn into a lavender expedition?"

"Wait," Rosie said. "I'm not finished. Those are all great choices, but my final vote goes to, drum roll, the Five Sisters of Lavender Lane. They're up in Canada, in Kelly's Cross on Prince Edward Island. It's such a great story. Five sisters who'd led really varied lives — I'm remembering clinical social worker, bank manager, artist, legal secretary, and maybe an antiques dealer. Anyway, their parents were from PEI, and in their sixties the sisters got together and took over the family property and started a lavender farm called the Five Sisters of Lavender Lane."

"That's actually pretty cool," Tess said.

137

"Maybe we should drop the Wildwater Walking Club thing and start calling ourselves the Three Sisters of Lavender Lane. Or we could get them to adopt us, and we could all be the Eight Sisters of Lavender Lane."

"I was just getting attached to The Wildwater Walking Club," Rosie said. She stopped and tilted her head forward and fluffed up her damp red curls like she was tossing a salad.

"You know," Tess said, "it's really interesting if you stop to think about it. There could be women on Wildwater Ways all over the place leading parallel lives. We could start an online community, maybe do virtual walks from one Wildwater Way to another. Oh, wait, get this, we reach out to everybody who lives on a Wildwater Way, and we get to use their mileage, too. I might have to pull in a world map for this, but don't worry, I know where I can order one."

I'd waited long enough. "Okay," I said in my best Fresh Horizons voice. "This is where groups start to fall apart. We're losing our focus. We can do all those things and more down the road if we want to, but for now, we'll have plenty of mileage as long as we use our frequent flier miles, so we need to think about one trip for three people and not go off on other tangents."

We walked through the seawall. It was dead low tide, or at least pretty close to it, so the water was anything but wild. But the good news was that meant all the best hard-packed walking sand was available. If I were still at Balancing Act, maybe I'd pitch a sneaker for beach walking. Little shields that kept the sand out of your sneakers when you walked through the dry, fluffy sand at the top of the beach? Or maybe tiny holes in the soles that let the sand drain back out, although there'd have to be a way to keep the holes from letting water in.

Or maybe I'd come up with a sneaker to make you feel like you were walking the beach when you weren't. Maybe instead of a gel insert for cushioning, it could have a sand-filled insole.

"Don't stop now," Tess said.

Rosie took a little skip in the sand to catch up to us. "Yeah, come on, you're doing great, Noreen."

"Thanks," I said. "Okay, Prince Edward Island would be a nice trip this time of year, especially if we took the ferry from Portland, and I'd love to meet the five sisters. But you need a passport to get into Canada now."

"You know where I stand on that," Tess said.

139

"Anyway, I think I have something even better." I took a deep breath and let it out. "The Sequim Lavender Festival."

"What's a *squim?*" Tess asked.

"It's a town in Washington state," Rosie said. "It looks like it should be sea-quim, but it's pronounced *squim.* You know, that's not a bad idea. It's the lavender capital of North America. I hear that festival is fabulous."

I'd learned a long time ago in team meetings that conviction could be contagious, so I made my voice sound really excited. "It's the perfect trip for us," I said, "and I know we'd have a blast. It's the third weekend in July, so the timing would work. I think we'll have enough frequent flier miles to get all of us to and from Seattle, even though it'll probably take double what it would if we'd booked our flights earlier."

"I hate that," Tess said. "It's such a rip-off. Especially to go to a place called Squid. They should at least change it to Calamari."

"*Squim,*" I said. "It means 'quiet waters.' "

"Ooh, sounds like a good time," Tess said.

"Wildwater meets quiet water," Rosie said. "I like it."

"We can rent a car and drive from the Seattle airport." I looked at Rosie. "You'll have a couple weeks to get caught up on everything." I turned to Tess. "And it'll still be a while before the school year starts. And it's really just a long weekend, so we won't be gone for long."

Neither of them said anything, so I kept talking. "Thirty-five thousand people from all over the world attend the festival, and eight separate lavender farms participate. Buses take you around to tour them all, so we don't even have to drive, once we get there."

"With thirty-five thousand people, you probably can't even drive," Tess said. "Plus, we should walk. That's the whole point."

I ignored her. "There are different demonstrations at each farm, everything from growing to cultivating to products made with lavender. Plus fields and fields of lavender and lots of other things like beekeeping, pottery, and craft demonstrations."

Tess pretended to snore.

"And there's a street fair going on at the same time, with a hundred and fifty different craft and lavender booths, plus music and food at both the fair and the farms." I closed my eyes for a second and tried to remember what I'd read last night. "Grilled lavender pepper sausages . . . sundried tomato lavender barbecued chicken . . . lavender lemon sorbet . . . white chocolate lavender raspberry cheesecake . . . honey lavender lemonade . . . lavender black currant champagne."

"Lavender black currant champagne?" Rosie said.

I went in for the kill. "Oh, and we can also tour six award-winning artisan wineries while we're there. It's part of the festival."

Tess stopped walking. "Wineries?" she said. "Oh, I am so there."

"It sounds perfect," Rosie said. "I can't wait."

"Okay," Tess said. "I'm almost on board. But how about we fly to New Orleans first, drop off the journals, and then continue on to Squid?"

"No way," Rosie said. "It would tack an extra day to either end, and I'm already pushing it time-wise, even without a detour. Why don't we just invite your teacher friend to meet us at the festival, and we can give her the journals there? She could probably use a break, too."

"You're completely missing the point," Tess said.

"Why don't *you* go then," Rosie said. "You can meet us in Sequim when you're finished. Noreen and I will be the two hotties at the bar drinking lavender black currant champagne."

"Thanks a lot," Tess said. She walked up ahead of us, and Rosie and I gave each other a look.

"Sorry," Rosie yelled.

Tess turned around. "You know," she said, "I'm just trying to make a difference here. My own daughter will probably never speak to me again, so I guess I thought . . ."

"Did something happen between you and Hannah?" I asked.

"I don't want to talk about it," Tess said. She turned and started walking again.

Rosie and I caught up with her. "Listen," I said. "I really think the best way to do this is to mail the journals. I'll help if you want."

Tess shook her head. "I know, I know. I'm always trying to save the world, and I really could use a weekend that's just about me. And fun."

"Exactly," came out of my mouth, exactly like I was my small-group career coach, Brock.

Tess sighed. "But after we go to Sequim, we have to do something about world peace, okay?"

I hadn't gotten around to doing my homework, so I tried to make up for it by getting to Fresh Horizons South early. I wasn't sure whether to sit in the small-group career coaching room and start writing my life story, or go into the office and try to get my hands on the career coaching DVDs. Maybe homeschooling was a better option for me. The more I tried to imagine it though, the surer I was that they'd still be sitting, unopened, on top of my DVD player a month from now, collecting dust along with my unwatched copy of *The Biggest Loser Workout.*

Since I hadn't ever actually signed up for the small-group sessions, maybe it wasn't too late to change my mind. I could just walk into the Fresh Horizons South office and register for twelve hours of private career coaching. But what if Brock turned out to be the private career coach, too, and it was essentially the same, just with more individualized embarrassment?

I stood in the hallway, surrounded once again by kiddie-size lockers, and tried to think it through. Maybe I'd just walk the cement block hallways for a while and get the rest of today's mileage in, and then go home. The deal Tess, Rosie, and I had made this morning was that, assuming we could find a hotel, we'd agree on the best flights to Seattle and book them right away while we could still get seats.

Then we'd be honor bound to walk at

least 10,000 steps a day each between now and when we left for Sequim. We were walking a little over half that on our morning walk, so we'd either have to add another loop together, or pick up the rest of the slack individually. I'd been doing pretty well for the last few days, but I wanted to make sure I didn't backslide.

"A quarter for your thoughts," a male voice said behind me.

I jumped.

"Sorry." One of the scruffy guys stepped up beside me. "I didn't mean to scare you."

"That's okay," I said. This was the guy with the lighter hair. Dick?

He held out his hand. "Rick," he said.

I shook it. He had a nice handshake, firm but not bone crushing, but also not one of those wimpy handshakes some men use with women, as if they think you're too delicate to handle a real handshake. A handshake like that is a big red flag.

"Hi," I said. "I'm . . ."

He smiled. It was a warm, friendly smile, backed up by good eye contact. And nice eyes, too, almost cat green. "I know, Noreen, but you're contemplating Nora, and Gloria's definitely not going to fly."

I switched into flirt mode, just so I wouldn't get rusty. "Impressive. Have you been taking notes or something?"

His smile got bigger. "Only the important things."

"So, what's your recommendation? You know, in the name department."

He let go of my hand and shook his head. "Boy, I don't know. I can barely decide what kind of coffee to order at Starbucks these days, not that they make it easy. I like Noreen though."

"Thanks," I said.

We just kind of looked at each other. "So," I said. "How was your après small-group coaching session tennis match?"

The smile was back. He was looking a little more put together with every smile. "I killed him," he said. "Ever play any Wii sports?"

I shook my head.

"Come on," Rick said.

We walked right past the Fresh Horizons South door. At the end of a long hallway, we stopped at a door with a sign that said SOUTH SHORE SENIOR CENTER LOUNGE.

"This can't possibly be good for my post-redundancy self-esteem," I said.

"Shh," Rick said. "I just have to make sure nobody's using it." He looked over his shoulder, then turned the doorknob carefully. He gave the door a little push and stuck his head inside the room.

"Coast is clear," he said. He reached in and flicked the light switch, then held the door open for me.

"Oh, right," I said. "Make me go first."

I tiptoed in. I was expecting card tables set up for bingo, but it was a real lounge. Padded red leather, or at least red leatherette, banquettes surrounded black button-top tables. A whole row of red recliners, with cutouts in the arms to hold drinks, no less, were lined up facing an enormous flat screen TV.

"Wow," I whispered.

"I know," Rick said. "I'm okay with getting old now. I mean, how bad can it be? Anyway, I think we're good till after lunch. I've never seen anyone in here at this hour. Meals on Wheels delivers to a café at the other end of the building, so they're all chowing down right now. And after that, they have a session in the activity room."

He walked over to a schedule on the wall and ran his finger down the list. "Well, what do you know, today's Senior Speed Dating."

"You made that up," I said.

"See for yourself." Rick walked over to a table and plugged a cord from a white rectangular boxlike thing into the TV. He placed another long thin gray thing on top of the TV. "The motion sensor," he said.

"What happens if we get caught in here?" I said.

He turned around and wrinkled his forehead. "I guess they ask us for our IDs, and when they find out we're not old enough, they kick us out. Can't be any worse than getting carded at a bar for underage drinking back in the day. Hey, maybe we can get fake senior citizen cards made. You know, I never thought about that until just this second."

"This is insane," I said.

"That's what makes it fun," he said. "Okay, ladies' choice. Tennis, boxing, golf, or bowling?"

"Bowling," I said, thinking bowling movements would be the most likely to register on my pedometer.

"Okay," Rick said. "But I have to warn you, it's totally addictive."

"I'll take my chances," I said.

He pushed a button and the huge TV screen faded to black. He browsed through several screens until a strange-looking cartoon guy appeared.

"What do you want your Mii to be?" Rick asked.

"My what?"

"Your Mii."

"I'm you?" I asked.

"No," Rick said. "Your Mii."

"That's what I said," I said.

Rick wrinkled his forehead. "Who's on first?"

I wrinkled mine. "What's on second."

We grinned at each other like idiots. It was possibly a bit premature, but I had a serious urge to kiss him.

"Okay," Rick said finally. "Moving right along. Another name for a Mii is an avatar. It's your virtual you — your designated bowler, if you will." He pushed some buttons until he came to something called the Mii Channel, then pressed Start from Scratch. "Okay, we're going to make you a designer Mii. Which one is your face shape?"

I pointed. "Maybe that one?"

"Eyebrow shape?"

"Before or after plucking?" I said. "You know, this is getting kind of personal. Is there any way we could just skip to the bowling part?"

Rick pushed a few more buttons and six cartoon characters appeared on the screen. "Sure, we can go with the default Mii's. Which one?"

"Lower right," I said.

"Done," he said. "I'll be top middle."

He picked up two little rectangular wireless remote controls and handed one to me. "Okay, you push the A button, right there, then swing your arm back and push the B button, right there, to let the ball go. And here's a trick I wouldn't share with just anyone. Release the ball high, so it drops on the lane before rolling, making sure you don't rotate your Wiimote."

"My what?" I said. "This is crazy. It's like learning a new language."

"Wait," he said. There was a little strap attached to the remote, or apparently the Wiimote, and he stepped closer and looped it around my wrist like a bracelet, then slid a little plastic Ziploc thing back to tighten it. His hair was still damp, and I could smell his shampoo, something fresh and citrusy.

He looked up and smiled. "You can't be too careful. There've been a surprising number of accidents with these things. More than a few television screens taken out."

"I bet," I said. I felt a flicker of disappointment when he let go of my wrist.

"Go ahead," he said. "Just bowl."

I took an awkward little swing back, switched direction, and pushed the button. "Oops," I said. "Gutter ball."

"Push this arrow to change the angle," he said. "And watch your Mii's movements for

150

the timing."

I hit three pins with the second ball. I handed Rick the Wiimote. He took an athletic step forward as he swung his bowling arm back gracefully.

"Strike!" I yelled. "Ohmigod, you're amazing."

"Thanks," he said. His thick hair, pale brown with paler strands of gray, was getting shorter and lighter as it dried, but it could still have used a good cut. He pushed a clump of it off his forehead. "Here's the thing though. Anybody over the age of twelve who's a pro at Wii bowling is quite possibly not living up to his full potential."

"You and me both," I said. "Come on, hurry up so I can have another turn."

After we finished the string, we sat down in two of the red recliners to take a break. I tilted mine back until my feet popped up in front at a comfortable level. "Wow, that's a workout," I said. I was dying to check my pedometer, but I didn't want to call undue attention to my midsection.

Rick tilted his recliner back, too. "Wait till you try the tennis," he said.

"So," I said a long minute later.

He looked up at the ceiling. "Divorced, two grown kids, homeowner, nonsmoker, Virgo, buyout."

I looked up at the ceiling, too. "Single, no kids, homeowner, nonsmoker, Libra, buyout."

"Movies, Indian over Chinese, everything but anchovies, no idea what's next."

I smiled. "Long walks, Thai over Indian, plain cheese, ditto."

He turned to look at me. He really did have great eyes. I also liked the way his forehead wrinkled when he was thinking about something. "Are you sure we haven't already dated?"

"It's a possibility," I said.

"I've never been more messed up in my life," he said.

"That would be another ditto," I said.

"There you are," a voice said from the doorway. Rick closed his eyes. "Hey, Mark," he said.

The guy named Mark walked into the room, followed by two more guys from our small-group coaching class.

"I can't believe you cut class," Mark said. "Your future's at stake here. At least what's left of it." He grabbed a Wiimote off the top of the console. "Okay, we're talking doubles tennis." He looked over at me. "You can rotate in or be the ball girl. Up to you."

"Thanks," I said. "But I was just leaving."

Rick stood up when I did. He looked at

me and shrugged.

I shrugged back. "See ya," I said.

I was just about to open the door, when Rick reached past me and turned the knob. He held the door open for me and pulled it closed behind us once we were both in the hallway.

"Don't you have a tennis game?" I asked.

"Match," he said.

I dusted off my flirty look and tried it on again. "Who's a match?" I said.

He grinned. "Time will tell. Can I call you later?" he asked.

"Sure," I said.

"Can I have your number?" he asked.

"Do you have a pen?" I asked.

"No, but I have a really good memory," he said.

"We'll see," I said. I gave him my cell phone number, just so he could reach me wherever I was.

I turned and walked away. I was trying to be cool, so it was a good thing my back was to him, since I had a smile on my face the size of Texas. I could feel him watching me the whole way down the hall. I sure hoped some of those walking benefits had made their way to my butt by now.

DAY 16:
12,759 STEPS

"Hello," I said, trying to make my voice kind of low and sexy without being obvious. Wow, it worked. I sounded like a cross between Sophia Loren and Marilyn Monroe. I'd read about a study that found that a woman's voice was sexiest when she was fertile, so maybe I was ovulating. Or maybe I was already pregnant, and this incredible voice was my first symptom.

"Nora," a male voice croaked. "It's Michael."

I didn't say anything. I seemed to be floating on a soft, fluffy cloud of lavender, rose petals, and mint, and I took a moment to breathe it all in.

"Carleton," he added.

I still didn't say anything.

"How's it going?" He coughed a loud, messy cough. "Well, I sure hope you haven't caught this cold thing that's going around. Listen, one of the reasons I'm calling . . .

do you remember that time I was at your place and I had the same kind of deal and you gave me some kind of cough medicine? It worked great, knocked me right out. Do you remember what it was?"

I took the receiver away from my ear and looked at it. Then I put it back to my ear again.

"Yeah," I said. My voice was rich, resonant, gorgeous. "I remember."

Michael launched into another coughing fit. "Great," he said when he finished. "What's it called?"

"Drano," I said.

I sat up in bed, and my dream pillow slid down to my lap. I tossed it on top of my alarm clock. "Back to the drawing board for you," I said in a voice that was ordinary and scratchy with sleep.

I was mostly relieved to realize it had only been a dream, but I also felt an embarrassing flicker of sadness that Michael hadn't really called. I pushed it away. He was old news.

It was still early, but since I was wide awake, I got up anyway. I made a strawberry-banana-yogurt smoothie for breakfast, then went outside to check on my lavender. My little plants were in full bloom. The Grasso and Munstead flowers were predictably purple, but the Hidcote flowers turned out to be pink. Even though it was ridiculous, I felt not only proud but also somehow personally responsible.

Still high on Rick's promised phone call, I'd stopped at Home Depot on my way home yesterday and bought a cute little bright green mulching rotary mower. A guy working there tried to talk me into a sit-down mower so I didn't have to work so hard, but I told him that was the point. Mowing my lawn would really rack up some mileage on my pedometer, plus I knew how proud Tess would be of me for choosing a mower that didn't pollute the air with noise or fumes. Though come to think of it, I'd seen her husband riding around their lawn on a sit-down mower. Maybe even Tess had to pick her battles.

After I got home and unloaded the mower from my trunk, I called and left a message canceling my lawn service. Then I checked unsuccessfully for phone messages. And then I went outside to mow.

I liked mowing my lawn. The mower made a soothing *clackety-clack* sound as the blades rotated, and I fell into a rhythm right away — a long swath down to the edge of the grass, then a little swing around, and back again with just the tiniest overlap of the strip I'd just cut.

Unfortunately, mowing the lawn gave me way too much time to think about Rick, and even though I'd been trying to resist, I'd been thinking about him pretty much non-stop ever since. I liked him. On the pro side, he was fun. He was cute. We were even astrologically compatible, though I had to admit I only believed in astrology when it told me what I wanted to hear. He seemed like a nice guy, and he was definitely a good bowler.

On the con side, he was a mess. I was a mess. So the ultimate question became: Could two messes ever be equal to more than the sum of their parts?

This morning I formulated a new set of questions: Why did Rick say he was going to call unless he was going to call in a timely fashion? If he wasn't going to call right away, he should have waited until the next time he saw me to tell me he was going to call. So what exactly had Rick meant when he said he'd call me later? Clearly not later today, since today had become yesterday already. Later tomorrow, which had turned into today? Later this week? This month? This lifetime? I was too old for this stuff. I should have turned the tables and told him

I'd call him later. Let him see what it felt like.

Tess stepped around the edge of her fence to my backyard. "Morning," she said. "So, what's the scoop, did you find us a hotel?"

"Oh, shit," I said. "I'm sorry, I completely forgot."

Rosie stepped off the path and into my yard. "We're probably not going to get one within a hundred miles anyway. You know, I think we should just go next summer instead. It'll give us more time to plan."

Tess let out a gust of air. "I really hate it when people tell you they're going to do something with you, and then they back out."

"I know," I said. "I think I hate that more than anything in the whole world. I mean, why even say it in the first place if they're not going to do it?"

Rosie looked at Tess, then at me. "Why do I think we're not talking about Sequim?" she said.

"Listen," I said. "It's my fault. You two go walk, and I'll try to find a hotel by the time you get back. I can always walk later."

"No way," Tess said. "First we'll walk and then we'll find a hotel. And then we'll book our flights. Today."

"I can't today," Rosie said. "I'm lucky to

158

get out for a quick walk. I've got plans that I have to finish drawing, and the lavender fields are choking in weeds."

"And then we'll go help Rosie weed," I said.

"Speak for yourself," Tess said. "I've got weeds of my own."

It was the quietest walk we'd had so far. Our rhythm seemed off, too, as if our strides didn't quite match anymore, and we stretched out into a single file on the sidewalk, even though we didn't have to. Maybe the honeymoon was over, and pretty soon we'd take turns making up excuses why The Wildwater Walking Club wasn't walking today.

It was going to be a hot one. It was just July and it already felt like August. I wiped some sweat off my upper lip with the sleeve of my T-shirt. Maybe Rick didn't want to appear overanxious. Or maybe he was having second thoughts. Or maybe for him, later meant tomorrow, the way next summer can mean this coming summer to some people and the summer of next year to other people.

Maybe I'd just call him and tell him not to bother calling me, because I really didn't need the aggravation. I mean, I was fine with him calling me, and I was fine with him not calling me. But what I really hated was not knowing whether or not he would call, and even assuming he would, exactly when it might be. I just couldn't take it. Maybe there's a point in your life when you've simply had enough of this kind of thing.

I stepped off the curb, and Tess yanked me back by my T-shirt. A car beeped.

"What are you trying to do?" Tess said. "Get yourself killed?"

Rosie, Tess, and I leaned over my computer and searched the Internet in the bedroom I'd converted into a home office. I would have dusted things off a little if I'd known I was going to have company, but other than that, it wasn't too bad. We'd dragged a couple of my dining room chairs in for Rosie and Tess to sit on, and I'd passed out bottled water all around. I wasn't Martha Stewart, but I thought I was doing okay in the hostess department.

We scrolled past a lavender-themed lesbian Internet chat line and a lavender-named historic railway run solely by volunteers in the village of Isfield in East Sussex, England. We learned that "laid out in lavender" could mean prepared for burial, since lavender was one of the herbs traditionally used to mask the strong smell of dead bodies, or it could also mean to show something in the best possible light. We found out that Adam and Eve may or may not have taken lavender with them when they were banished from the Garden of Eden, and that long ago, women used to throw their laundry over lavender bushes so it could absorb the scent as it dried.

"Do you think I could have sea lavender in my garden?" I asked.

"Sure," Rosie said, "but it's not really lavender. It's actually statice." She took over the mouse and surfed up a picture.

Eventually we moved on to finding a hotel. Nothing. Not a single available hotel within a hundred miles of the Sequim Lavender Festival.

"Bummer," I said. "I'm really sorry. I blew it."

"I'm sure a day didn't make a bit of difference," Rosie said.

"Wouldn't you know," Tess said. "Just when I was starting to get used to the idea."

"All right," I said, "let's think for a minute." I propped my elbows up on the desk and rested my head in my hands. One of the things I'd learned at work was that there was usually a solution if you just backed up, reassessed, and then approached the problem from a slightly different angle.

It was so quiet in the room you could almost hear our brains ticking. Outside, we heard a distant *cock-a-doodle-do*.

"Oh, Rod," Rosie said, "keep it down, will you."

"I thought roosters were only supposed to crow to greet the day," Tess said.

"Try telling Rod Stewart that," Rosie said.

"I've got it," I said. "I'll print out a list of hotels and bed-and-breakfasts in the area. We'll split it three ways and just keep calling until we find one that's had a cancellation. I bet lots of people book their hotel early and then something comes up."

"Let's just go to New Orleans instead," Tess said.

"I can't," Rosie said. "I've got way too much to do without visiting teachers I don't even know. And I really think we should wait until next year to go anywhere."

"Never mind," I said. "I'll do it myself."

The minute they left, I printed out a list and curled up on the couch in my living room and started calling. Just on the off chance that today was Rick's idea of later and in case my call waiting wasn't reliable, I made sure I used my home phone and not my cell.

On the fifth call, to an all-suites hotel just

off Highway 101, I hit pay dirt. "Good afternoon," a friendly woman's voice said. "Sequim Suites, how may I help you?"

"I'm hoping you can conjure up a hotel room for my walking partners and me for the lavender festival. We have our hearts set on going and we all really, really need to get away. One of us even has a lavender farm way over here on the East Coast in Massachusetts, and I just took a buyout from my company and it's the first vacation I've had in —"

"You're not going to believe this," the woman said.

"What?" I said.

"I just had a cancellation not five minutes ago. Technically, I'm supposed to check the waiting list . . ."

"Oh, please," I said. "Please, please, please. I'll bring you a pair of sneakers. Balancing Act. The Walk On By — top of the line. What size shoe do you wear?"

I called Tess and Rosie right away, and they came back over after dinner. I poured them each a glass of white wine. "It's not lavender black currant champagne," I said.

"It'll do," Tess said.

"To hot times in Sequim," Rosie said. We clinked our glasses.

"I can't believe the woman who answered

the phone wears an eight and a half," I said. "I mean, how lucky can you get?"

"I can't believe you got us a hotel room," Rosie said. "And a suite, no less."

"No way am I sleeping on that pullout sofa," Tess said.

"We'll take turns," I said. "Come on, let's spend those frequent flier miles."

It took almost two hours, but eventually we worked our way through the online frequent flier reservation maze, and got all three of us on the same flights, both ways no less.

"What a workout," Tess said. "They sure don't make it easy. I can't believe how many miles it took. And how about that fuel surcharge — such a rip-off."

"But we did it," Rosie said. "That's the important thing. Ohmigod, how am I ever going to take that much time off?"

"Not a problem," I said. "I'll come weed for you tomorrow."

"Really?" Rosie said. "You'd do that?"

"Sure," I said. "As soon as we finish walking. And lifting and stretching."

After they left, I went into my kitchen and stared at my phone for a while. I closed my eyes and willed Rick to call. I went into the bathroom, washed my face, slathered on some moisturizer, brushed my teeth, gargled with mouthwash.

Just as I was walking to my bedroom, my cell phone rang.

"Wow, that was quick," I said out loud. I took my time walking to the phone. UN-AVAILABLE, my caller ID said, which was probably true, but I thought I should talk to him anyway. My heart took an extra beat as I reached for the phone.

"Hello," I said, trying unsuccessfully to conjure up my sexy dream voice.

"How're your windows working for you?" a rich male voice said.

I knew I should just hang up. "Okay, I guess," I said.

"Did you know that hands down the best thing you can do to increase your home value is to install tilt-to-clean vinyl replacement windows?"

I closed my eyes. "Really?" I said, just to hear him talk some more. I imagined him handsome, but not too, with kind eyes and a killer smile. I mean, everybody had to make a living, and who knew, he might make big bucks selling tilt-to-clean windows. Not that money was the most important thing.

"I kid you not. You'll pay them off in one to five years with just the energy savings alone. And that's without factoring in the sizeable tax rebates you can receive for making your home more energy efficient. And best of all, our personalized, professional estimate is free, and if you hurry you can just make the deadline on our thirty percent off special."

I'd heard stories about a woman my age at work who was paying some guy in his thirties for regular "massages" that included more than a massage. Maybe it had all started with a phone call like this.

I was lonely, but not that lonely. "Thanks anyway," I said before I hung up. "But windows are the least of my problems."

DAY 17:
10,013 STEPS

"I'll be over as soon as I change," I said to Rosie. The three of us had just finished working out, and Tess was already on her way back to her house.

"Are you sure?" Rosie asked.

"Absolutely. I've got nothing else planned for the day." Actually, I had nothing else planned for most of the rest of my life, but why go there.

"Thanks," Rosie said. "I'll meet you out in the lavender field."

I'd just replaced my sweaty, white walking T-shirt with a ripped-up old red one, and I was putting on an old pair of sneakers I didn't mind getting dirty, when my phone rang.

One shoe on and one shoe off, I hobbled into my kitchen. Sherry's name peered out from my caller ID. I wasn't sure I wanted to talk to her, but I figured I might as well get it over with, instead of worrying about whether or not to call her back.

"Hello," I said, as if I didn't already know who it was.

"Hi, Noreen, it's Sherry."

"Oh, hi, Sherry." I felt totally phony and it wasn't just about the caller ID. "How's it going?"

"Fine. I'm at work, so I have to make this quick. I was just wondering if you were planning to go to O'Malley's tonight."

I looked at my calendar. It was Wednesday again. Who knew. "I hadn't really thought about it," I said.

"Well, I was just thinking if you were already planning on going out, maybe we could skip O'Malley's and meet at Lemongrass instead. Remember the place where we had drinks and appetizers last time? Near that mall?"

It couldn't possibly be a good idea, but I also couldn't think of an easy way out. "Sure," I said. "What time?"

"Five-thirty?"

"See you then," I said.

I grabbed a handful of walnuts and pushed my back door open. Hannah was leaning against the fence that separated our properties, talking on her cell. She jumped when my door slammed.

I waved as I walked across my backyard.

"I'll call you right back," Hannah said into her phone. She clicked it off, then looked up at me. "What?"

I pointed to the path to Rosie's house. "Nothing. Just saying hi."

"It's a free country," she said. "I should be allowed to talk on my own phone."

I kept walking. "Have a nice day," I said.

Rosie was already weeding when I got to her house. An old, faded purple bandana covered most of her curls. I wondered if it had belonged to her mother.

"Wow," I said. "It's like a sea of purple around here. And I just can't get enough of the smell."

"Thanks for reminding me," Rosie said. "Sometimes I actually forget to smell the lavender. You get so used to it, you know? Here, jump right in." She pointed to a wheelbarrow. "If it's not lavender, it goes in there. The weeds are brutal this year. All that rain in June. We've got some sand down for mulch, but it doesn't do much. We can't use bark mulch — it holds in too much moisture and causes rot."

Rod Stewart strutted past us, stopping occasionally to scratch and peck at the ground. The Supremes followed him in a single file that was so perfectly spaced it looked almost choreographed. I kept waiting for them to break into the poultry version of "Stop! In the Name of Love."

"Not again," Rosie said. "Don't you dare eat my lettuce," she yelled. She lowered her voice again. "Just in case you were wondering where the expression 'fly the coop' comes from, they're amazing escape artists. Let me know if they're bothering you."

Maybe it was all that walking together, but Rosie and I fell into an easy weeding cadence, standing a few rows apart and working from left to right.

"Will the lavender still be in bloom when we get to Sequim?" I asked.

Rosie laughed. "Of course. They plan the festival around the peak of the bloom season. Theirs is a couple weeks after ours."

"So this is past peak?" I asked. I looked out over the rows and rows of bushy plants covered in spikes of flowers. Most of the flowers were some shade of purple, though a few plants had pink blooms like my Hidcote, and even white. Bees and butterflies were everywhere, as well as an occasional hummingbird, something I only remembered seeing in photos. The bees were making me a little bit nervous, but as long as I stayed out of their flight patterns, they didn't seem interested in me.

Rosie adjusted her purple bandana and

left a streak of dirt under one ear. "Yup. Enjoy it while you can. Another few weeks and the show's pretty much over, though some of the early bloomers will have a second, smaller flowering, which you can help along if you cut them back fast once the first one is over. Anyway, I should be harvesting. The best time is as soon as the blooms open."

I looked around. "It seems like such a shame to pick them."

Rosie pulled a big leafy weed, shook the dirt off the roots, then tossed it into the wheelbarrow. "Yeah, especially when I'm not really using the harvest. Most of the stuff in the shop has been sitting there for a while. I should at least change out last year's dried bouquets and check to make sure nothing has gone bad. Not that we get many customers anymore."

An older man, who looked just like Rosie, but with only a hint of red left in his yellowy white curls, came out to join us.

"Hey, Dad," Rosie said. "Noreen, this is my father, Kent Stockton. Dad, Noreen Kelly, one of the neighbors I've been walking with."

I held out my hand, and he kissed it, dirt and all. "Now, there's a nice Irish name," he said. "Can I get you two girls a sandwich?" he asked.

"Right, Dad," Rosie said. "Like you've ever made a sandwich in your life."

He grinned.

"I've got to get going anyway," I said. "I'm meeting someone for dinner."

"Wait," Rosie said. "At least let me give you a few more lavender plants. You can dig them in yourself and water them, and I'll check on them before we walk tomorrow. Just let me dump these weeds in the compost and we'll load up the wheelbarrow."

Rosie filled the wheelbarrow with lavender plants, and threw in some lavender moisturizer and a kit for making lavender scones. "Everything else is in the kit — all you have to do is add the buttermilk. Oh, and the egg. Do you want me to grab one from the Supremes?"

"I don't think so," I said.

Rosie's dad grabbed the handle of the wheelbarrow. "I'll wheel it home for you, little lady," he said. "It'll do me good to get some exercise. And that way I can wheel it right back and save you the trip."

"Thanks," I said. He was adorable, sweet, and gentlemanly. Why didn't they make men like this in my dating demographic?

"Great," Rosie said. "See you in the morning, Noreen, and thanks so much. And Dad, if you see the chickens, will you shoo them back this way?"

"Will do, my darling daughter." Rosie's dad lifted the handles of the wheelbarrow and started to sing in an old-fashioned baritone as he pushed it along. "Lavender's blue, dilly dilly. Rosemary's green. When I am king, dilly dilly. You shall be queen."

My eyes teared up. Until that moment, I'd completely forgotten my own father used to sing a version of that same song to me when I was a little, little girl. I missed him all over again.

Kent Stockton and I were almost to the end of the path when we heard the first scream.

It was a woman's scream, and it sounded like it was coming from the direction of my house.

My mother was still screaming when we found her. She was standing up on one of my dining room chairs while Rod Stewart and the Supremes circled her like covered wagons in an old western.

"Have you got some breakfast cereal handy?" Rosie's dad asked.

I was already heading for the Special K. As soon as I had the box in my hands, the chickens abandoned my mother and made

173

a beeline for me. I threw the box to Rosie's dad, who caught it and started shaking it like he'd done it a million times before.

He reached his free hand up to my mother. "Kent Stockton," he said.

"Get them out of here," my mother yelled. "Now!"

"A pleasure to meet you," Rosie's dad said. "Perhaps I can make you a sandwich later."

"Mom," I said, once my mother had finally gotten off the chair and had a little bit of time to settle down. "What are you doing here?" Even with the screaming and the chickens, the two large suitcases camped out in my front hallway had not escaped me.

My mother reached up to stroke the earrings she was wearing. They looked like turtles. Or maybe flattened armadillos. "Why aren't you at work?" she asked. "Is something wrong?"

Leave it to my mother to find a way to turn the tables. "Why did you leave my front door open?" I countered.

"I was just airing things out a little," my mother said. She was sitting on my couch, and I was across from her on a chair. "How was I to know you had livestock issues?"

"I thought you were on Nantucket," I

said. "I was just making plans to go see you." This last part wasn't quite true, but I had come as close as thinking about calling my sister to plan a visit.

"You know I don't like strange guest rooms," my mother said. "Anyone could have slept there. There was a damp smell, too."

"Mom, it's an island. It's supposed to smell wet."

"Your sister had to go home for a day anyway. Jenny broke a wire on her braces and Jason forgot something he couldn't live without. They dropped me off on the way back. I told her not to wait. Good thing I know where you hide the key."

I'd completely forgotten about Sherry. I looked at my watch. "Mom, I'm supposed to be meeting someone for dinner."

My mother sighed a long, martyred sigh. "Sure, dear, go right ahead. Far be it from me to get in the way of your love life. I'll just find something in the freezer and pop it in the microwave. I don't need much."

Sherry kept her cell on the table as we talked.

I couldn't resist nodding at it. "Waiting for a call?" I asked.

"Not really," she said. We each took a sip

of our wine.

"So," she said.

"So," I said.

"What's it really like not to be working?"

"It's great," I said. "Well, it's sort of great and sort of disorienting. Why, are you thinking of taking a buyout?"

"Maybe," she said. "Rumor has it that the VRIF won't be on the table much longer. Plus, the company's changing so much. Everybody's posturing, embellishing their job descriptions. You know, trying to make themselves look valuable so they don't get edged out by Olympus. I heard an assistant who stuffs papers into folders for meetings is now calling himself the Director of Portfolio Development."

I smiled. "That's actually fairly brilliant."

Sherry shook her head. "It just not the same there. And it's anybody's guess who'll be left at the end of the year anyway."

I nibbled at a spring roll. "I'm sure you'll make the right decision," I said.

We each took another sip of our wine.

"So," Sherry said. "Are you seeing anyone these days?"

This was a tough one. On the one hand, if she should happen to mention it to Michael, I wanted him to eat his heart out with jealousy. On the other hand, Rick hadn't exactly called yet, and just in case he never did, there was always the off chance that Michael would miss me, dump Sherry, and apologize for weeks, even months, until I finally forgave him.

"Here and there," I said. "How about you?"

Sherry leaned forward. I braced myself. "Yeah," she whispered. "But we have to keep it on the down low. He works on campus. You know . . ."

I took another gulp of my wine.

"I know, I know," Sherry said. "You never think you're going to do it, until you do it. But I don't think I'll be there much longer anyway, so it's really just a technicality. And where else do you meet anyone but the office anyway?"

A better person might have suggested Fresh Horizons small-group counseling sessions, but I just nodded. Maybe I was such an awful person I wanted to keep all the unemployed guys to myself. In a minute I'd be getting territorial with the tilt-and-clean vinyl replacement windows salesman.

Sherry sighed. "Have you ever met someone you feel like you've known forever? You know, you have all the same references from the past, and you have so much fun sharing all your old goofy stories?"

I was starting to get a sore neck from all the nodding, but I didn't know what else to do.

"Oh, God," Sherry said. "He had me in stitches the other night. When he was in high school, his hair was so wavy — he called it a tragedy of epic proportions."

Until that moment, I'd never really understood the expression about your eyes bugging out of your head, but I could feel mine doing just that.

Sherry didn't seem to notice. "He had to wash it every night before he went to bed and sleep with one of his sister's nylon stockings pulled down over his head."

"So he could get that cool surfer dude look?" slipped out of my mouth before I had time to stop it.

Sherry just nodded and reached for her wineglass. She took a quick sip and started to laugh. "He's so funny. He told me about a girl in his junior high who lost her garter belt in the hallway. He took it home and slept with it for years."

My jaw actually dropped. "He wishes," I said. "That sounds totally made up to me."

Sherry ran her fingers through her hair. She had new blond highlights, and she looked like she'd dropped a few pounds, too. "No, he's not like that at all. He's really honest, probably the most honest man I've ever met."

After I finally said good-bye to Sherry, I parked my car at the bottom of Wildwater Way and took a flashlight out of my glove compartment. I circled around my street in the dark until I reached my step quota for the day. At the moment, it seemed like the only thing I could control in this crazy, crazy world.

I was on my way back to my car, when I saw another car idling just behind mine. I froze. Maybe someone had been watching my every move, waiting until I got my mileage in before he mugged me. My heart kicked into overdrive.

Hannah came tiptoeing down the street, flip-flops in hand and her white shorts glowing under the streetlights. The car window rolled down, and music and girls' laughter spilled out.

"Shh . . . ," Hannah whispered. "Come on, you guys, my parents will completely kill me if they catch me."

I waited until they'd pulled away, then climbed into my own car. Technically, I knew I should tell Tess. But then Tess would tell Hannah I'd seen her, and I'd be right in the middle. And did I want to be responsible for Hannah missing more of her last sum-

179

mer before college? I mean, I'd done my fair share of sneaking out myself when I was Hannah's age, and I'd turned out okay.

I drove right by Tess's driveway and pulled into my own. When I let myself into my house, it was like traveling through a time tunnel. My mother was sitting on my couch waiting up for me, just like I really was back in junior high, with or without my garter belt. "Hi, Mom," I said. "I hope you found something decent to eat."

"So when am I going to get to meet that boyfriend of yours?" she said.

I froze. Here it came. First the boyfriend, or lack thereof, then the job, or lack thereof. When I finally got around to calling my sister, I was certainly going to give her a piece of my mind. I mean, nice of her to just dump my mother on my doorstep without any warning. She could at least have given me some time to get my stories straight.

"Why don't you invite him to dinner tomorrow night? I'll do the cooking. I'll give you a grocery list in the morning, unless you want me to drive you to work and keep the car."

I had half an urge to tiptoe back out and try to catch up with Hannah and her friends.

DAY 18:
12,222 STEPS

"She just showed up at the door without any warning?" Tess asked. Rosie and I had already checked on my new lavender plants, which I was thrilled to learn I'd planted correctly, and we were all walking down Wildwater Way.

"Actually, she was standing on top of one of my dining room chairs when I found her."

"My dad said Rod and the girls scared the bejesus out of her," Rosie said. She sounded just like her father when she said it. "And that she was screaming bloody murder." Rosie was up in front of us, and she turned around and started walking backward, like a student guide on a college tour. "Sorry about that. Is she okay?"

"She's fine," I said. I wondered how fine she'd be once she found out I didn't exactly have either a job or a boyfriend to invite to dinner. It crossed my mind that it might make things easier all around if I just kept walking forever.

Tess took a big leap forward and grabbed Rosie before she collided with a fire hydrant. "Thanks," Rosie said. She turned around and started walking again.

We took a right at the corner. "Well, I e-mailed her," Tess said.

"Who?" Rosie and I both said at once.

Tess unhooked her reading glasses from the front of her T-shirt and pulled a folded piece of paper from the pocket of her shorts. "The teacher from New Orleans," she said. "Who else? You know, the one who teaches the class Hannah's class adopted? Anyway, I got an auto-reply e-mail message that sent me to her blog."

I pushed aside a guilt-inducing image of Hannah driving off with her friends.

Rosie looked over her shoulder. "Do we have to get into this again? I've already told you New Orleans is out."

"It's one of those care sites," Tess said. "Listen to this." We crossed the street and took a left to our side street shortcut. Tess unfolded the paper, and Rosie and I got on either side of her, so we could look over her shoulder while she read.

Another Betty Crocker double Bake-Off yesterday. The next big dose of cancer-eating Kool-Aid will be tomorrow, and drum roll, my highly anticipated dog scan (teaching third grade causes one's sense of humor to regress, as some of you know) will take place on August 1. Say a little prayer for me that day, if you get an extra minute.

So far so good this round. Just a little tired. What keeps me going is my daily visit to my classroom, which has never looked better, especially in the summer. Each day I write a note to my students on a new date in my plan book, and then I visualize myself alive and well and reading it to a room full of little hellions. These kids know loss; Katrina was their teacher. But they don't need any more of it, so I'm trying my best, for them and for me.

I'm already up to October, picturing a cool, crisp fall in NOLA, not that we usually get one here, and me standing in my classroom, cancer free. Thanks for your messages of hope and support — they mean more than I can say.

Yours,

Annalisa Grady, aka Ms. Grady the

Great

"Stop," I said. "I can't see where I'm going." Somehow, we'd made it to the beach parking lot, and we all started wiping our eyes with the sleeves of our T-shirts.

"Geez," Rosie said. "You could have at least brought some tissues, Tess."

"Poor Ms. Grady," I said. "God, I hope she makes it."

"You can call her Annalisa," Tess said. "She's not your teacher."

Rosie sniffed. "It's a beautiful name," she said. "So melodic."

Tess folded up the paper and put it back in her pocket, and we all started to walk again.

"Bummer," I said.

"No shit," Tess said. "I must have known she needed us. Life is so unfair. She tries to make a difference in the world, and what does she get for her trouble?"

"It's really, really sad," Rosie said, "but I'm still not going."

"Fine," Tess said, "then I think we should bring her with us to Sequim. We could pool what's left of our frequent flier miles and maybe each take out an airline credit card if we don't have enough. They always give you bonus miles for that. And I bet our suite is probably plenty big enough to have a cot brought in. We'll give her a bed, of course."

"I'll sleep on the cot," Rosie said. "My

legs are the shortest."

"I don't want to be pessimistic here," Tess said, "but it could be Annalisa's last trip."

I waited till we'd made our way through the opening in the seawall and onto the beach. A perfect little family — mother, father, cute toddler girl, and cute toddler boy — were already camped out with beach chairs and coolers, the kids digging in the sand with little plastic shovels.

"Here's the thing," I said. "Even if we overlook the obvious question of why she'd want to go on vacation with three women she doesn't know, she's having radiation *and* chemo. She can't just pack up and leave."

"I'm sure they give her the weekends off," Rosie said. "It's not like she'd be gone for more than a few days."

"But she doesn't feel well," I said. "I'm sure the last thing she needs is a plane ride."

"You don't know that," Tess said. "And just to set the record straight, I *do* know her. We have an established e-mail relationship."

"Okay, invite her," I said. "Can you e-mail her through the care site?"

"I already did," Tess said.

"Good," Rosie said.

We walked the rest of the beach in silence.

When we got back out to the parking lot,

Tess stopped to tie one of her lavender laces. I watched a seagull soar through the blue, cloudless sky.

"Kind of puts your own stupid stuff in perspective, doesn't it?" Tess said.

The smell of fresh-baked lavender scones greeted me as I opened my front door. I'd almost managed to forget about my mother.

"You'd better get a move on," she yelled from the kitchen, "or you'll be late for work. And make sure you shut that door behind you. We don't want a repeat of yesterday."

I closed my eyes. I could feel a headache creeping its way across my left temple. "I took the rest of the week off," I yelled. Surely my sister would be back to get her by the weekend. Or I could drive to Hyannis and drop her off at the Nantucket ferry, or maybe even take the ride over with her and stay for a visit. Like for an hour or two. Nothing against my sister, but I just didn't really feel like talking to anyone who might possibly ask questions. At least until I got my life back on track again.

My mother poked her head out from the kitchen. "You didn't have to do that just for me, honey."

"I wanted to, Mom," I said. It was kind of true. If I had been working, and my mother had been considerate enough to warn me that she was coming, I really might have wanted to take a few days off to spend them with her.

My mother came over and gave me a little peck on the cheek. "Well, then," she said, "you can help me cook. Come sit and have a nice scone, while we decide what to make for dinner to impress that fellow of yours."

"Who?" I said.

"Oh, you," my mother said. "Such a kidder. You get that from your father, you know."

I wondered if I could track down the window sales guy who'd called, and if so, whether my mother would catch on if he spent the entire dinner trying to sell us vinyl replacement windows that tilted out for easy cleaning.

"Too bad," I said. "Wouldn't you know he's away on business all week. He'll be so sorry when I tell him."

I walked into my kitchen and peeked out the window. My mother had already discovered my clothesline. She seemed to be systematically washing the contents of both suitcases and hanging them out to dry in my yard. My mother had some surprisingly racy underwear for a woman her age, I thought. Maybe it was a Florida thing.

Even though I'd just mowed it yesterday, I was fighting the urge to mow my lawn again, just to get out of the house. I wondered if it were possible to become addicted to lawn mowing.

My mother followed me into my kitchen. "I think we'll make coq au vin anyway," she said. She popped two scones onto plates, and placed them on my little kitchen table.

I picked one up and took a bite. "Mmm. This scone is amazing. Chicken in wine, right?"

My mother filled my laundry basket with another load of wet clothes. "*Mais oui.* Your father loved coq au vin. It was our romantic dinner. We'd wait until all of you were in bed and light some candles. . . ."

"Sure," I said quickly, hoping to steer her away from an overshare. "Feed us tuna noodle casserole and save the good stuff for yourself."

"Since you've got the day off, you can do the shopping," my mother said. "Write this down."

I opened a drawer and pulled out a little pad of paper and a pen. I leaned back against the kitchen counter.

"Two small chickens, thick-sliced bacon, baby carrots, mushrooms, pearl onions, garlic, chicken broth, bay leaves, thyme, olive oil, salad greens, and a baguette. Oh, and don't forget, we'll need two nice bottles of red wine, one for us and one for the chickens."

"Don't say that too loud in this neighborhood," I said.

The doorbell rang at six o'clock on the dot. "Can you get that, honey?" my mother yelled.

Rosie's dad was standing on my doorstep, wearing a crisp, button-down shirt and holding a big bouquet of lavender.

My mother came up beside me. "Come in, come in, Kent. Aren't you the sweetest man in the world. First you rescue a damsel in distress, and now you bring her flowers."

Kent Stockton stepped into my hallway and gave my mother the bouquet.

"Am I missing something?" I asked.

My mother handed me the lavender. "Can you find a nice vase for these, honey, and give the coq au vin a little stir while you're in the kitchen? Oh, and you can get us a drink, too. Is red wine fine for you, Kent? It will complement our dinner."

"Lovely," Rosie's dad said. "Then I can compliment you while it's complementing our dinner."

"Oh, you," my mother said.

189

I stood at my stove and chugged most of a glass of red wine while I stirred the chicken with my free hand. One quick jump up on a chair and some screaming, and presto, even my mother had a boyfriend. Bearing flowers, no less. Even if they were from his poor forgotten dead wife's garden.

Nice of my mother to warn me.

I knew it was too late to suddenly remember dinner plans of my own, plus Rosie's dad was a sweet man, and I didn't want to hurt his feelings. I'd just have to get through it.

As soon as we were all seated around my dining room table, my mother held up her wineglass. "To good food and good company," she said.

"To chickens and lovely ladies," Rosie's dad said. "Thanks for inviting me, Lois."

My mother smiled. "Call me Lo," she said. Never in my life had I heard anyone call my mother anything but Lois. She was wearing a low-cut black top I'd never seen before. Who was this strange woman, and what had she done with my mother?

Rosie's dad raved about the coq au vin. It was pretty good, but the pearl onions really got on my nerves. What was the point of all those stupid little onions?

I took another gulp of wine. I poured

another glass. I started counting backward from one hundred.

"May I please be excused?" I said in a little girl's voice when I'd finished.

I was hoping for a laugh, but my mother's eyes never left Rosie's dad's. "Sure, dear," she said.

DAY 19:
10,307 STEPS

I woke up with a serious coq au vin headache, but I dragged myself out of bed anyway. I knew the only thing that would help, besides about a gallon of water, was a nice long walk. In a world full of disappointment, walking was becoming the one thing I could actually count on.

Sometimes the first half mile or so was a little bit of a struggle, but then I got caught up in the conversation, or the beautiful day, or the soothing feeling of just putting one foot in front of the other, over and over and over again. Then the endorphins, those lifesaving opiatelike chemicals, would kick in, and I'd think, wow, maybe I really can make it through another day after all.

I choked down some vitamins, two Advil, plus a smoothie, drank some more water, and headed out to my driveway. Tess was already in my garage recording her mileage on the map.

"Can you believe we've only made it to West Woohoosett?" she said. "And, yes, of course there's really a Woohoosett. It's named after the red-billed Woohoosett — you can hear those damn birds woohooing all over town."

"Did we walk through East Woohoosett on our way?" I asked.

"Absolutely. Don't you remember? It's the wildest part of town. Anyway, good thing we had those frequent flier miles, or we'd be lucky to cross the Massachusetts state line." Tess looked up. "Geez, what happened to you? Have you been out partying with my daughter?"

"No," I said. "With my mother."

Rosie stepped into the garage. "And my father," she said. "He had a great time last night, by the way."

"Are you two having parties without me?" Tess asked. "I think that could get awkward."

"Of course not," I said. Even though we'd never actually talked about it, the lines seemed pretty clear to me. We walked together and then went back to the rest of our lives. The exception was anything involving our trip to Sequim. Over the years I'd learned that instant new best friend relationships often fizzled after a short burst of too much information, too much time together. Friendships that lasted needed time and space to evolve, and it was nice when everybody just got that.

"Noreen's mother invited my father to dinner, that's all," Rosie said.

We filed out of the garage and started to walk. I moved up ahead of them on the sidewalk, hoping to give my head some time to clear. I'd had three glasses of red wine, if you didn't count what was in the coq au vin, which was one critical glass over my limit. The older I got, the less I could get away with doing that. I wasn't sure if I'd become more sensitive to alcohol or less accepting of feeling like shit. It didn't seem fair somehow. Just getting through dinner with my new mother and her date should have been suffering enough.

Rosie was a little quieter than usual today, I thought. I knew I was. Tess filled the space created by our silence. "So," she said. "I haven't heard back from Annalisa yet. Maybe she gets a lot of e-mail, or maybe she's saving her energy for her classroom. Or maybe she's off having some fun before she goes for chemo on Monday."

We crossed over to our side street. "So," Tess continued. "I started shopping for the writing journals. I mean, it's not like she's going to say she doesn't want them. And I can just buy extra, since I don't have a head count. Anyway, I found these really cute ones at a good price, fluorescent green with orange stars all over them. I thought I could hand-letter *Be the Star Ms. Grady Knows You Are* on each one."

My eyes filled up with tears. I blinked them back.

"But they weren't lined, and third graders do better with journals with lines, so I'm going to keep looking."

We walked for a while without anybody talking.

"Don't all jump in at once," Tess said. "Am I boring you or something?"

"Sorry," I said. "I'm just not feeling very talkative today."

Rosie didn't say anything.

We walked the rest of our usual route in an unusual silence. It was exactly what I needed. I tried to take in the perfectly cloudless summer sky, to enjoy the hint of coolness that would be gone in another hour or so as the sun heated up the day. My calves and thighs felt so much stronger than they'd been a couple weeks ago, and I found myself swinging my arms to intensify my workout.

"Well, that was fun," Tess said when we

were back in front of her house. "Ciao." She gave us a wave over her shoulder as she walked away.

I looked at Rosie. "Is she mad at us?"

Rosie shrugged. "She'll get over it. Every day can't be perfect."

Rosie and I went into my garage and stretched on the mats. Then I started walking Rosie back to the path, the way I always did.

Rosie stopped at my lavender patch and bent down to check the plants. Some of the little blooms were going by already. It was sad, if you thought about it, how soon the good things were over. I'd been pinching the dead flower spikes off, just like Rosie had shown me, so each plant would put its energy into becoming a stronger plant for next year, instead of trying to keep a flower alive when it was on its way out. It seemed like there might be a big message for me in there somewhere.

"I don't quite know how to say this," Rosie said. She was still looking at my garden.

"What?" I said.

"It's just that my father hasn't been a widower very long, and well, he hasn't dated since my mother died, and I just want to make sure . . ."

"Oh," I said. "Don't worry. My mother's

a really nice person. And she hasn't dated since my father died either, at least I don't think she has. Plus, it's probably not even real dating. It's more about companionship at their age, isn't it?"

Rosie stood up. We both looked at my clothesline, where my mother's racy underwear dangled like a Siren's call.

"Oh, boy," I said.

"Maybe we should just stay out of it," Rosie said. "Or maybe we should sit them down and have the condom talk."

I was still looking at my clothesline. "Hard to tell," I said.

It was probably morbid curiosity that propelled me to my Friday small-group coaching session. That and the fact that I really needed to get out of my house. My mother was purging and rearranging my kitchen cabinets. She was also singing to herself and driving me crazy. I left just before I drowned in "Moon River."

When I got to Fresh Horizons South, I sat in the parking lot, the air-conditioning in my car blasting, and planned my entrance carefully. Too early and I might have to have an awkward conversation with Rick. Too late and the whole class would look at me when I walked in, and I wasn't sure I was up to

197

the scrutiny today. My headache was gone, and I'd taken the time to blow-dry my hair and put on some makeup and a decent outfit, but I was still a little bit shaky in the self-esteem department.

With four minutes to go, I locked my car and headed for the small-group coaching classroom. Even though I'd tried to put him out of my mind, the kiddie-size lockers in the hallway made me think about Michael again. I mean, if he had the social skills of an eighth grader, he could have at least had one of his friends call me to break up for him. And to think I'd thought all that retro stuff was cute. Maybe it was a fine line between retro and regression. It seemed to me that, as we got older, maybe we all started thinking about our childhoods more and more. And that was probably okay. What I needed to watch out for were the men who *became* children again.

I held my head high and opened the Fresh Horizons South classroom door. Rick looked away as soon as he saw me. It took every ounce of willpower I had not to get right in his face and yell, *Oh, grow up.*

I sat in a chair on the other side of the semicircle. I stared out the window, not really seeing anything, until Brock walked in and set up his video camera.

198

Brock shut his eyes and let out three quick puffs of air. He opened his eyes again, tilted his chin up, and threw his shoulders back. "Welcome," he said. "Welcome to all of you, and make that welcome back if you've been here before. My name is Brock, and I'll be your Fresh Horizons certified small-group career coach . . ."

". . . for the next ninety minutes," half the class said right along with him.

"Let's begin with a question," Brock said. He was wearing my favorite pale pink shirt and a pair of gray pinstriped pants I hadn't seen before, and he looked extra adorable. Since I seemed to be attracting children instead of men into my life, maybe I should set my sights on a boy toy like Brock. At least he still had all his hair and his testosterone.

I crossed my legs and flashed Brock a big smile.

He looked right through me as if I didn't even exist. If we were standing on a corner, he'd probably offer to help me cross the street.

Brock clapped his hands. "What's your biggest investment?"

"The house my ex-wife got?" the scruffy guy named Mark said.

"Our small-group coaching sessions?" one

199

of the women said in a flirty voice. Clearly I was not the only one having Brock fantasies.

Brock clapped his hands three times. "When you make," he said, "a serious, fully conscious decision to invest in yourself, it will be the biggest investment you ever make."

It hit me like a ton of bricks. I closed my eyes and repeated it to myself. I'd never really thought about it that way. For all the hours I'd logged in on my career, it really wasn't the same as putting the work into myself. I was pretty sure I'd never, ever made a decision like that.

Brock moved on to the video part. Fortunately he didn't get around to calling on me, because I'd checked out of the classroom to take a stroll down memory lane. I retraced every bit of my life that I could remember. My first stacking game, the one where you were supposed to put the brightly colored plastic rings on the post in order of decreasing size, and which I hurled across the room on a regular basis. The time my brothers got real Adidas sneakers and my sister and I got fakes with one less stripe, and as outraged as I was, I never even fought for our right to equal footwear. My short fingers and their disastrous piano lessons. The horseback riding lessons I started when tennis got too hard. The year I sort of ran for class treasurer. My college application essays. My career. My relationships.

I didn't think I'd ever given anything my all. I wasn't sure why — fear of failure, fear of success, or maybe I was constitutionally a slacker — did it really matter? Whatever the cause, what it all boiled down to was that if I didn't start believing I deserved a better life, then I sure as hell didn't have half a chance of getting one.

I jumped out of my chair as soon as the session was over. I was several steps down the hallway before I changed my mind and turned around.

Rick was just coming out of the classroom. "Can I talk to you for a minute?" I said.

He looked around for an escape route. "Actually," he said, "I've got a tennis match scheduled. . . ."

"*Actually,*" I said, "this will only take a minute. Maybe even less."

"Uh-oh," one of the other scruffy guys said as he walked by us.

"Oh, grow up," I said.

"Here's the thing," I said when Rick and I were alone. "You had your chance. You could have called me Monday, Tuesday, Wednesday, or Thursday."

He wrinkled up his forehead. "I really

meant to," he said. "Time just got away from me."

"Even this morning. But you didn't."

I looked at my power watch, then up again. "I don't have time for this," I said. "I'm working really hard at moving forward in my life, and I think part of that is surrounding myself with the right people."

I tried to look Rick in the eyes as I said it, but it takes two sets of eyes for that.

"I'm sorry. It's not you," he said finally. His green cat eyes made contact for a second, then darted away. "It's just that I can't seem to get my act together lately."

"So I just want to make it perfectly clear," I finished, "that the offer has expired."

"Okay, then," Rick said.

"Okay, then," I said.

I turned and walked away.

DAY 20:
14,111 STEPS

Rosie was already standing out by my lavender patch when I got there.

"Morning," I said. "Feels like it's going to be a hot one."

She looked up at my kitchen window. "The weather's not the only thing that's hot, from what I hear." She lowered her voice to a whisper. "Date. Tonight. Dinner *and* dancing."

"Really?"

Rosie was still whispering. "Just act surprised when she tells you, okay? I don't want to get in trouble."

"What," I said, "you mean like grounded?"

We started walking around to the front to meet Tess. Rosie stopped to pull a weed that was tall enough to be leaning up against my house. "It's weird, isn't it, how it all turns around? It's like the roles sort of reverse, but not completely, so in a way it feels like you're the parent now, but you're also still the kid."

I'd almost pulled the exact same weed yesterday, but at the last minute I'd doubted myself and started wondering whether it might really be a good plant, after all.

"Yeah, it's totally strange," I said. "But at least you *have* some parenting experience."

"That's a good point," Rosie said. "Not that most of parenting isn't just a crapshoot. What's that old saying? Even a broken clock is right twice a day."

Tess must have been looking out her screen door, because she opened it as soon as we got to my driveway. She was wearing a white terry cloth bathrobe.

"Not today," she yelled. "I've been up all night."

The door slammed shut. "What do we do?" I asked.

"Same thing we did that day you faked sick," Rosie said. "We walk, and then we show up at her house later and make sure she's okay."

Tess's door opened again. "And don't come back and bug me later," she yelled. "I'm not in the mood."

"So much for that theory," Rosie said.

Nothing against Tess, but it turned out to be much easier for two people to walk together than three. No moving forward and

204

back in the little fairness dance we'd created, no changing partners so the same person wasn't stuck up front doing a solo for too long. The conversational logistics were less complicated, too: simply wait till the other person stopped talking and dive right in.

"This is really selfish," Rosie was saying, "but I spent the whole night tossing and turning and wondering what would happen if things worked out between your mother and my dad. I mean, there's room downstairs and we could probably add a little kitchenette, but I don't think I could handle living with one more person. Both my kids have friends over all the time, plus my husband's crew is always in and out. My personal space is practically nonexistent already."

"Well, they're certainly not moving in with me," I said. "My social life is nonexistent enough without a handicap like that. Maybe we could ship them off to my mother's place in Florida."

We walked for a while, considering. "I guess that could work," Rosie said, "but I've kind of gotten used to having him around. And here's the thing: I turned my life upside down, uprooted my husband and kids, so my father didn't have to move out of his house. If he moves to Florida with your mother, then what the hell are we doing there?"

I stepped in front of Rosie to go through the opening in the seawall. We stopped at the top of the beach just long enough to take in the view. Sailboats were zigging and zagging all over the place, and closer to shore swimmers were already venturing in. The beach day began earlier and ended later on the weekends.

We started walking again. I had a sudden vision of my mother careening off a cliff. "Is your father a good driver?" I asked.

"A little bit of a lead foot, but his reactions are still pretty good. Why, do you think we should have your mother drive instead?"

A piece of sea glass twinkled up at me, and I bent down and picked it up. "Probably not," I said. "My father did most of the driving."

Rosie took a little catch-up hop. "Okay," she said. "How about my dad drives, and we wait and see how their second date goes before we worry about living arrangements?"

"Sounds like a plan," I said. I blew out a puff of air. "Well, now that we've prematurely worked out our parents' relationship . . ."

"No kidding," Rosie said. "If we spent even a quarter of the time focusing on ourselves that we do worrying about everyone else's lives . . ."

"Why do you think that is?" I asked. I really wanted to know.

Rosie bent down and picked up a small dried-up starfish, each orange-brown leg stretched out in a different direction. "I like to think it's because I'm such a kind, loving, unselfish person." She laughed. "But if I'm really honest with myself, I think I spend a lot of time hiding behind the never-ending needs of my family. It keeps me from having to think about what I want out of my own life."

My mother finished making my breakfast as soon as I came in the door from walking with Rosie. This part I could get used to.

I sat down across from my mother at the kitchen table. "Thanks," I said. "I haven't had soft-boiled eggs and toast triangles in years. I completely forgot about the egg cups you sent me that time. Easter, wasn't it?"

My mother nodded. "It was your favorite breakfast when you were a little girl. The yolks had to be just right, so you could dip the corners of your toast in."

I dipped. "Yum," I said. "Perfect. Not too hard and not too gooey."

My mother sipped her tea and watched me eat. She was wearing white capris and a bright purple sleeveless top with matching purple flip-flops. Her freshly dyed dark hair was tucked behind her ears, and pink and purple parrot earrings dangled from her earlobes. I tried to make myself say something nice about the earrings, but I couldn't quite get there.

I took a deep breath. "Mom, was I always a little bit lost? I mean, was the writing on the wall from, I don't know, like, birth?"

"Where did that come from?" my mother asked.

I shrugged and took another bite of my perfectly cooked egg. There are parts of yourself you don't really want to revisit. But, if you have to, it's better to have your mother do the reality check than, say, your first boyfriend, or the kid you punched out on the playground when you were five.

My mother took a sip of her tea. She was probably trying to think of the best way to break it to me that I'd always shown signs of being not only a late bloomer, but a non-bloomer. Maybe she'd even known when she was pregnant that the baby growing inside her wasn't quite like her other three.

I suddenly really wanted to know. How had my sister and brothers managed to thrive, while I'd floundered and floundered some more, and how soon had she been able to feel it in her all-knowing mother bones?

"You know, honey, your father and I never played favorites. We loved all four of you the same."

I guess that was supposed to make me feel better, but I wondered if it might have cost me some pity points along the way. I stirred a toast point around in my egg yolk.

"But you were always the spunky one. Nothing ever got in your way for too long. You just backed right up and came at it again, full steam ahead. Your father used to tell everyone you were going to be the first female astronaut."

"Ha," I said.

My mother looked around my kitchen. "Look at all you've accomplished. A big job, a house of your own, and in a nice neighborhood."

"Don't forget the livestock issues," I said.

She smiled. "I was seventy-one before I learned how to pay the bills. Your father always did it. I was barely twenty when we were married. I'd never killed a bug I couldn't coax out of the house. I'd just lock it in a room until your father got home from work and took care of it. I'd never cleaned a clogged drain, washed the car, lived alone."

I pushed my egg away and took a sip of my coffee. "It's a blast, isn't it?"

My mother shrugged. "It takes some getting used to." She lifted up her mug and used her other hand to square her place mat with the edge of the table. "Honey, your whole life you were fine as long as you knew what you wanted. Sometimes it took you a while to decide, that's all. You were good at almost everything you tried. Choice is a wonderful thing, but it can also be confusing. Things were different when I was your age."

"When you were my age, you were already a grandmother." It was a slight exaggeration, but it was practically true.

"Oh, stop," my mother said. "Youth lasts a lot longer these days."

"Sometimes forever," I said. I was thinking of Michael, Rick, possibly all men. Maybe even me.

I closed my eyes and blew out three quick puffs of air. "Mom, I'm not working. I took a buyout from my company." My eyes teared up. "And I don't know what I'm going to do next."

My mother reached out and put her hand over mine. "You'll figure it out, honey. Do you need a little loan to tide you over?"

"No, no, I'm fine. They're giving me my full base salary for eighteen months."

"Well, then it would be silly to work if they're giving away all that free money, now wouldn't it?" She patted my hand a few times. "Something will come up the minute you stop worrying. My mother always used to tell me a watched pot never boils."

This didn't quite seem like a brilliant job hunting strategy, but I let it go. Just to clear the air, I said, "Mom, remember what I said about my boyfriend being away on business? Well, he's not. I don't actually have a boyfriend right now."

"Don't worry, sweetie," my mother said. "A friend in my complex has a single nephew who lives in Boston. I could give her a call."

I slid my hand out from under my mother's and started patting hers. "Thanks, Mom," I said. "I'll let you know."

"Have a good time," I yelled from my doorway as I waved at my mother and her date backing out of my driveway. Boyohboy, talk about a role reversal. How many times had my parents waved at me this way?

I pulled the door shut behind me and started walking down Wildwater Way by

211

myself to finish the rest of the day's mileage. I was thinking about my father. He'd died suddenly, a massive heart attack in the middle of a golf game. *What a way to go,* we all said, even though we were devastated. I mean, if you have to die, better to be fine one minute, doing what you love to do, and gone the next. With luck, he never felt a thing.

The tough part was we'd never had a chance to say good-bye to him. Not even my mother. They'd been inseparable for over fifty years, raised four kids together, never spent more than a night or two away from each other. How do you move on from that? But, clearly, my mother had. She was the one with the date tonight.

Instead of the usual right, I took a left at the bottom of Wildwater and started winding up and down the newer developments off High Street. I'd lived here for years without checking out any of these streets. When I was working, I got in my car, drove to work, drove home, and pulled my car into the garage. If I had shopping to do, I'd do it on the way home, or get back in the car and drive to the store. It would never have occurred to me to wander around on a Saturday night by myself. If I didn't have a date, I would have made plans with a friend, or stayed in.

It was still light out, and the streets of Marshbury were as safe as any can be in this crazy world. I'd taken the extra precaution of bringing my cell phone with me. I stayed on the sidewalks when they were available, and when they weren't, I made sure I was facing the traffic, just in case I needed to jump out of the way of some nutty driver. I really liked this solitary wandering. It was a nice balance to the teamwork of our morning walks, where every little twist and turn was a group decision.

I passed Tess's house on the way to mine. I looked up at the second-floor windows, imagining Hannah safe and sound in her own room. I'd definitely say something to Tess if I saw her sneaking out again.

I spent the rest of the evening flipping through a book Rosie had loaned me about tussie-mussies, or Victorian speaking bouquets. Apparently the Victorians exchanged symbolic flower arrangements instead of letters, a way of subtly and gracefully expressing one's repressed feelings. Oh, those daring Victorians.

I wondered if, back in the day, Michael might have sent me a dark and dreary breakup bouquet, which actually would have been a step up from just disappearing. Then I could have wandered my cutting garden in my long dress and button-up boots, shears in hand, carefully considering each bloom, and poking stem after stem through a hand-crocheted lace doily as I created my tussie-mussie answer.

Tussie-Mussie Fuckie-Youie Bouquet

geranium = you are childish
rosemary = remembrance
thyme = courage
sunflower = pride
ginger = strength
anemone = forsaken
harebell = grief
marigold = despair
dill = lust
candytuft = indifference
yellow carnation = rejection
meadow saffron = my best days fled
bittersweet = truth
dark crimson rose = mourning
ice plant = your appearance freezes
    my heart

Day 21:
10,556 STEPS

"Isn't this the most divine lavender?" My mother said as she greeted Kent Stockton's bouquet with an early morning sniff.

"Mmm," I said. Lavender usually meant devotion, but it could also mean luck — Victorians were as cryptic as they were repressed. Either way, I guess it wasn't a bad first-date message.

I followed her outside and watched her hang our freshly washed sheets and towels on my clothesline. I took a sip of the coffee she'd made for me, even though she only drank tea.

"So, how'd your date go?" I asked. I'd tried to wait up for her, which seemed only fair, since she'd always done it for me, but I conked out sometime right after ten. Must have been all that walking.

My mother took a wooden clothespin out of the little basket. The sheet she was holding flapped in the wind. I grabbed one end and looped it over the line. I held it steady until my mother pinned it down.

"Thanks, honey." My mother tucked some hair behind her ears. She had earrings on already, panda bears this time. I didn't quite get this wild animal motif. Maybe she'd been to the zoo lately. "Kent is a delightful man and quite the dancer. We had a grand time."

I wondered if I'd ever have a grand time with a man who was quite the dancer. Or quite the anything. I walked over to check out my tiny lavender plants. There were only a few stray flowers left, but I could see shoots of new, paler gray-green growth where I'd pinched the spent blooms back. I rubbed my fingers along the leaves and then held them under my nose. The scent was as intoxicating as ever.

"This is a marvelous clothesline," my mother said. "You'll have to get me one just like it for Christmas. Though I think I'd prefer one that's a little bit jazzier, if you can find it." We both looked up at the beige retractable plastic case Tess had screwed into the side of my house. "Maybe you could find one with a touch of animal print on it?"

At least that meant she wasn't planning on still being here at Christmas. "Sure," I said. "I'll look around for some penguin clothespins, too." I mean, better on clothespins than on her ears, if you asked me. "Wait, are you allowed to have a clothesline at your complex? It's actually illegal around here — some kind of community ordinance."

"We passed a law in Florida not too long ago. The entire state can let it all hang out now."

"Wow," I said. "That must be quite the sight."

My mother grinned. "Well, I have to admit, we've gotten a bit competitive at my complex. We've all been upgrading our intimates."

I burst out laughing. "So, that explains it. I thought you'd just turned into a wild woman."

"Nothing wrong with putting a little spice in your undies," my mother said. "You should think about it. There's a woman in my complex who does home lingerie parties. I'll have one next time you're down."

"Great," I said. "Can't wait." I hoped this didn't mean my mother had been going through my drawers when I was out.

I pinched off a little sprig of lavender and handed it to my mother. "Did you think about Dad last night?" I asked.

My mother held it under her nose and sniffed. "Of course I did, Noreen. I talked about him quite a bit, and Kent talked about his Rosalie."

"Aww," I said. "Her name was Rosalie? Rosie must have been named for her — her real name is Rosemary, you know."

"Of course I know. We talked about our children half the night."

My mother tucked the lavender behind her ear. Maybe the panda earring would think it was breakfast. She bent down and pulled a damp pillowcase from my laundry basket. "Lavender's blue," she sang, "Rosemary's green. . . ."

I wondered if she was thinking about my father or Rosie's.

"Yes, I'm fine," Tess said. "My daughter is grounded again, that's all. And since she was already grounded for life, let's hope reincarnation isn't just a pipe dream. And no, I don't want to talk about it."

Tess walked up ahead of us on the sidewalk. Rosie rolled her eyes in my direction. "Good time?" she asked.

"Great," I said. "How 'bout at your end?"

"He's totally crazy about her," Rosie said.

"Ditto," I said. "Oh, and get this, my mother's definitely not a hootchie mama.

Apparently Florida has turned into a right-to-dry state, and everyone at my mother's senior complex is buying slutty underwear to impress the neighbors."

"Well, there's no way I'm sending my father to Florida then," Rosie said. "We'll have to come up with something else. Did you hear they're going bike riding today?"

Tess turned around. "What are you two, new best friends?"

"Sorry," I said. Rosie walked up ahead and Tess dropped back next to me. "So where did you get my retractable clothesline again? I want to decorate one to surprise my mother. Sort of a bon voyage present when she goes back to Florida."

"That's subtle," Tess said. "We gave our son a new cell phone and a check for the first month's rent to get him out again the last time he moved home. The hardware store, right on Main Street. You know, you could start a nice little side business selling air-drying paraphernalia. Plus, you'd make a real difference in the world. Clothes dryer fires account for over fifteen deaths and four hundred injuries annually."

"I'm not going to ask how many of them you were personally responsible for," I said.

Rosie turned around. "No way. If you start any kind of business, I mean, take my lavender, please."

The last thing I wanted to do was ruin this beautiful day by thinking about what I should or shouldn't do next. Plus, I still had over seventeen months of full base salary coming to me. We turned left and spread out across our side street.

"Have you heard from Annalisa?" I asked.

"Nothing yet," Tess said. She reached into her pocket and pulled out a folded sheet of white paper. "But here's what she posted Friday afternoon."

I showed up at the hospital all bright-eyed and bushy-tailed, as my grandfather (a squirrel) used to say, but I didn't get my chemo. A national chemo holiday, you might ask? No, my platelets and hemoglobin were too low for Kool-Aid (or chemo). But they didn't send me away empty-veined. I got two units of blood instead, and I'm sure I'll be feeling like Superwoman and leaping tall buildings in no time. I go back for a recheck next week.

The friend who drove me was kind enough to stop by my school. She sat outside while I went into the classroom. I found myself thinking about a student from a few years ago. Tough, tough life. He lost his mother, and not long thereafter his father ran off with a girlfriend and left him with his grandma. This little boy was hurting.

One day he finally got a math concept (converting between hours and fractions of hours, as I remember) he'd been struggling and struggling with, so I praised him up and down, and told him it was a good day, a day to remember.

"It was just one minute," he said. "What's the rest of the day gonna do for me?"

"Sometimes you only get one good minute a day," I said. "You just have to make the most of it."

So, I made the most of my one good minute today and wrote another note to my precious students.

"Ouch," I said. "Someone should invent a sunscreen that doesn't sting your eyes when you cry."
We were all wiping our eyes with the sleeves of our T-shirts as we walked. "I wish

my kids had Annalisa for a teacher," Rosie said. "Or maybe I don't. God, I hope she's going to be okay."

Tess folded up the paper and put it back in her pocket. "Maybe the e-mail I sent through her care site got lost in cyberspace. If I don't hear from her by tomorrow or Tuesday, I think I'll try again. I guess it's too late for us to bring her with us, but maybe she can come with us next time. And I'd like to at least get those journals in the mail before we leave for Sequim."

"Do you believe it's this Thursday?" I said.

"Crack of dawn," Tess said.

"Ohmigod," Rosie said. "How am I ever going to get everything done before I leave?"

As soon as I got back from walking, I told my mother I was going over to do some weeding at Rosie's. She invited herself along, big surprise. We changed into gardening clothes, and my mother followed me down the path.

"This is lovely," she said. It felt about ten degrees cooler under the dense shade of the trees, and our feet barely made a sound as we walked along the carpet of pine needles.

The path ended, and we stepped into Rosie's world. Her two sons, unmistakable in their resemblance to Rosie and her dad, even though they both had dark hair instead of red, were running around with a bunch of friends. They were all screaming and shooting one another with squirt guns. Rod and the Supremes were scratching away in the middle of the vegetable garden.

I looked at my mother. "Are you okay with the chickens being loose?"

My mother winked. "I think I'm feeling a bit faint. Kent may well have to rescue me again."

Rosie poked her head out of the little lavender shed. She brushed some cobwebs from her hair and wiped her hands on her jeans.

She took a little skip toward us and held one hand out to my mother. "I'm so happy to meet you, Mrs. Kelly."

"Lo," my mother said. "Call me Lo."

We followed Rosie inside the shed, and my mother oohed and awed over every little thing. "Lovely," she said. "Just lovely."

"More like overwhelming," Rosie said. "I don't even know where to start anymore."

"You girls get out of here," my mother said, as if we were ten and she was shooing us out to play. "Just tell your father I'm here, Rosie honey, if you don't mind. We'll have this little doll house in shipshape condition in no time. And after that, we've got a nice little bicycle ride planned."

Rosie made a fist and pulled her elbow down as we walked away. "Yes!" she whispered. "Who cares if your mother buys her underwear at Frederick's of Hollywood? I totally love her."

"Hey," Michael's voice said behind me. "You look great. I didn't know you wore dresses, Nora."

I turned around to make sure he was really standing there. He was wearing jeans and an old leather belt with a rusty metal peace sign. His shiny brown hair still didn't have a single strand of gray, and his eyes were still the color of a chocolate bar. He was shirtless. And flowerless.

"I didn't hear the doorbell," I said.

"Your mother saw me coming," he said.

"That makes one of us," I said.

He didn't say anything.

"I thought you were sick," I said.

"I'm a fast healer," he said.

"Must be nice," I said.

He held out a bottle of white wine. "It's cold."

I pushed past him without taking it. "Let's just get this over with," I said.

He and my mother clinked glasses. Michael held his glass up in my direction. I ignored him and took a sip instead.

"Thanks for inviting me, Lo," Michael said. "It was really nice of you."

"Nobody calls her Lo," I said. "Ever."

"Why are you acting like this?" he whispered.

"What?" I whispered. "You actually have the nerve to ask me that?"

"I miss talking to you," he whispered.

"Good," I whispered back.

"There's been lots of stress at work," he whispered. "I really needed to focus more on the job."

I just looked at him.

"And I didn't feel it was appropriate for me to stand in the way of a potential someone who could offer you a full-time relationship."

I still didn't say anything.

He sighed. "And I didn't want to hurt your feelings."

"Good-bye, Michael," I yelled, so loud it hurt my ears. I gave him a little push, and my hand went through him and disappeared into the cold night air.

I sat up in bed. My dream pillow landed in my lap with a plop. I picked it up and lobbed it across my room. "Not helping," I whispered.

Day 22:
10,123 steps

Brock closed his eyes and let out three quick puffs of air. He opened his eyes again, tilted his chin up, and threw his shoulders back. "Welcome," he said. "Welcome to all of you, and make that welcome back if you've been here before. My name is Brock . . ."

". . . and I'll be your Fresh Horizons certified small-group career coach for the next ninety minutes," most of the class said.

"Before you know it, you won't even have to show up," the scruffy guy named Mark said. "We'll be totally self-sufficient."

"Ha," I said.

"My second ex-wife was a ballbuster, too," he said.

I shuffled the notes in my hand. I'd stayed up late last night, working on my story, and I'd gone over it several times in my head while we walked this morning. Today was my last small-group session until after we got back from Sequim, and I wanted to give it my best shot.

As soon as Brock finished setting up his video camera, I put my hand up.

He looked at me without one iota of anything that could be even loosely interpreted as sexual attraction. "Yes?" he said.

"Can I go first?" I asked.

"Kiss up," somebody said.

A man walked into the room and stood just inside the doorway. He was freshly shaved, and his hair was perfectly brown, without a strand out of place. Either I was still dreaming, or it was Michael.

"Nice suit," the messy guy closest to the door said.

"Thanks, man," Michael said. He sat down beside him.

"Ready?" Brock asked.

I licked my lips and nodded.

Brock pushed a button on the video camera. He lifted one hand over his head and brought it down like the clapper on a movie set. "Go," he said.

It took a major effort, but I managed to pretend Michael didn't exist. I looked right at the camera and smiled. "My name is Noreen Kelly," I said. "I'm good at a lot of things. I'm smart and caring, and I have excellent problem-solving skills. I'm a good leader. My problem has been that I've been afraid to take risks, and I sometimes have a hard time figuring out what I want.

"What I do know so far is that I don't want to be bored anymore. I think I want to do something more cutting edge than traditional, and it has to have an appropriate amount of stretch. Plus I have to feel energy and passion for it. And I also know I want more fun in my life."

Everybody actually clapped when I finished. Michael gave me a little wave.

"Excellent," Brock said. "You're well on your way to making an investment in yourself. Keep up the good work, and before you know it you'll be behaving the Fresh Horizons way and exercising choice on your own behalf."

Once again I waited for Brock to break into a tap dance and start singing the Fresh Horizons theme song. Still, it felt pretty good.

Brock turned to Michael. "Welcome," he said. "Just speak clearly, look into the camera, and tell us about yourself. Hey, weren't you at Fresh Horizons North this morning?"

Michael shrugged. "Maybe."

Somebody snickered.

"Hey," Michael said. "Nothing wrong with keeping busy."

Brock lowered his hand like a clapper. "Go," he said.

Michael ran a hand through his perfect hair and smiled at the camera. "My name is Michael Carleton," he said. "I just took a buyout. For the last eighteen years I was employed by Olympus, most recently as Senior Brand Communications Manager."

"Okay, fine," Brock said. "Tell us about you."

"I reported to —"

Brock put up one hand. "No, tell us about you."

"I was responsible for —"

"No, no, no." Brock clapped his hands once for each word, which made him look like a toddler having a tantrum. "You're regurgitating your résumé. Tell us about you. Who you are. What you hate. What you love. What you're good at. What you hope you never have to do again for the rest of your life. Tell us the story of Mike Carleton."

"Not Mike," Michael said. "Michael."

I couldn't resist. "Tell us the story of Not Mike Michael Carleton," I said.

Everybody but Michael laughed. One of the scruffy guys reached over and gave me a high five.

"Listen," Michael said. "I had no idea it

would be like this. All I want to do is find another job."

As soon as the session was over, I made a dash for the door.

Michael was right behind me. "Nora, wait."

I turned. "What?"

"I was hoping you'd be here," he said.

"Oh, please," I said. "Get over yourself. I certainly have."

I stopped at the hardware store on my way home. I bought two retractable clotheslines. One was for my mother. I thought I might decorate the other for Annalisa. I could ask Tess to send it to her when she sent the journals. I knew I didn't know her, but she just seemed like the kind of person who might appreciate a clothesline. Perhaps there was even a way she could use it in her classroom. Maybe to hang up the kids' artwork while it was drying?

I also bought a kind of paint that the woman behind the counter assured me would stick to plastic. I chose a rainbow of colors, plus some foam brushes. I couldn't believe how excited I was. I hadn't done a crafts project in practically forever. I used to love bringing make-your-own-jewelry and decorate-a-birdhouse kits with me when I visited my nieces and nephews. But they'd gotten older, so I couldn't use them as excuses anymore, and it somehow seemed really embarrassing to buy them for myself. I mean, it could escalate, and before I knew it I'd be the crazy maiden aunt crocheting those hoop skirt doll covers for the extra roll of toilet paper.

My mother was off somewhere when I got home — with Rosie's dad, no doubt. I brought the two retractable clotheslines into the garage and covered a section of the floor with old newspapers. I left one boring beige plastic clothesline cover alone and painted the other a bright turquoise. I opened the garage doors so it would dry faster. I headed into the house to pull my suitcase out of the attic and start thinking about what I was going to take for clothes to Sequim.

After I got as far as moving my suitcase from the attic to my bedroom, I decided I'd earned a break. I brought an iced tea into the living room and sat on the couch. I put my feet up on the coffee table and sipped. On the one hand, it was kind of nice to have my house to myself. But, on the other hand, if my mother weren't here, I wouldn't be sipping freshly brewed iced tea. So, it was sort of a trade-off. Maybe life was just like that.

I looked out my window. Hannah, wearing short shorts and a tiny bathing suit top, was just heading out to check the mail. She opened the mailbox, which was empty, then turned back to the house suddenly, as if someone had called her name. She shook her head in disgust, then held her middle finger up. Not a quick flash of the bird but openly, defiantly, for all the world to see.

I could remember being her age so clearly. The eternally raging hormones, the profound impatience, the intense urge to get the hell out of this honky-tonk town because I just couldn't take it anymore. The world was filled with such stupid people back when you thought you knew it all.

Not that I still didn't think there were lots of stupid people in the world, but the difference was that, in the years since I was Tess's daughter's age, I'd been one of them myself just often enough that I wasn't so quick to judge. At least I hoped I wasn't.

I finished my tea and walked the glass back to my kitchen. I went into the guest room and rifled through the top dresser drawer. Even my mother's underwear was folded into neat little piles. Apparently I didn't get her neatness gene. Maybe it skips a generation.

I felt a little bit guilty snooping, but it was

232

for a good cause. I chose a snazzy leopard-print bra and carried it out to the garage. I looped it from the corner of a low shelf, and it dangled like a flag from some very hot country. Then I sat down cross-legged on the floor and picked up one of the retractable clotheslines. I shut one eye and held my thumb up toward the bra.

I dipped a small round brush in buttery caramel paint and dotted it haphazardly all over the beige plastic cover. I looked at the bra again for inspiration while I gave the paint a chance to dry. I dipped another brush, this one slightly bigger, into some coconut husk-colored paint and surrounded the dots with uneven, not-quite-closed circles.

I sat back and admired my handiwork. I was pretty damn good at leopard, if I did say so myself. And not only that, but I'd created what might well have been the world's first matching bra and clothesline set. Maybe a leopard could change her spots after all.

"Genius," I said out loud. "Total, unadulterated genius." I stood the retractable clothesline up on its square metal bracket so it could dry without messing up my paint job.

I went to town on Annalisa's clothesline

next. I painted bright yellow stars randomly all over the turquoise background. Then, with a black Sharpie, circling around the edges in tiny block letters, I wrote over and over and over: *Shine On.*

I was crying when I finished, though I thought it was somehow as much about me as about this woman I didn't even know.

Hannah poked her head into my garage. "You okay?" she asked.

I wiped my eyes with the sleeve of my T-shirt. "Fine," I said. "Your mother is sending journals to some kids in New Orleans. You know, that classroom your class adopted?" I held up the turquoise clothesline carefully, so I wouldn't smudge the stars. "Anyway, I made this for them, too."

Hannah glared at me. "What?"

I reached for something to get rid of that look. "Well, you know, the teacher is sick and . . ."

"Of course I know," Hannah said. "I'm a *mentor.* It's like totally none of my mother's business. Why does she always try to take over my life? It's so annoying."

Hannah took a deep breath and sighed dramatically. Suddenly, her voice changed completely. "Ooh, can I paint some of those for the New Orleans kids? They'll totally love them."

She pointed to a pile of shoelaces. The white shoelaces Tess, Rosie, and I had removed from our Walk On Bys were sitting on top of the tangled web of laces Rosie's mother had dyed purple.

"Sure," I said.

"Ohmigod," Hannah said a few minutes later. "I haven't done this in, like, forever." We'd managed to separate about a dozen pairs of laces, and we were painting them in matched sets.

"You're really good at it," I said.

"Thanks," Hannah said. "You, too. You've totally got the animal print thing down."

"Thanks," I said. I reached for a lavender lace and dipped a brush in some turquoise paint. "Now I'm working on an abstract wave motif for new laces for the walking group your mother and I are in. We call ourselves The Wildwater Walking Club."

Hannah rolled her eyes. "Weird." She stood up. "Can I leave mine here while they dry? Then I'm going to mail them myself, so my mother doesn't try to take credit."

"Absolutely," I said. "Just come back and get them whenever you want. I never lock the garage door."

Hannah looked over her shoulder. "Okay. And, um, if my mother asks, I just left, okay?"

235

I was still thinking about what I should have said while I cleaned up the paints and went into the kitchen to wash my hands. As soon as I turned off the water, the doorbell rang.

I tiptoed to the door and peeked out. The mailman was standing on my front steps.

When I opened the door, he held out a certified letter. "Sign here," he said.

"What is it?" I asked.

"A certified letter," he said.

"Do I have to?" I asked.

"Only if you want to read it," he said. Even though he was wearing shorts, beads of perspiration dotted his upper lip.

I stood there, considering. Had anyone in the entire world ever received good news via certified letter? I squinted, but I couldn't read the return address without my reading glasses.

The mailman sighed.

I signed.

I retraced my steps out to the garage, where I'd left my reading glasses, and then carried the letter to my kitchen table. Town of Marshbury, the return address said. Maybe I'd messed up on my property taxes. I turned the envelope over and opened it.

Dear Noreen Kelly:

This CEASE AND DESIST ORDER is to inform you, as well as any and all occupants of 14 Wildwater Way, Marshbury, Massachusetts, that you are in direct violation of the Marshbury Community Clothesline Ban Ordinance.

Sec. 10-6. FULL AND COMPLETE CLOTHESLINE BAN In order to protect residents from bombardment of the senses, offense of sensibilities, and the lowering of property values, clothes drying apparatus of any kind is hereby banned from all outdoor property. Furthermore, clothes drying apparatus installed indoors shall be completely screened from inadvertent view of passersby.

Within twenty-four hours of signing for this notification, you are ordered to wholly remove any and all clothes drying apparatus from your property, including clothes, lines, and pins. Failure to do so will result in a fine of $200 (two hundred dollars) for the first offense, and $500 (five hundred dollars) for each subsequent violation.

Yours Truly,
The Marshbury Board of Selectmen
Making it in Marshbury since 1783

DAY 23:
10,642 STEPS

"Yeah, I got one, too," Tess said. "Idiots. Small town, elitist, clothes-minded idiots. I mean close-minded."

"Clothes-minded was actually pretty good," I said.

"I'd sure like to know who the looky-loo was that dropped a dime on us, that's for sure," Tess said. "And don't think I won't find out."

"Looky-loo?" I said. "Well, twenty-three skidoo to you, too."

We were in my garage recording yesterday's mileage on the map.

"Okay," Tess said. "That just about brings us to Quichickichick, where the female to male ratio is seven times worse than anywhere else in the partially inhabitable world."

"Ooh, what are these?" Rosie said.

"I've been decorating clotheslines," I said. "Not that I think you should start worrying about my social life or anything."

Rosie picked up the retractable clothesline I'd painted like a leopard. "This is so your mother," she said. "Though you might not want to leave her bra hanging in the garage much longer. If your garage door stays open for more than a minute, you could get tarred and feathered and run out of town."

"Oh, shit," I said. "I forgot to put it back. She'd kill me if she thought I'd left her best bra in the garage where nobody can even see it."

Tess picked up the other clothesline and turned it sideways to read the writing.

"That one's for Annalisa," I said. "I thought you could send it to her when you send the journals."

"Nice," Tess said, "but I think it might take away from my journals."

Rosie rolled her eyes.

"I was just trying to make a contribution," I said.

"Sometimes less is more," Tess said.

"Sometimes more is more," I said. "Especially if you live in New Orleans."

Tess and I stared at each other.

"All right," I said. I sighed an exaggerated sigh. "I was just thinking it would make it easier for her to hang her students' artwork up when school starts again. She'll probably still be really tired."

"Fine," Tess said. "We'll send the clothes-line. Hey, wait, you totally manipulated me just then, didn't you?"

"Somebody had to do it," Rosie said. She leaned over and picked up one of the decorated shoelaces. "These are adorable."

"You don't mind that they were your mother's shoelaces?" I asked.

"Of course not," Rosie said.

"Hannah decorated some of them, and I made these for us. We don't have to wear them if you don't like them."

Tess and Rosie were already sitting down, untying their sneakers. "Of course, we have to wear them," Rosie said. "It's the Wildwater Way."

I waited for Tess to ask me what time Hannah had left. I wondered what I would say.

Tess picked up one of Hannah's laces and shook her head. "It's like one minute she's twenty-two, and the next minute she's two. Just get me through the summer."

"These look great, Noreen," Rosie said. "Nice job. Come on, let's get a walk in. I have about three trillion things to do before we take off."

I walked up ahead of Tess and Rosie and started swinging my arms. I breathed deeply, trying to stay in the moment and really appreciate all the fresh air, even if it was almost eighty degrees out already. I'd probably been outside more in the last month than I had in the last two years. It was amazing just how much of your life you could live without coming into contact with nature. I'd spent years and years going from house to car to office to car to house. What kind of a life was that?

Rosie walked up ahead, and Tess dropped back beside me.

"So, have you taken down your clothesline yet?" I asked.

"Oh, please," Tess said. "Stop worrying. Just unhook it and let it retract. It'll all blow over by the time we're back from Sequim. I went through the same kind of thing last year when we put colored lights outside at Christmastime."

"You mean we're not allowed to put up colored lights?" I said. "That's ridiculous." Not that I'd ever put up any kind of lights, but still. "What did they do?"

"Nothing," Tess said. "By the time the board of selectmen got their act together to send me a fine, it was January and the lights were already down. So I just didn't pay it. They never did a thing. I can't wait till this Christmas. I'm thinking one of those ten-foot inflatable snow globes with strobe lights and disco carols. . . ."

"I don't get it," I said. "I really like having a clothesline. And if it's good for the environment, and if I don't mind my neighbors seeing my underwear . . ."

We crossed over onto our side street and Rosie skipped up beside me. "I'm just being devil's advocate here, but what if your neighbors mind seeing your underwear?"

"Then I think they should stay in their stupid houses and not look," Tess said. "Green is the new black, and clotheslines have gone from tacky to chic. Now we just have to wait a decade for our provincial little town to wake up and smell the lack of pollution."

"Maybe we should try to get the ordinance changed," I said. "Can we get it on the ballot for the next town meeting or something? Couldn't we go to a selectmen's meeting and try?"

"Have you ever been to a selectmen's meeting?" Rosie asked. "You can actually die of boredom."

"I know," Tess said. "We could just wrap up all the selectmen and women . . ."

"Selectpeople," Rosie said.

". . . whatever, tie them all up in clothesline, and leave them dangling somewhere.

We wouldn't hurt them. We'd just make our statement, followed by a quick getaway to Sequim."

"You know," I said. "One of my regrets is that I've never really taken a stand. Activism doesn't have to be just about the big things, you know."

"Hey, don't lecture me," Tess said. "Who's the card-carrying member of Project Air Dry here?"

"I don't think we need to tie anybody up or anything," I said. "But what if we just started a petition? Or we could make some signs and hang them up all over town?"

"I think there's an ordinance against that," Rosie said.

My mother was dressed in black and green spandex and talking on the phone in the kitchen when I got back from walking.

"Lovely to talk to you," my mother said. "Here she is."

She picked up my old bike helmet from the counter and held out the phone to me.

"Bike ride with Kent," she mouthed.

I nodded. "Be careful," I mouthed.

My mother kissed me on the cheek.

"Hello," I said.

"It's me," Sherry said. "You don't want to go out tonight, do you?"

243

"Hi," I said. "Sorry, I've got a trip coming up, and I haven't even started packing. How 'bout I give you a call when I get back?"

Sherry gulped back a sob.

"Okay," I said. "Not a problem. How about Splash at six-thirty?"

"Thanks," Sherry said. "See you then."

As soon as I hung up the phone, I got busy. I gift wrapped the two retractable clotheslines. I put my mother's in the back of my closet. I'd been thinking she would just naturally go somewhere else when I left for Sequim, but I wasn't seeing any signs of her requiring a going-away present yet.

I left Annalisa's in the garage. The plan was that Tess would add it to the box of journals and pens in the morning and mail the package before we left for Sequim. I circled back around to my kitchen to grab a glass of water. I stood at the counter, drinking and looking out my kitchen window. My lavender was barely flowering, and now my clothesline was gone. Or at least coiled up and tucked against the side of my house.

Change was in the air.

Sherry was already seated at a table when I got to Splash. She looked up at me with sad, puffy eyes.

I slid into the chair across from her. "Are

you okay?" I asked.

"That guy I was seeing," she said. "He broke up with me."

"Jerk," I said.

A glass of white wine was already waiting. I took a sip. It looked like Sherry was already working on her second glass.

"Wait," I said. "He actually broke up with you?"

Sherry looked at her cell phone, which was sitting in the middle of the table. "He just stopped answering my calls."

"Maybe . . . ," I said. We each took a sip of our wine.

I took a deep breath. "Listen," I said. "I should have told you this last time. I know it's Michael Carleton you were seeing."

Sherry opened her eyes wide. "How?" she said.

"Because I was sneaking around with him, too. I should have told you when I realized it, but I was jealous. I'm so glad you didn't take a buyout unless you were sure you wanted to, because he'll never leave to go cross country with you in a van, even if he said he would, and by the way, that was my garter belt, and he never slept with it. He didn't even know me in junior high."

Sherry put her glass down on the table with a *thunk*. "What an asshole," she said. "I can't believe I fell for him."

"It happens," I said.

Sherry took another sip of her wine. "Well, we can't let him get away with it. I know, I'll leave a message saying I have something life or death to tell him, and he has to meet me. And then when he shows up, we'll both be waiting. . . ."

I shook my head.

Sherry leaned forward over the table. "Okay, I'll send an e-blast to everybody in the sneaker industry. It's too late to stop his buyout, but we can make sure he never gets a foot in the door again."

"He's not worth it," I said.

Sherry's eyes teared up.

I held up my glass. "To better choices next time around."

She clinked her glass to mine.

I took a sip, then picked up my menu.

"Come on," I said. "Let's eat."

Sherry gave her cell phone one more glance, and then she reached for her menu.

Day 24:
10,873 STEPS

"We have to do it before we leave," Tess said. "It'll be like throwing ourselves a bon voyage party. I'll mail the journals and glitter pens . . ."

"And the retractable clothesline," I said.

". . . and the retractable clothesline. Then tonight we'll paper the town with right-to-dry signs and hit the road with our tires squealing. We won't tell a soul, so nobody can rat us out even if they want to."

"There's no way I can add one more thing to my day," Rosie said. "I'll be lucky to get out of my house by morning as it is."

"Okay," Tess said. "Noreen and I will do it. Just be on standby in case we need you to bail us out or anything."

That got my attention. "You're kidding, right?"

Tess shrugged. "Whatever it takes to fight the good fight."

We stepped through the opening in the

seawall. The tide was really high today. "Just think," I said, "the next time we set foot on a beach, we'll be looking at a different ocean."

"Cool," Rosie said. "But can we pick up the pace a little? I've got a gazillion things to do."

We finished our walk in record time. Just as I was reaching for my door, my mother opened it. She was wearing a big white T-shirt and black leggings. Silver humpback whale earrings dangled beneath my former bicycle helmet. Rosie's dad was wearing the same outfit, minus the humpbacks.

My mother gave me a big smile. "Oh, hi, honey. I left your breakfast on the stove. You can pop it in the microwave if it's not hot enough. Kent and I are going to ride our bikes to the Y for a tai chi class."

I hoped that didn't mean she'd paid for a lifetime membership. "Hi, Mr. Stockton," I said.

He kissed my hand. "Kent. Lovely to see you, Noreen. Come on, Lo, we need all the chi we can get at our age."

"Oh, you," my mother said.

While I ate my breakfast, I did some thinking. How was it that other people seemed to have no problem having relationships? Even my own mother knew how to do it. Was it that they knew what they wanted? Or maybe they knew what they didn't want and stayed open to the rest.

I found my dream pillow in my bedroom. Carefully, using some tiny nail scissors I found in the bathroom, I snipped out the stitches at one of the smaller ends. Then I curled up with Rosie's tussie-mussie book and a legal pad. I took my time, flipping through each section, trying to work with plants I'd be able to recognize from the photographs and could find either in my garden or at the supermarket.

I wasn't able to find all the ingredients, but I thought I'd found enough of them to get my dreams moving in the right direction. As soon as I finished stitching up the pillow again, I put it right into my suitcase, so I wouldn't forget it. My clothes would smell great by the time I got to the lavender festival. I smiled at the thought of eligible men from all over the world catching the scent of my dreams and flocking behind me everywhere I went.

I was just about packed by the time my mother came home long enough to change her clothes. "So, Mom," I said, "are you planning to stay here while I'm in Sequim? I'm just wondering."

> ## Dream Pillow Reinvented
>
> lavender = devotion, luck, happiness
> mint = warmth
> pink rose = friendship
> thyme = courage
> lemon balm = understanding
> honeysuckle = passion
> fern = sincerity
> almond blossom = hope
> freesia = trust
> dogwood = durability
> dandelion = time and love

"Why wouldn't I?" my mother asked.

"No reason," I said. "I was only thinking everybody else might start to get mad because I'm hogging your whole visit."

My mother opened my refrigerator and grabbed a bottle of water. "Not to worry," she said. "Jimmy and Kevin are going to bring their families by for dinner this weekend, so they can meet Kent."

"Gee, make yourself at home," I said.

"Thanks, sweetie." She came over and kissed me on my cheek. "Oh, and honey, if I'm not home by the time you go to bed, have a wonderful trip, okay?"

I was almost asleep when I heard the knock at my door. I opened one eye enough to read the green numbers on my alarm clock: 9:32. Maybe my mother was having an early night and had forgotten where I hid the key.

I kicked the covers off. I pulled the hem of my T-shirt down as I tiptoed to the door.

Tess was standing on my front steps, dressed all in black and holding a basket of markers and a big pile of poster boards.

I opened the door. "Do we have to?" I said.

Tess pushed past me. "You weren't asleep already, were you?"

"Don't be ridiculous," I said. I yawned. "I just figured you'd changed your mind, so I got ready for bed."

"Well, get unready then." Tess started spreading sheets of white poster board across my dining room table. "And shake a leg — I don't want to be up all night. Unlike my daughter, I need at least a few hours of sleep to be functional."

I went back to my bedroom and threw on an old pair of jeans.

"Are you trying to get us arrested?" Tess asked when she saw me. She shook her head. "We're talking basic black here."

It didn't seem worth the fight, so I went back to my bedroom and found some black

251

exercise pants and a black T-shirt.

FIGHT FOR THE RIGHT TO AIR DRY, Tess had already written in huge green letters on a poster board by the time I got back.

I grabbed another green marker and thought for a moment. HANG TOUGH, I wrote.

"Hey, you're good at this," Tess said.

"Thanks," I said. I thought some more. CLOTHESLINES ARE THE NEW COOL, I wrote.

"Eh," Tess said. She chewed the end of her marker for a moment. DO YOUR PART TO STOP GLOBAL WARMING — FIGHT THE MARSHBURY COMMUNITY CLOTHESLINE BAN.

I yawned. "Not too catchy," I said. I drew a clothesline in a few quick strokes. HANG IT UP, I wrote, BAN THE BAN.

"Okay, fine," Tess said. "You're better at this than I am. Come on, we don't have to be brilliant. We just have to get this done."

There were four poster boards left. Tess handed me two. A CLOTHESLINE IS A THING OF BEAUTY, I wrote on the first one. THERE'S NOTHING LIKE THE SMELL OF YOUR SHEETS FRESH OFF THE LINE, I wrote on the second. It was a little bit wordy, but it was important to invoke all the senses in a campaign, and I thought if

252

we could get people to actually smell the sheets, we'd be well on our way.

"Ooh, wait," I said. I grabbed one of Tess's poster boards. WAKE UP AND SMELL THE SHEETS, I wrote.

"Hey, that was my poster board," Tess said. DON'T TELL ME HOW TO DRY MY CLOTHES AND I WON'T HAVE TO TELL YOU WHERE TO GO, she wrote on the last one.

"Are you sure people aren't going to know you're responsible for this?" I said.

Tess was already putting the posters into a pile. "You mean, *we're* responsible for this," she said. "Come on, let's hit the road."

Tess had her hunter green minivan all backed into my driveway and ready for a quick takeoff. When I opened the door on the passenger side, a jug of laundry detergent fell out. I jumped back before it could break a toe.

"What are you trying to do, kill me?" I said. I bent down and picked up the big plastic container. "Don't tell me we're going to stage a public wash-in or something . . ."

Tess was beside me, sliding open the side door of the van so she could stash the posters. "Much better than that," she said. "Trust me."

"Ha," I said.

253

Tess pulled out of my driveway and put her blinker on to take a left at the end of Wildwater Way. I felt a lump under my foot and reached down to pull up a roll of clothesline. "What's this for?" I said.

"To hang the posters," Tess said. "It'll make them more visually evocative." She reached around in the space behind the hump between us and pulled out two black ski masks.

"Tell me you're kidding," I said. "It's still at least seventy-five degrees out."

Tess put one ski mask in her lap and handed me the other. "So, don't put it on yet. We have time."

I placed it on the dashboard. "No offense," I said. "But this isn't exactly a female gangster kind of vehicle."

"Hel-lo, it's called camouflage," Tess said. "You want to hide in a suburb, you drive a green minivan."

I thought we were heading for Main Street, but Tess pulled into a parking space at the town common. She yanked her black ski mask over her head.

"Where did you even get these?" I asked.

Tess grabbed mine from the dashboard and handed it to me. "My son went through a ninja warrior phase," she said. "I saved these and a couple of his weapons. I have a memory box for each of my kids."

"Sweet," I said. I pulled the mask over my head. It was hot and scratchy, and it smelled like attic.

"Grab the clothesline," Tess said. "And there should be a Ziploc bag filled with clothespins and a roll of duct tape, too. Check under the seat if you don't see them."

"Why do we need duct tape if we have clothespins?" I asked.

"It's good to be prepared," Tess said. "Just in case."

"In case what?"

Tess ignored me. We got out of the minivan. Tess walked around to get the posters, and I reached back into the van and rooted around until I found the clothespins and duct tape. Then I shut the door and looked up through the holes in my ski mask. The moon was almost full, and the whole sky twinkled with stars. It made me think of Annalisa. I hoped she was doing okay. I hoped I'd get to meet her one day, which was crazy, but probably no crazier than standing around wearing a ski mask on a hot night in July.

The side door closed with a click. There was one other car, down at the far end of the single row of parking spaces that flanked one edge of the town common. Tess walked right up to it and banged on the windshield with her knuckles.

Under the light of the silvery moon, we watched two teenagers pop up from the backseat. I had a sudden, random feeling one of them was going to be Hannah.

"Get the hell out of here, or I'll call both your parents," Tess growled in a voice that scared even me.

"Whoa," I said. "Shouldn't they at least find a secluded place to do that, like we used to?"

"Don't get me started," Tess said.

"Would you really call their parents?" I asked. "I mean, if Hannah was in that car, would you want somebody to tell you?"

"I'd rather they offered to keep her for the rest of the summer," Tess said.

I followed Tess across the common. She was taking big, purposeful steps, and I took a couple of Rosie-like hops to catch up with her.

Lots of New England towns have village greens at their centers, and even I knew that the town common was the pride and joy of Marshbury. It had huge statues, stone benches, and an enormous fountain. Plus plaques honoring soldiers who'd been killed in wars. And gorgeous trees and gardens dotting a vast stretch of manicured lawn.

But what I was really noticing most right now was its location. The Marshbury common was shaped like a big triangle, with a well-traveled road running along each of its three sides.

"Tess," I whispered. "We are sooooooo going to get caught."

Tess put the stack of posters on the ground and reached for the clothesline I was holding. "Okay," she said. "Take this end and head down to that tree over there. . . ."

"Can't we go somewhere a little less conspicuous?" I said. "Maybe we can duct tape them to telephone poles around town. I'll drive and you can jump out of the car —"

"No way. They'll get totally lost in all the yard sale signs. We have to hang them all together to make a big statement. Half the town will drive right past here tomorrow morning on their way to work."

A car drove past now and put on its high beams. I ducked. "Okay," I whispered. "Just hurry."

My heart was beating like crazy, but I wrapped my end of the clothesline around a tree. Tess looped hers around the neck of some Revolutionary War guy, who was about the same size. She tore off a piece of duct tape and covered his eyes with it, then stood on her toes and gave him a kiss on his bronze cheek. "Keep it under your hat, big boy," she said.

"Tess," I whispered. "Hurry."

We got all the posters clothespinned on as fast as we could, and when we finished, they stretched across the width of the common.

Tess stepped back for a better look. "No one's going to miss them in the morning, that's for sure," she said.

"Come on," I said. "Let's go."

I was more than ready for a quick getaway, but Tess walked to my side of the minivan with me. She opened the door and pulled out the laundry detergent.

"What's that for?" I said.

"Follow me," Tess said.

I was too curious not to. We headed right for the fountain. It was huge, plenty big enough to have a wading party in, and kids and dogs were always splashing around in there whenever I drove by on a nice day. Three enormous verdigris elephants stood on their hind legs in the center, spraying water out of their trunks.

Tess unscrewed the cap and started pouring the detergent into the fountain.

"Ohmigod," I said. "Tess, I bet we can get into serious trouble for this."

Tess kept pouring. "Relax. It's hypoallergenic, biodegradable, nontoxic, and free of petroleum solvents. It doesn't clean for shit, but it sure makes great bubbles."

Day 25:
4877 steps

We'd hired an airport shuttle service to pick us up at 3:30 and drive us to Logan Airport for our 6 A.M. flight. We'd all decided that if you factored in the cost of airport parking and aggravation, plus the fact that we could split it three ways, the shuttle was definitely the way to go.

I'd expected Tess to be already out in her driveway, giggling and singing "I'm Forever Blowing Bubbles" in the dark, but when I rolled my suitcase outside, I was alone. Seeing the same stars that had witnessed us vandalizing our town common gave a dreamlike mantle to our adventures last night. Not seeing Tess made me wonder if I'd somehow gotten the day wrong.

I was just about to run back in to check my calendar, when Tess's front door opened. She stood there for a moment under her outside light, talking to someone behind her. Finally she walked out the door with her carry-on. Her husband followed, rolling a suitcase behind him.

I felt a little bolt of jealousy. Must be nice to have a semicute, loyal husband who got up at this insane hour to say good-bye to his wife, even though he'd be exhausted at work all day. I tried to picture someone loving me enough to wake up at 3:30 A.M., but I couldn't quite get there.

I dragged my suitcase across the grass to Tess's driveway.

"I don't think I can go," Tess said.

"What?" I said.

"Of course you can," her husband said. "I'll handle it."

"What's wrong?" I asked.

"Hannah hasn't come home yet," Tess said. "If she's okay, she is so completely grounded for her next nine lives."

A white van pulled into Tess's driveway. Her husband put his arms around her and kissed her on the lips. "Love you," he said.

"Love you, too," she said. "Call me the minute she gets home. No, make her call me. No, don't. I don't want to ruin my trip. Never mind. You figure it out."

The driver got out and put our suitcases in the back of the van, and Tess and I climbed in. Rosie was waiting on High Street, at the end of her long dirt driveway.

"Woo-hoo," she said as she jumped into the seat behind us. "I'm out of the house!"

Nobody said anything.

"What happened?" Rosie said.

I turned around. "Hannah's not home yet," I said.

"She'll be fine," Rosie said. "God, I so don't want to let Connor and Nick be teenagers."

Nobody said a word until we got to the Marshbury common. "Well, will you look at that," the driver said. "I don't know how I missed it on the way into town. Must have still been half asleep."

Tess's and my posters were softly lit by the stars, the moon, and the streetlights. They flapped gently in the predawn breeze. We'd done a great job on the lettering. All of the posters were legible as we drove by, even WAKE UP AND SMELL THE SHEETS, which had slipped out from under one of its clothespins. You just had to turn your head sideways to read it.

But it was the bubbles that really got your attention. Overnight they'd multiplied and taken on a life of their own. They'd overflowed the fountain and surged across the manicured grass of the common. They looked like a cross between a seriously late snowstorm and an effervescent tidal wave.

Rosie poked me between the shoulder blades. Hard.

In front of us, the driver shook his head. "Stupid kids," he said. "Wait till the cops get their hands on them."

Tess gave her husband one last call before the flight attendant made us turn off our cell phones. "Nothing?" she said. "Okay, call Kayley's house and see if she came home last night. If Kayley's home, have them wake her up, and make her call everyone she could possibly be with. And then try you-know-who's house, just in case they're back together again. There's still time for me to get off the plane. Okay, okay. I'll call you from Atlanta."

I had an aisle seat. Tess was across from me on the other aisle, and Rosie had the window seat beside me. I glanced over at Rosie. She was ghostly pale and white-knuckling both armrests.

"Are you okay?" I asked.

Rosie shook her head. "I hate to fly," she whispered.

Tess leaned over the aisle to get a look at Rosie. "Don't worry, sweetie pie," she said. "I have Valium." Tess reached under the seat, unzipped her carry-on, and pulled out a Baggie filled with pills.

"Here, switch seats with me," Tess said. I switched.

"How's she doing over there?" I whispered once we'd reached cruising altitude.

"Sleeping like a baby," Tess whispered back. "Get ready, though, she's got an aggravating little snore."

"Good thing you packed your Valium," I said.

Tess pulled a magazine out of the seat pocket in front of her. "Like I believe in pharmaceutical drugs. It was one of my vitamins. Magnesium. I have to take it with my calcium pills so I don't get constipated."

"Seriously?" I said.

"What, calcium doesn't do that to you?"

I shook my head. "No, I mean you didn't really give her Valium?"

Tess leaned across the aisle. "Once I gave my husband one of the kids' old vitamins and told him it was Viagra. Smurf blue and probably ten years old."

The woman behind me leaned into the aisle. "It worked?" she whispered.

"Like a charm," Tess said.

As soon as we landed, Tess called her husband. "Thank God," she said. "Oh, puhlease, a likely story. Yeah, yeah, okay. Right, don't let her out of the house for a second. Okay, work, but call and double-check she's really on the schedule. No, I don't want to talk to her. I'm trying to have a vacation, not that she hasn't ruined it already. Okay, okay. I will. I won't. Okay, call you later. Love you, too."

"She's all right?" Rosie and I both said as soon as Tess hung up.

"Fine," Tess said. "At least until I get my hands on her."

Eventually they let us deplane, and we rolled our carry-ons along the ramp and into the terminal.

"I still don't get how you can fly from Boston to Seattle and have to go through Atlanta," Tess said. "It's a total waste of fossil fuel."

"Look on the bright side," I said. "We got here early, plus we have an eighty-three-minute layover. This airport is huge. I bet we can get four thousand steps in before we have to board."

Rosie yawned. "No way. You two walk. I'll sit and watch our carry-ons."

"Slacker," I said.

"Sorry," Rosie said. "It's just that I've always been really sensitive to drugs. . . ."

Tess grabbed one of her elbows. "I think we'd better keep you walking then. We don't want any drug overdoses on this trip."

We bypassed the tram and the moving

sidewalk and kept walking, even on the escalators. We checked out some great stone sculptures from Zimbabwe while infectious Zimbabwean music played overhead, a tribute to the African roots of a large percentage of Atlanta's population. I thought it was great that more and more airports were supporting artists and giving travelers something to look at while their flights were inevitably canceled or delayed.

Fortunately ours was almost on time. Better yet, by the time we'd grabbed something to eat at the Atlanta Bread Factory and found our seats on the plane that would actually take us to Seattle, we'd dragged Rosie around for 4,133 steps. I flipped my pedometer closed. "Wow," I said, "not bad."

Tess turned to check on Rosie. "How're you doing, kiddo? Need another dose?"

"I don't know if I dare," Rosie said. "Okay, but just a half this time."

A little more than nine hours after our first plane took off, our second plane finally landed in Seattle.

The seat had flattened my hair into the back of my head, maybe permanently. I tried to fluff it up with one hand while I pulled my carry-on with the other. "Boy, am I tired," I said. "I can't believe we still have to pick up our rental car and drive to Sequim. Maybe we should have planned to spend tonight in Seattle."

Tess finished resetting her watch. "That wouldn't have made any sense at all. It's only noon here, plus we're heading in the opposite direction."

"I'll drive," Rosie said. She was rolling her suitcase ahead of us like a race horse. "I feel great. I haven't slept like that in years. I am so getting my own Valium prescription when we get back."

"Nice art here, too," I said. We looked up at a row of suitcases and one guitar case suspended high above us. They had holes drilled through their centers and a metal bar threaded through, and they were twisted at random angles.

"That's such a great piece," Rosie said, "although I feel a little bit sorry for that poor guitar case. I'm trying to decide if I like this or the sea creatures embedded in the walkways at Logan better."

"Apples and oranges," Tess said. "This one is much edgier, and the sea creatures are more, I don't know, aquatic." She stretched her arms overhead. "You know, except for my stiff back, it almost feels like we've spent the day museum hopping. Come on, let's go get our rental car."

"Why is everybody in our line?" Rosie asked a few minutes later. There were five rental car counters lined up side by side across from the baggage claim carousels. Each of the other lines had about three people in them, while the line in front of Nationwide stretched back endlessly.

"I picked it because it was the cheapest one online," I said.

"By how much?" Tess said.

I shrugged. "Maybe a dollar or two. Per day."

"People think it's all about sexual predators, but this is how you really get in trouble on the Internet," Tess said. "From now on, always go with the second cheapest offer."

"Welcome to Sea-Tac," the woman at the rental car counter said an eternity later. "This your first time?"

Rosie yawned and handed the woman her license. "Yes," she said. "We're heading to Sequim for the lavender festival."

"Oh, you're going to love it," she said. "Here, let me find it on the map for you. Where did you say you were going again?"

Tess started to giggle. Then I did. "Bathroom," Tess said.

We were still laughing when Rosie found us outside the bathroom. "It wasn't that funny," she said.

"Ohmigod," Tess said. "It was the funniest thing I've heard in my whole life."

"Then you need a better life," Rosie said.

"No shit," Tess said.

Tess and I started laughing all over again.

"When did you two become new best friends?" Rosie asked.

The airport was south of Seattle, so it turned out to be a pretty easy two hours to Sequim. We drove south until we got to Tacoma, then headed northwest toward the Olympic Peninsula. On the map, the Olympic Peninsula looked like an arm reaching out across the Strait of Juan de Fuca and waving to Victoria, British Columbia.

Right around Gig Harbor, Rosie read a sign out loud: "CORRECTIONAL FACILITY, DO NOT PICK UP HITCHHIKERS." She fumbled with her left hand until we heard the click of all four doors locking.

I flipped through my travel guide. "That's the Washington State Corrections Center for Women."

"If they make it this far, I say we pick them up," Tess said. "They probably just need somebody to believe in them."

"You sure you don't want to stop and do some quick volunteering?" I asked. "It says here they have a great Prisoner Pet Partnership Program."

"Don't encourage her," Rosie said.

We were quiet until we came to the Hood Canal Bridge.

"Wow," Tess said.

"Will you look at those views," Rosie said. "Just incredible."

"It's the third largest floating bridge in the world," I read. "It connects the Kitsap Peninsula to the Olympic Peninsula."

"I can't believe these huge trees," I said a while later.

"Doug firs," Rosie said.

"Doug Fir," Tess said. "I think I dated him in college. Tall guy, right?"

Sequim was a surprise. I'd expected just a quaint little village, but it was a lot more spread out than I'd pictured, hugging the highway the way towns in Vermont did. Then it stretched through farmland out to the ocean. It felt both familiar and completely foreign to be near the ocean, but in full view of whitecapped mountains.

"Wow," Tess said. "It's like New England in an alternate universe."

"And how about that lavender," Rosie said. "Look, even the gas stations have perfect displays of lavender."

"Ooh," I said, "what's that kind of lavender called with the dark pink bunny ears?"

"Spanish lavender," Rosie said. "It's not a

true lavender, but isn't it great?"

She pulled our cramped white rental into the Sequim Suites parking lot.

"And what's the one over there that looks like a punk rocker?" I pointed to a big clump of purple lavender with one pale pink section running through it like a streak.

Rosie laughed. "It's probably a hybrid trying to revert back to its original self."

"Wherever you go, there you are," Tess said. "I hate that."

I leaned out my window for a closer look. "How do you know it's not just becoming the color it's always wanted to be?"

Rosie put the car in park. "Geez, we definitely should have gone for the standard instead of the midsize."

"Well," I said, "they don't make it easy. I thought the midsize sounded bigger."

"Well," Tess said, "obviously if it was cheaper, it was smaller."

"Okay," I said, "next time you get the car."

"Come on," Tess said, "let's check in and go drink our dinner."

"It's only three-thirteen," I said.

"Not for me," Rosie said. "I haven't changed my watch yet. Hey, do you think I dare have a glass of wine? I mean, do I still have Valium in my system?"

Tess was already yanking our suitcases out

of the car. "Come on," she said. "I want to check my e-mail. Maybe there's something from Annalisa."

The woman behind the reception desk, who had great cheekbones and a slightly gap-toothed smile, was about our age. Her name was Nancy, and she couldn't believe I'd remembered her sneakers. "Are you sure?" she kept saying. "You know, I would have given you the room anyway."

The lobby was bursting at the seams with people. "Is it always like this?" Rosie asked.

The woman tucked the sneakers behind the counter. "Just for the festival," she said. "Wait till you see it tomorrow."

I zipped up my suitcase again, and we headed for our suite. Tess sat down on the couch and pulled her laptop from her carry-on. Rosie turned on the television, and I started unpacking.

"Nothing," Tess said.

"Wow," Rosie said. "High sixties, low seventies for the whole weekend. Hey, can you check Marshburytownonline.org for the weather at home? I just want to make sure it's hot and muggy, so I can gloat."

"Holy shit," Tess said a minute later.

"That bad, huh?" Rosie said.

"Holy shit," Tess said again.

Rosie sat down on the couch beside Tess,

and I dug in my suitcase for my toiletry case. Once I got myself relatively organized, I'd kick into vacation mode for the rest of the weekend.

"Noreen?" Rosie said. "You might want to come over here for a minute."

I sat down on Tess's other side. "What?" I said.

Rosie pointed.

On Tess's computer screen, right below the local weather forecast and above the recap of the last Marshbury selectmen's meeting, was a blurry close-up of me taking off my black ski mask. There was an arrow on my nose. Tess clicked on the arrow, and the video started. A hazy but identifiable me followed a ski-masked and unidentifiable Tess and her laundry detergent over to the fountain.

The video panned the length of clothesline long enough to read our signs, cut to the duct-taped mouth of the Revolutionary statue, to a sea of bubbles, and then back to the beginning again. "In a stunning reversal of roles, on the Marshbury town common, under the cover of darkness," the voice-over said, "two as yet unidentified older adult female vandals were caught on cell phone camera by a couple of quick-thinking teens, who happened to be in the area."

"Ohmigod," I said. "Tess, you can tell it's me."

"Did you see how wide my hips look?" Tess said. "But, come on, *older?*"

DAY 26:
6425 STEPS

The next morning at breakfast, the three of us checked out the people sitting at the other tables.

"I don't know," Tess said. "Seems like an awful lot of whiteheads here."

"Stop," I said. "There but for a bottle of dye go I — and you, too." I looked around. "I don't think most of them are that much older than we are."

"Ohmigod," Rosie whispered. "Don't look now, but over there."

Tess and I turned to look. A couple was unloading the contents of a canvas bag onto their table: his and her seven-day vitamin dispensers, soy milk, ground flaxseed, and finally, a bag of prunes.

"Are three enough?" Tess whispered. "Are six too many?"

"They call them dried plums now," I said. "It's all in the spin."

"Shoot me," Tess said. "If I ever walk into

a restaurant with a bag of prunes, please just shoot me. And in the meantime, I hope we can at least manage to stay up a little bit later tonight. I can't believe we were all asleep by six-thirty."

Rosie took a bite of her lavender pear pancakes. "Cut us some slack," she said. "It was really nine-thirty. But you're right, we should have at least gone for that second glass of wine. Mmm, these are delicious."

"I had the best dream last night," I said. "It must have been my new dream pillow. I waded into the middle of the Marshbury common fountain and climbed up on a big soapbox. . . ."

"Great symbol," Rosie said.

"Thanks," I said. "I'm a good dreamer. Anyway, I gave this incredible clothesline speech. It was like I was channeling Sally Field in *Norma Rae*."

Rosie took another bite of pancake. "Love that movie."

I tried my lavender coffee cake. Amazing. "Yeah, me, too. But, back to my dream speech. I opened with that line about well-behaved women never making history."

Tess stirred some lavender honey into her tea. "What was I doing?"

I took another nibble of lavender coffee cake. Beyond amazing. "You weren't in it."

Tess put her mug down on the table. "What do you mean, I wasn't in it? The whole clothesline thing was my idea."

"It was my dream," I said. "I have every right to be in charge of it."

"Settle down, you two," Rosie said. "I do enough refereeing when I'm home."

We studied our festival brochures silently.

"Okay," I said. "It looks like the street fair opens at nine, and then the farm buses begin service to the farms from the street fair bus stop at nine-thirty, and the farms open at ten. There are four buses, A, B, C, and D, and each one goes to two of the eight lavender farms, and they run continuously till six."

"Whatever," Rosie said. "We'll just follow you."

"When does the winery tour start?" Tess asked.

"It's self-guided," I said. "So we can go anytime."

"That's ridiculous," Tess said. "They drive you to the lavender but make you drive yourself to the booze?"

"Wait," I said. "It says you can also taste the local wines at the Wine & Beer Garden at the street fair. *A selection of two wines from each winery will be available for tasting and purchase.*"

"I like that," Tess said. "It's so much more efficient. If you factor in street fair shopping and eating, it's total multitasking."

"But the whole point is to see the vineyards," Rosie said.

"No," Tess said. "The point is to drink the wine."

Tess's and Rosie's brochures were back on the table, and they were focusing on breakfast. I took another bite of my rich, buttery, exotic coffee cake.

"Okay, what else should we do while we're here?" Tess asked.

"Who made me the social director?" I asked.

"You have great leadership skills," Rosie said.

"So do I," Tess said. "But I'm on vacation."

I flipped my brochure over. "Ooh," I said. "There's a Puffin Sunset Marine Dinner Cruise. Let's see, a two-hour tour, expect to see tufted puffins, rhinoceros auklets, and other seabirds."

"I love puffins," Tess said. "Whenever we took the kids to the aquarium, they were my favorite. Maybe we should go there sometime, just the three of us."

"Right," I said. "Like I'd go anywhere near water with you and your laundry detergent ever again."

"I didn't even think of that," Tess said. "Bubbles in the aquarium would be genius. Imagine all the media coverage we'd get. We'd just have to figure out where to put the puffins."

As soon as we finished breakfast, we headed for the street fair. The closer we got, the more we could smell the lavender.

"It's like being wrapped in lavender," Tess said. "It's so sensual. Kind of sexy and relaxing at the same time."

"I can't figure out if it's more floral or woody," I said.

"Musky," Rosie said. "To me, it's almost musky. Hey, did you know that the riverside washerwomen in Provence were called *lavandières*? They used to sing a song about while there are still clothes to wash, who needs men."

"That's so twisted," Tess said.

"I don't know," I said. "Maybe we could stay here, find a river, and become Sequim *lavandières.* I read in the brochure that the Sequim-Dungeness Valley gets less than twenty inches of rain per year. It's so close to Seattle, you'd think the weather would be the same, but they actually call this area the blue hole. The microclimate is remarkably similar to Provence. That's why lavender grows so well here."

"I can show you how to make lavender water," Rosie said. "It's great to spray on your sheets and towels before you put them in the dryer."

"Excuse me?" Tess said.

"Sorry," Rosie said. "I meant before you hang them on the line. You can also add it to the final rinse in your washing machine. Or spray it on your pillow before you go to bed, to give you peaceful dreams."

Lavender Water

2 cups distilled water
2 oz. vodka or isopropyl alcohol
15 drops lavender essential oil

Mix all ingredients and pour through a funnel into a glass container you've sterilized by placing it in boiling water for 4 to 5 minutes.

"If you splash some on your temples, it's supposed to help overcome exhaustion," Rosie said. "It's a natural insect repellant, too, and you can also use it as a mouthwash."

"What can't lavender water do?" Tess said. She stopped and looked at her pedometer. "Twelve hundred and three steps from Sequim Suites to the street fair," she said. "That's great. If we do five roundtrips a day, we've got. . . ."

Rosie and I looked at each other.

"Twelve thousand and thirty," Tess said. "Boy, do you two need to do elementary school over again."

We each paid our fifteen dollars for the farm tours at the ticket booth and pinned on our FESTIVAL SUPPORT buttons. "I can't believe this is for all three days, including transportation," Rosie said. "I bet Provence is way more expensive."

"They probably gave us the senior citizen discount," Tess said. "I bet it's the only price they have."

"Knock it off," I said. "There are plenty of younger people here."

I looked around to be sure. There were families with strollers, clumps of friends, plus couples of all ages and sexual orientations, most wearing shorts and T-shirts.

We joined the throng milling past rows of booths set up under colorful umbrellas along both sides of Fir Street. "Is it my imagination," Tess whispered, "or are there lots of gay people here? Not that there's anything wrong with that."

Two women walked by wearing identical purple outfits and holding hands. "I think it's a lavender thing," I said while I looked at my power watch. "Okay, I say let's do a quick walk up and down the street to check it out and then jump on the first bus to the farms."

Even before you open your mouth, your feet are always a dead giveaway that you're not from around here. After a stroll past the booths, we climbed aboard Bus B with a bunch of T-shirted people. I'd expected mostly locals, but the range of accents and footwear was fascinating. The woman diagonally across the aisle in front of me sounded Australian and was wearing an Italian two-toned red patent leather Italian sneaker, maybe Zagmani.

Across from her, a single fluorescent green and orange Puma Argentina was air-tapping in the center of the aisle. Last I'd heard, Puma Argentinas were hot in England, and neon colors were growing in popularity in Europe and heading this way. The Onitsuka Tiger, the Japanese sneaker worn by Uma Thurman in *Kill Bill,* were all the rage in the Netherlands at one time.

My head was filled to the brim with sneaker factoids I'd never need again. The first rubber-soled shoes, called plimsolls, were made in the early 1800s or possibly as early as the late 1700s. Goodyear made the first canvas and rubber Keds in 1892. Sneakers were mostly worn by athletes until Hollywood picked up on the fashion, first in the 1930s and then in a big way in the 1950s when James Dean started wearing his signature jeans, a T-shirt, and sneakers.

I closed my eyes and listened to the chatter on the bus, accents blending together like the countless styles of athletic shoes, the myriad layers of the scent of lavender. I could pick out a voice that sounded like home behind me, plus a couple of southern accents up in front. I'd read that the Pacific Northwest accent was subtle but sounded slightly creaky, and unlike the rest of the country, people who lived there pronounced the vowels in *caught* and *cot* exactly the same. I listened some more, but I didn't hear anyone creaking, or talking about caught *or* cots.

My phone rang. I fished it out of my purse. UNAVAILABLE, the screen read.

"Hello," I said. Tess and Rosie looked over at me.

"It's Michael," Michael's voice said.

"Why are you calling me?" I said.

"Boy, do you have a double," he said.

"What?" I said.

"Yeah, a dead ringer for you. She even lives in Marshbury. It's all over the local news. Some nut and her friend covered the common with bubbles. They must have used one of those bubble makers."

"Laundry detergent," I said.

"Oh," he said. "I didn't see that part."

"Listen," I said. "I have to go. I'm in Sequim and my bus is just pulling into the lavender farm."

"Where?"

I flipped my phone shut.

"I am so dying to know who that was," Tess said.

Since Tess was sitting beside me on the bus, it was easy to elbow her.

"Ouch," she said.

"It's all over the news," I said.

"Relax," Tess said. "They'll never find you here."

"Us," I said. "They'll never find *us* here."

"Wow," Rosie said as soon as we stepped off the bus. "Lavender fields forever."

There were rows and rows of undulating lavender, in gorgeous shades of purple, blue, white, and pink, stretching out as far as the eye could see. Most were in full bloom, but some of the bushes had been sheared to a mushroom shape, with bunches of lavender tied into bouquets and resting crisscrossed over the top.

"That's to show a harvest in progress," Rosie said. "Over there is where you pick your own." Sure enough, there was a sign that said U PICK — $5/TWIST TIE.

"I don't get it," Tess said.

"You get as big a bouquet as you can get the twist tie around," Rosie said.

"Ooh, I love a challenge," Tess said.

My cell phone rang again. I fished in my purse and pulled it out. UNAVAILABLE, my caller ID said.

"Hello," I said.

"You hung up before I had a chance to say what I needed to say," Michael said.

"Fine," I said. "Shoot."

"Okay, well, it's just that I've been wondering if we should give it another try. I've missed you. And, man, I just don't know what to do with myself since I stopped working. I get up, I make coffee, I read the paper —"

"No thanks," I said. "But maybe you should give Sherry a call."

There was dead silence on the other end.

"Sorry," I said. "That was beneath me. Okay, here's the thing. You had your chance, and you totally, irrevocably blew it. I've moved on. And now I'm in the middle of an amazing vacation with some fabulous new friends. So if you'll excuse me . . ."

As soon as I hung up, Tess put an arm over my shoulder. "We are fabulous, aren't we? And you have a much more interesting social life than I gave you credit for."

"Come on," Rosie said. "Let's go get a snack. We've got twenty minutes before the essential oil distillation demonstration starts."

Tess rolled her eyes. "Yeah, don't make us late for that," she said.

Tess smiled at two men who were wearing sandals and white socks pulled up to their shins and talking in some unidentifiable language. "Cute guys around here, especially if you like bald heads and ponytails. Maybe you should ask somebody for a date, Noreen."

"Or you could," I said. "Though, who knows, if I wandered around by myself, I might meet my soul mate coming out of the Porta Potti."

Tess leaned back on her elbows. "Go ahead," she said. "We'll wait here. Don't worry, what happens in Squid stays in Squid."

We were stretched out at the edge of a huge field of lavender. "It's almost like Dorothy in her field of poppies," I said. "Pretty soon we're all going to start getting sleepy and have to curl up and take a nap."

"And probably get trampled to death," Tess said as a woman tripped over her foot and excused herself. "Dorothy had a lot more personal space in that poppy field."

"They're all great, but I think this is my favorite farm so far," Rosie said. She sat up and looked around. "Look, it's like a series of Monet paintings — everywhere you look, there's a new composition. I mean, whoever owns this farm has vision."

"And let's not forget the business angle," I said. "They sell everything but lavender kitchen sinks in that gift shop."

"And I totally love that picture of Jimi Hendrix over the cash register," Tess said. "Who says brain cells lost in the '60s don't regenerate."

My phone rang. I flipped it open. UN-AVAILABLE, it said.

I shook my head. "What," I said.

"Noreen? Hi, it's Rick."

"Rick," I said.

"Listen, I know I'm past the expiration date, but when I didn't see you at group today, it just hit me that I might never see you again. I mean, you sure sounded ready to graduate last time. So, anyway, I was hoping you'd like to go out tonight."

"And do what?" I asked, because I was curious.

"Wii tennis at the senior center?" he said.

I didn't say anything.

"Kidding," he said. "I was kidding. Dinner. A movie. Dinner and a movie. None of the above. Whatever you want to do."

"I can't," I said. "I'm in Sequim."

"What's a squim?"

"It's a town in Washington State. I'm here with some friends at a lavender festival."

"How about next week?"

"Let's talk about it next week," I said.

"So will I see you in group on Monday?" he said.

"Maybe," I said. "Depends on how tired I am. Maybe Monday or maybe Friday."

"Okay, well, have a good time. See you next week, Noreen."

"Different guy?" Rosie said after I'd closed my phone again.

"Mmm," I said.

"You know," Tess said. "I used to feel a little bit sorry for you, but now I'm not so sure."

"Come on," Rosie said. "Even I've had enough lavender for the day. Let's go find a winery."

This time I drove, while Tess and Rosie

opened up winery tour maps.

"Okay," Tess said. "We've got our choice of seven award-winning artisan wineries."

"Just pick the closest one," I said. "It's not like we know anything about wine anyway."

"Speak for yourself," Tess said. "*Sideways* is one of my favorite movies."

"Okay," Rosie said. "Let's try the 'small family-owned winery on a wooded shoulder of Lost Mountain, in the Olympic foothills.' It's right in Sequim. Okay, head west on 101."

"What a great spot," I said when we pulled into the parking lot. What I was really thinking was what a romantic place to bring a date. The weathered wood building had a secluded, tree-canopied patio tucked in next to it. If I ever came back again, I wondered who'd be with me.

The tasting room was dark, almost like the inside of an oak barrel.

"Have you ever done this before?" I whispered. I wasn't sure whether to pretend to be just looking or to make my way boldly up to the wine bar.

The woman standing behind the bar must have known we were rookies. "Step right up," she said with a big smile. We each paid a small tasting fee and she handed us a menu. "You can choose any five wines to sample. We've got them listed in the best order for tasting, starting with the lightest, pinot grigio, and moving toward our boldest cabernet sauvignon. We specialize in robust reds made without sulfites."

She turned to pour for three women standing next to us at the bar.

"This is so cool," Rosie whispered. "I'm dying to spit in that big brass spittoon."

"Don't waste it," Tess said. "I think they only give you half an ounce with each pour."

We decided to skip the whites and jump right into the robust reds.

"That's what we did, too," one of the women standing next to us said. "You here for the lavender festival?"

We nodded.

"I have a small lavender farm in Massachusetts," Rosie said. "I'm ready to pack it up and move it out here. They're really on to something. You put eight lavender farms together and suddenly there's a culture."

One of the women laughed. "We were just plotting how we could move here from Ohio and start our own winery."

"Nice jacket," Tess said to the one who'd spoken.

"Chico's," she said. "Love that blouse."

290

"Thanks," Tess said. "J. Jill."

"Ohmigod," one of the other women said. "We found the best Target on the way up. I got these great exercise pants marked down to practically nothing."

"Gotta love Tarjay," I said. I tried to check out their feet to see if they were wearing sneakers and, if so, what kind they were, but it was too dark. "Are you walkers?"

"Kayakers," Chico's Jacket said. "We did three hours of sea kayaking on Dungeness Bay this morning. Talk about an upper body workout."

"Wow," I said. "We're planning to walk the Dungeness Spit out to the lighthouse while we're here." When she didn't look that impressed, I added, "Five miles each way."

"Over rough terrain," Tess said.

Rosie rolled her eyes. "On our hands."

Everybody laughed. I took a sip of our second wine, a cabernet franc, or cab franc, as I'd know enough to call it from now on.

The tallest of the three women reached for a cracker. "Whatever you do, don't miss the REI flagship store in Seattle while you're out here. It's got a sixty-five-foot climbing wall."

"Only sixty-five feet?" I said.

Day 27:
17,777 steps

Tess added some more lavender honey to her tea. "I can't believe we couldn't even stay awake for the puffin cruise last night," she said. "We're a disgrace."

Rosie took a bite of a tiny doughnut sprinkled with lavender sugar. "These are so good," she said. "No we're not. We just had a busy day. And we've got another one today."

Tess shook her head. "And I still can't believe we haven't found lavender black currant champagne anywhere. Maybe it's a bait and switch."

"Maybe it's a drink," Rosie said. "You know, you muddle lavender and black currants together and then add champagne."

"Too much work," Tess said. "We're on vacation."

"I'm dying to learn how to make lavender wands," I said. I took another sip of my lavender iced tea. "I thought my muslin lavender sachet bag came out great yesterday."

"Boring," Tess said. "I thought this was going to be a little bit more of an adventure, not a crafts session. Although I'm planning on making lavender halos with ribbon streamers on the first day back at school. The kids will love it, and halos couldn't hurt in terms of setting the tone for the year's behavior. I think I'll send the directions to Annalisa when I hear from her."

"Nothing yet?" Rosie asked.

"I'll check again later," Tess said. "Did you see that lavender pasta salad at that farm café yesterday? I am so having that for lunch. We might have to tack an extra five thousand steps on today. I was finally back into my old jeans before we left."

"I think I'll go for the lavender chicken tahini wrap this time," Rosie said. "And I really want to try a piece of lavender cheese-cake at some point. I'll just throw out my old jeans, if it comes to that."

I held up my finished lavender wand for the instructor to admire. "This is the coolest thing ever," I said. "I want one for each of my drawers, and I think I might even hang one from the rearview mirror of my car. And my mother is so going to want one for her lingerie drawer."

"I'd almost forgotten how to make these," Rosie said. "My mother used to make them every year. Be sure the ribbon is pulled really tight, because it will loosen up as the lavender dries. And if the scent starts to fade, you just have to squeeze the wand, and it will renew."

Tess held hers up. "They're actually kind of phallic," she said, "not that I'm complaining. Can we go do some more wine tasting today? If we start early, we might be able to get to the rest of the six wineries."

"Maybe," I said. "Let's go back to the hotel, drop this stuff off, and pick up the car."

We grabbed the C bus to the street fair, then hoofed it back to the hotel from there. Rosie sprawled out on the cot and checked her pedometer. "I feel great," she said. "The air, the lavender, the food . . ."

"The fabulous company," I said.

"The fabulous company," she said.

Tess was firing up her laptop. "Check the news," I said on my way into the bathroom. "That video can't still be up, can it?"

"Oh, no," Tess was saying when I came out.

"Damn," I said. "It's still up?"

"Oh, no," Tess said again in a tiny voice.

"What?" Rosie said. She sat down beside

Tess on the couch.

I was afraid to sit down. Maybe Hannah had been arrested, or worse. I should have told Tess I knew she was sneaking around. The point wasn't whether or not Hannah would have ever spoken to me again. I should have done it to keep her safe. And because Tess was my friend.

I made myself sit down on Tess's other side. A message filled her computer screen.

This update is being posted by Annalisa Grady's family. As some of you know by now, Annalisa passed Tuesday evening. She was surrounded by her loved ones, and she died peacefully in her sleep.

Among her final requests was that we tell everyone at this care site how grateful she was to her sister teachers and friends for their loving support. We thank you, too, more than we can ever say. Annalisa was a very lucky woman to be able to call so many people from all over the world her friends. Although she was no longer able to post, her delight in reading your messages continued until the end. Know that they made all the difference.

Annalisa's wish was that her remains be cremated, and that in lieu of flowers, donations be made to a fund for teaching supplies started in her name. Information for donating to and applying for funds from the Ms. Grady the Great Memorial Fund follows this message.

As those of you in the New Orleans area already know, a memorial service will take place Sunday at 3 P.M. in Annalisa's school gymnasium. Annalisa asked that we celebrate her life and not mourn her death, so if you're near NOLA, we hope you'll come on down. If not, please close your eyes and say a prayer for our Annalisa.

Tears were burning my eyes and streaming down my face. "Ohmigod," I said. "I can't believe it."

"It just sucks," Rosie said. She pulled a travel pack of tissues from her purse and passed them around. "She was so young. Wasn't she?"

Tess blew her nose. "I'm not sure," she said. "I think she was probably our age. But we have to go."

"Go?" I said.

Tess was already searching for flights.

"The memorial service. We have to go to Annalisa's memorial service."

"Do you have any idea how much it would cost us to fly from Seattle to New Orleans tomorrow?" I said. "Plus, we'd have to buy another ticket back to Boston, too."

"Maybe we can get a bereavement fare," Tess said. "I think we just have to show a copy of the death certificate."

"Tess," I said. "You can't get a copy of Annalisa's death certificate. You barely knew her."

Tess slid her laptop down to the coffee table and closed it like a coffin. She put her elbows on her knees and buried her head in her hands. Rosie sniffed. I blew my nose.

Tess lifted her head up. "If this were the movie of our lives, we'd go."

Rosie smiled. "It would be the montage part. Everything would go all slow motion and we'd be running to make the plane. And then there'd be scenes from Annalisa's life, and our lives, too."

"And music," I said. "Maybe 'Stairway to Heaven.' "

"No, that's all wrong," Rosie said. "Minnie Riperton's 'Lovin' You.' You know, the one with the bird sounds. I bet Annalisa liked that song."

" 'Let It Be' by the Beatles," Tess said. "I

think that would be classy. I like the line about whispering words of wisdom."

"I wish I had some," I said. I could feel my lower lip start to quiver again, and I bit down on it hard.

"So what do we do then?" Tess said.

I blew my nose again and thought about it. "We buy a couple bottles of local wine. . . ."

"And a corkscrew," Rosie said.

"And a corkscrew," I said. "And we take them down to the Five-Mile Dungeness Spit. We walk the whole way out, and we celebrate Annalisa's life. We'll stay there as long as it takes. All night, if we have to."

Tess pushed herself to her feet. "I'm in," she said. "But maybe we should make lavender black currant champagne instead. I think Annalisa would like that."

Nancy, our sneaker-clad friend at the front desk, talked the bartender in the lounge into selling us two bottles of champagne and drew directions to the Dungeness Spit on a hotel map for us. She circled a description in a brochure and gave us that, too.

"You can't drink there," she said. "It's a national wildlife refuge."

"Don't worry," Tess said. "We wouldn't dream of it."

"Watch the tides," Nancy said. "And the light."

"Don't worry," I said. "We live near the beach."

Culinary lavender was easy to find at the street fair, and at the far end we finally found a farm stand with black currants.

Tess slipped the little green cardboard box of black currants into a plastic bag and tied it tight.

Rosie unzipped her backpack again. "I'm so glad I brought one of the kids' back-packs," Rosie said. "But we're going to have to take turns carrying it. Between the water and the champagne, it's pretty heavy."

"Okay," I said. "It says we head west on Highway 101, then turn north on Kitchen-Dick road."

"There's a joke there," Tess said. "But I'm not in the mood."

"Do you think we should bring food, too?" Rosie asked. "Just to absorb the cham-pagne?"

"We'll be fine," Tess said. "We'll have a late dinner when we get back. I'm too sad to eat."

Tess put the backpack on when we got to Kitchen-Dick Road, and I read from the directions. "Continue three miles to the Dungeness Recreation Area."

We were quieter than usual, and instead of our alternating dance of one up front, two behind, we walked single file. We stopped about midway for water, and I took over the backpack.

At the Dungeness Recreation Area parking lot, we took another water break. Normally, we would have checked our pedometers, but I guess we were all too busy thinking about Annalisa.

We walked up a gradual hill and passed a campground. We made a stop at the restrooms, refilled our water bottles at the water fountain, then paid our fee at the Dungeness National Wildlife Refuge entrance booth.

"I'll count you all as one family, so that'll be three dollars," the man in the booth said. "Just put the money in the slot right there."

"Thanks," Rosie said. "That's really nice of you."

He looked at his watch. "You're only going to have time to make it to the overlook. That's three-eighths of a mile. It's about another five miles out to the lighthouse, so it's too late for that today. The refuge closes promptly at dusk. You sure you don't want to come back tomorrow instead? I'll give you a full refund."

"Nah," Tess said. "We're big spenders."

"Watch the light," the man said, "and don't stay out there too long."

We were definitely walking against the traffic. We spread out across the trail when we could but had to keep stepping right to make a single file so people could walk by us on their way out. There were families, couples, and groups of friends. Most of them looked pretty exhausted.

The forested trail dropped steeply but gracefully as it meandered down to the water. "This is gorgeous," Rosie whispered.

I read the little plaques at the base of the plants as we passed them. Oceanspray. False lily-of-the-valley. Douglas Fir, Tess's old boyfriend, was the only one I recognized.

We took turns peering through two big telescopes when we got to the overlook.

"Will you look at those mountains," Rosie said. "So amazing."

"And that's some wild water," Tess said. "Wow, the lighthouse is a long way out. I mean, is this the mother of all sand spits, or what?"

I sat down on a bench and took out my brochure. "It says the lighthouse closes at dusk, too. But they also have picnic tables out there."

"Wouldn't they be closed if the lighthouse is closed?" Rosie said.

"That's ridiculous," Tess said. "How can you close a picnic table?"

"We're pretty fast walkers," I said. "We'll be back before we know it."

"There's probably no better place in the world to drink a toast to Annalisa," Tess said.

"It's totally insane," Rosie said. "Come on, let's do it."

We made our way carefully down a steep hill, then picked up our pace as we walked onto the spit. The crashing of the waves was unexpectedly loud, and the wind whipped our hair all over the place.

But the driftwood was the biggest surprise. Huge weathered logs, even whole trees, plus tons and tons of smaller pieces of sun-bleached driftwood were scattered all along our path. They seemed to anchor the narrow strip of sand somehow, as if maybe without all these huge hunks of wood, the spit would simply wash out to sea.

"It's almost like a sculpture garden," Rosie said.

"Or a graveyard," Tess said.

Four women with white hair and matching purple fanny packs were just coming off the spit. "What a workout," one of them yelled.

"Too late to make it now," another said

when they got closer. "It'll be dark before you know it."

"We wouldn't dream of it," Tess said. She pointed to me. "My friend just left her jacket on a rock back there."

"Brown," I said. "With a hood."

We tried to stay on the packed sand close to the water and away from the piles of rocks higher up, which slipped and slid under our feet and made the going tough. We walked quickly, swinging our arms and stretching out our legs. My calves were a little bit tight, but other than that, I felt great. It was amazing to think that not so very long ago, I wasn't sure if I could walk a lap around Wildwater Way.

Now I knew that the hardest part of any workout was just putting on your sneakers. Once you got started, all you had to do was keep placing one foot in front of the other, no matter what was or wasn't happening in your life, no matter how happy or sad you were. I'd taken that first step because I'd wanted to look better. I'd wanted my clothes to fit. But it hadn't taken me long to figure out that the biggest benefit was less about vanity than it was about sanity. Walking always helped.

A bald eagle soared overhead. A harbor seal stretched out on a rock.

"Aww," we all said as it slithered off the rock and dove into the water.

The spit kept turning to the right, so all we could see ahead of us was water.

"I'll feel better when we can actually see the lighthouse," Tess said. "I know it's out there, but it still seems like blind faith. Not to sound religiously incorrect or anything, but it really is a little bit like walking on water."

"I wish I could tell how much longer we have till sunset," Rosie said. Off to our left, an orange-glow sun was looking suspiciously low over the snowcapped mountains.

Finally, we saw the lighthouse and a couple of other buildings up ahead.

Rosie stopped walking. "Okay, I know we're more than halfway there, but I think if we turn around now, we can still make it back before dark."

Tess stopped and looked around. "We're almost there," she said.

"I really think we should go back," Rosie said.

Ahead of us, the lighthouse beckoned. It was a tall lighthouse, with an expanse of rolling green lawn all around it.

"You can't ever go back," I said. "If this were a movie, that would totally be the best line." I started jogging toward the lighthouse.

"Come on," I yelled, "it's the Wildwater Way!" And then I looked back, just to make sure Tess and Rosie were behind me.

"You know," Rosie said. "This is kind of fun, once you get past the sheer terror stage."

"How bad can it be?" Tess said. "We have champagne."

"And we have cell phones," I said. "I'm sure we could get the Coast Guard to rescue us if we had to."

"I'm just going to pretend we're camping," Rosie said.

We finished making a loop around. There were three buildings, including an unlocked bathroom with running water.

We sat down at the picnic table, and I popped a bottle of champagne. Tess pulled out three plastic cups, and we added some lavender flowers and some black currants to each one.

"Pardon my fingers," Rosie said as she mashed everything in the bottom of the cups. "Silly me, I forgot to pack a muddler."

I poured in the champagne, and we all picked up our cups. "To Annalisa," Tess said. "Who gave so much to so many. May her memory live on forever."

We touched plastic cups and drank.

"Hey, this is really good," I said.

"I wish you'd met her," Tess said. "I wish *I'd* met her. I wish she were alive and sitting right here with us."

"I know," Rosie and I both said at once.

"I am so getting a mammogram when I get home," I said. "I'm way overdue."

"I'm almost afraid to get one now," Rosie said. "I'm not sure I'd want to know."

"I'm getting a full-body scan," Tess said. "Whether I need one or not."

We sipped for a while in silence. The mountains stretched out across the horizon, and the ocean surrounded us in this perfect piece of paradise. An incredible array of birds careened and squawked overhead.

"I think we're going to miss the puffin cruise again," Tess said.

"Maybe it'll stop for us here," I said.

We both started to laugh like crazy.

"It's not that funny," Rosie said. She poured some more champagne.

Tess ran her finger around the edge of her cup. "I guess all the clichés are true. You never know when your time might be up."

"You've got to live every day like it's your last," Rosie said.

"You have to appreciate every single mo-

306

ment on Kitchen-Dick Road," I said.

Rosie and I laughed this time. Tess just took another sip of champagne.

"You okay?" I asked.

"My daughter hates me," she said.

"Of course she does," Rosie said. "She's supposed to hate you. It's developmental."

Tess shook her head. "She thought she was pregnant. I mean, can you believe it? We had all the right talks, I gave her all the right books, she knew how to get birth control."

"What happened?" Rosie said.

"She finally got her period," Tess said. "And then she accused me of trying to kill my own grandchild, because I talked to her about her choices."

"She'll get over it," Rosie said.

"Maybe," Tess said. "But here's the thing. These kids are all so entitled. They just assume we'd like nothing more than to turn the basement playroom into an apartment and invite the boyfriend over to play house. Everybody's doing it. I know this one woman whose sixteen-year-old daughter is pregnant, and her son's girlfriend and their baby just moved in, too. It's like an enabling epidemic. I could see the writing on the wall. I don't want to be the babysitter. I want my own life."

She put her head on the table and started to cry, small sobs at first, then big, ragged ones. Rosie reached across the picnic table and stroked her hand. I was sitting next to Tess, so I patted her on the back.

"There are lots of couples out there looking for a baby to adopt," Rosie said softly.

Tess whipped her head up. "Oh, please," she said. "She can't even give away her old toys."

"I had a baby at her age," Rosie whispered. "It was tough, but I kept him. You make your bed . . ."

"With your husband?" I asked.

Rosie shook her head. "Different one," she said. "Anyway, he's all grown up with kids of his own now."

"That must have been tough," Tess said. "What did your parents do?"

"My mother was okay, but my father didn't speak to me for almost a year," Rosie said. "He'd just leave the room when I came to visit."

"I wouldn't have dared tell my parents I was pregnant," Tess said. "And what kind of parent would I have been back then? I'm not even that great now."

Rosie leaned back on her elbows. "You do the best you can with what you have to work with, I guess. My son and I kind of grew up together."

I closed my eyes. "Tess," I said. "I saw Hannah sneak out one night. And that time we were decorating shoelaces together? She told me to tell you she'd just left if you asked."

Tess didn't say anything.

"I'm really sorry," I said. "I should have told you right away. I don't know, maybe I thought it wasn't my business, or that you'd yell at me. But I really think I just wanted Hannah to think I was cool."

Even if Tess never spoke to me again, I felt better. At least I thought I did.

Tess chugged the rest of her champagne. She stood up. "Do you want to know why I'm such a do-gooder? Because volunteering is so much easier than having to look at the way you've screwed up in your own life."

She paced a lap around the picnic tables, then sat down again. "Wait till I get my hands on her," she said. She reached over and gave me a quick hug. "Brave woman," she said. "Once I told a friend of mine her daughter threw a wild party while she was away, and she told me I was just jealous because her daughter was more popular than mine."

"Sorry I didn't tell you sooner," I said.

"But you told me," she said. "Thanks."

We moved down to the edge of the water and sat on a big piece of driftwood. We put our champagne glasses on the ground and pulled our lavender wands from Rosie's backpack. They were a little bit smooshed, but we straightened them out as best we could and waved them around like sparklers as we watched the sunset. It was a truly amazing sunset extravaganza — fiery orange with streaks of purple over a navy blue sea, with a backdrop of white-tipped mountains.

As the sun disappeared, we tried a chorus of "Let It Be," but we couldn't quite pull it off, so we switched to "Walk On By."

"It doesn't really fit, but I think she'd understand," Rosie said when we finished. "It's our only song. We'd probably never make it as a girl group."

Across the Strait of Juan de Fuca, the city lights of Victoria twinkled over at us. Above us, a zillion stars lit up the endless sky.

"Good-bye, Annalisa," we said. "Shine on."

Day 28:
15,295 STEPS

"Noreen," Rosie whispered. "Are you awake?"

"Yeah," I whispered.

"Me, too," Tess said.

"I'm freezing," Rosie said.

Tess and I each grabbed one of her hands and started rubbing. It was pitch-black in the restroom. We were leaning back against a metal railing in the alcove outside the single bathroom. Every time I moved an inch, I had to warm up the railing all over again.

"That's what you get for being so skinny," Tess said. "Real women have body fat."

"Boyohboy, could I use a pillow," I said. "And a sleeping bag. Or a fire, a big roaring fire."

"Why didn't I think to bring a flashlight?" Rosie said. "Can you believe I actually took one out of this backpack before I packed it?"

I pushed myself up to a standing position and felt my way over to the light switch.

Tess and Rosie put their hands over their faces as soon as the fluorescent lights started flickering.

"It's not just the cold," Rosie said. "I'm really, really hungry."

"Wait," I said. "I might have something."

I rooted around in the backpack until I found a candy bar.

"Bless you," Rosie said. "What kind is it?"

"Lavender dark chocolate," I said. "What else?"

"Here, give me that backpack," Rosie said. "I packed a nail file, too, in case one of us broke a nail."

"No wonder the damn thing was so heavy," I said. I opened the wrapper and carefully scored the chocolate bar with the nail file so I could break it into three equal pieces.

Tess held hers out to Rosie. "Here, take mine. I have a slow metabolism."

"No," Rosie said. "You have it. Ohmigod, this is the best thing I've ever eaten in my entire life."

I took tiny bites and savored each rich, lavender-laced bite as it melted in my mouth.

"Wait," Rosie said. "Doesn't this remind

you of that *I Love Lucy* episode. . . ."

"The one in the Swiss Alps," I said.

"When they get caught in the avalanche," Tess said.

"I loved *I Love Lucy*," Rosie said. "I had such a crush on Ricky."

"Fred was highly underrated," Tess said. "He was always there for Ethel. And I loved how he called her Honeybunch."

I popped the last tiny bit into my mouth. "That's it," I said. "I've had enough adventure. It's forty-something degrees in this bathroom and it smells." I pulled my cell phone out of my pocket. "Shit. No service."

Rosie and Tess pulled their phones out, and Tess put her reading glasses on. "Nothing," Tess said.

Rosie held her phone away from her and closed one eye. "Bingo," she said. "Four bars."

"Who do you have?" Tess asked.

"AT&T," Rosie said.

Tess shook her head. "If we make it out of here alive, I am so changing my cell provider."

Rosie pushed herself to a standing position. "Who should I call? Nine-one-one?"

There was a knock on the restroom door.

Tess jumped up. "Find a weapon," she whispered.

Rosie grabbed a plunger from the bathroom stall.

There was another knock on the restroom door, this one louder.

"Just a minute," I said in a singsong voice.

The door opened, and two scared-looking women shined flashlights in our eyes. Both were holding long wooden pool cues.

"Well, that was fun," Tess said. "I haven't played pool in ages."

Rosie handed the backpack to me, then started swinging her arms again. "Who knew they let people stay in the Dungeness Lighthouse. We should definitely try to get on the list for next year."

"I can't believe we never thought to knock on the door," I said. "Although in our defense, it's not like we saw any lights on in there. Except the one on top, of course."

"That's because they were in the game room in the basement," Tess said. "I can't believe there's a game room. And a television. I'm not sure that's quite fair somehow."

"At least they had bunk beds," Rosie said. "I don't know about yours, but mine was surprisingly comfortable."

"Yeah," Tess said. "It's not that I don't love nature, it's just that I want amenities.

It was really nice of them to let us stay. And I think they meant it when they said they'd come visit us in Marshbury, too."

"I have plenty of room," I said. "They can stay with me."

"I still can't believe that thing they told us," Rosie said, "about black currant champagne being made with ordinary crème de cassis. All that muddling for nothing."

"It was worth it," Tess said. "I know Annalisa appreciated the gesture."

The wind whipped our already wind-matted hair around, and the sun was moving higher up over the mountains to our right. To our left, we could see a huge cruise ship way off in the distance, maybe on its way to Alaska. The tide was going out, giving us more and more packed hard sand to walk on.

"How about the looks on their faces?" Tess said. "I mean, how scared were they?"

"We were pretty scared ourselves," I said.

"Not me," Rosie said. "I had the plunger."

"You know what the best part is?" I said. I checked my pedometer. "All that walking we did yesterday, and look at us today. I mean, my legs are a little tight, but other than that, I'm ready for the next adventure."

The sixty-five-foot REI climbing wall was

called the Pinnacle, and they gave us pagers so we could shop while we waited for our turns. We'd considered a spin or two around the mountain bike test trail instead, but after packing, checking out of the Sequim Suites, and making the two-hour drive back to Seattle, we were running a bit low on energy.

"Shopping always works," Tess said. "It's the world's best pick-me-up."

"Food is better," Rosie said. "And it's a lot less work."

"Tie breaker," Tess said. "Come on, Noreen, which is better, shopping or food?"

"Shopping for food?" I said. "Ohmigod, look at this." I held up a beautiful teal jacket called a power hoodie. The name alone might have made me buy it, but I also thought it would be perfect for walking my way through the next season.

I looked at Rosie and Tess. "Maybe we should have a Wildwater Walking Club uniform?"

"Nah," we all said. Tess picked out a jacket in orange and Rosie found one in sage.

Our pagers went off before we had time to do any more damage.

The climbing wall was a scarily realistic rock sculpture encased in a tall glass box attached to the store.

We looked up. Way up. "Maybe it's just because I'm short," Rosie said, "but sixty-five feet is a lot higher than it sounds."

"We'll be fine," I said. "It says here you only have to be eight years old to climb it."

"I was a lot braver when I was eight," Tess said.

We were each assigned to a friendly outdoorsy-looking staffer, who helped us into our safety gear and "belayed" us by holding on to ropes attached to our harnesses by metal hooks called carabiners.

We all made it at least partway up our beginner's route, and more importantly, all the way back down in one piece. It was truly terrifying, even after I discovered that the trick to rock climbing is not to look down. Because if you look down, you'll realize how certifiably insane you are.

I stepped out of my harness and handed it to a woman my age. She looked scared.

"You'll be fine," I said. "Just don't look down."

"We totally rocked it," Tess said as she stepped out of her harness. "I bet we have just as much upper body strength as those kayak women at the winery. Maybe even more."

"I wouldn't mind doing some kayaking," Rosie said, "just to break it up. And we should definitely check out the REI trip-planning area on the way out."

I massaged the front of my thighs, where I could feel the lactic acid already starting to build up in the muscles. I knew I'd be sore, but I'd also lived up to the challenge. I felt feisty and fabulous.

Finding a parking place at Pike Place Market turned out to be a bigger challenge than the REI climbing wall. Eventually we found a garage way up the hill, then practically rolled our way back down to the waterfront. It was worth it. The market was a sprawling maze of vendors' stalls and mul-tileveled old buildings. We sampled chocolate-covered cherries at Chukar Cher-ries and pepper jellies on crackers at Mick's Peppourri. We took turns putting pennies into Rachel the Pig, the unofficial Pike Place Market mascot piggy bank.

We wove our way through a waterfront teeming with people, then started climbing back up the hill, trying to decide where to grab something to eat before we headed for the airport.

"Ooh, let's go there," Rosie said. She pointed to a purple sign that said PURPLE CAFÉ AND WINE BAR.

"How perfect," Tess said.

"Do you have a good cab franc?" I said to

impress the gorgeous waiter when he came over to our table.

He smiled and flashed brilliantly white teeth. "Sorry, we're all out of wine." Behind him, an enormous round multistory wine rack took up the whole center of the room.

"Cut it out," I said.

He burst out laughing. " 'Cut it out,' " he said. "You sound like home. Massachusetts, right?"

"Right," I said.

"I went to school there," he said. "If you love Boston, you'll totally love Seattle."

"We do," we all said at once.

"Let me see if I can find you some wine," he said.

We looked around the room while we waited. Really handsome waiters glided around the room, and same-sex couples occupied many of the tables.

"Is this a gay bar?" Rosie whispered.

"Seems like," I said.

"What is it about the color purple?" Tess asked our waiter when he came back. "I mean, why do gay people get their own color? Straight people don't have a color."

"Cut it out," our waiter said as he put our wineglasses down in front of us. "You people don't have your own color yet?" He hugged his round tray into his chest and

319

considered. "Okay, you can have blue. It's right next to us on the color wheel."

"What a fun trip," Rosie said when we were finally back at the airport. "You'd think I'd be lavendered out, but I'm not. I'm almost looking forward to weeding mine tomorrow."

"You know," Tess said, "last night was actually a good thing. It got us on schedule for the red-eye. I can't believe we get into Boston at 10:42 A.M. I think this will be the first all-nighter I've pulled since college."

"I can't wait to check on my garden," I said.

"I wonder if my daughter has managed to escape yet," Tess said.

"Speaking of families," Rosie said, "I wonder if our parents are still a hot item."

"And I wonder," I said, "if I'm still the most wanted woman in Marshbury."

"You have to admit," Tess said, "that has a nice ring to it."

"Come on," Rosie said. "We have just enough time to hit ten thousand steps for the day before they board the plane. And then may I please have some more Valium? I promise I'll pay you back."

DAY 29:
10,232 STEPS

We'd slept most of the plane ride home, so we decided to have the driver drop us all off at my house. That way we could get a walk in before we reentered our lives.

We turned to look when we passed it, but all was quiet on the Marshbury common. The posters and clothesline were gone. Crystal clear water gushed from the three bronze elephants' trunks in the fountain.

"Let's just throw our stuff in your garage," Rosie said when we turned into Wildwater Way. "I'm dying to see my family, but if I go home first, I won't get out again until tomorrow."

"Yeah," Tess said. "I could definitely use some endorphins before I face my daughter. Plus, we should write down our mileage before we forget. It's never too soon to start stockpiling miles for the next trip."

"Maybe we can go to Cape Cod Lavender Farm later this week," I said.

"And visit the Five Sisters of Lavender Lane next week," Rosie said. She sighed. "I can dream, can't I?"

As soon as we finished recording our mileage, I carried my stuff into the house. There was a note from my mother. *Gone to Nantucket with Kent,* it said. *Watch out for the chickens.*

We all used the bathroom, grabbed bottles of water from my refrigerator, and headed out on our usual walk.

We saw the first clothesline while we were still on Wildwater Way. It was stretched across the front yard of a huge yellow colonial with black shutters, and big white sheets were blowing in the wind. Between two sheets, a sign was attached with clothespins. It said BAN THE BAN.

"Ohmigod," I said. "They stole my line."

"No pun intended," Rosie said.

Just before we crossed the street, we saw another sign: HANG IT UP: FIGHT FOR THE RIGHT TO AIR DRY was tacked to a telephone pole.

"This is so cool," I said. "Look what we've started."

"Excuse me," Tess said, "but I'm the one who started it."

"Excuse me," I said. "But I'm the one who could still get arrested."

"Well," Rosie said, "I want in. I'm still wiped out from that Valium, but as soon as I take a nap, I'll put up a sign at the end of my driveway. Oh, don't worry, I really will pay you back as soon as I get a prescription, Tess."

We walked through the seawall. It felt good to be walking on our own beach again. I kind of missed it.

"Actually, it was only magnesium," Tess said. "It wasn't really Valium."

"What?" Rosie said.

"It's called the placebo effect," Tess said.

"She once gave her husband a Smurf blue vitamin and told him it was Viagra." I giggled. "It worked like a charm."

Rosie turned and started race-walking in the other direction.

"Rosie," Tess said.

"Leave me alone," Rosie said.

I ran a few steps after her. "Rosie," I yelled.

"Both of you," she yelled without turning around.

Tess and I finished our walk, but we didn't say much. Rosie's luggage was gone when we got back to my garage. Tess grabbed hers and started rolling it across the lawn to her house.

"It'll blow over," I said. "We're all exhausted."

Tess just kept rolling.

I went inside, jumped in the shower, then brewed some coffee and ate a yogurt and an apple. I checked the clock over the stove. If I hurried, I had just enough time to make it to my Fresh Horizons South small-group counseling class.

I didn't have the energy to try to impress anyone today, and I wasn't even sure if I wanted to, so I just blow-dried my hair and threw on jeans and a T-shirt and a little bit of makeup.

I drove to Fresh Horizons South and pulled into the parking lot. Just as I was getting ready to open the car door, there was a knock on the passenger window. I jumped.

Rick smiled through the glass. He had a brand-new haircut, and he looked freshly shaven and distinctly unscruffy. I pushed the button and rolled down the window.

"Can I come in?" he asked.

"To the car?" I asked.

His cat green eyes held mine. "Well, you could take it more symbolically, I guess, but I'm okay with the car."

I flicked the unlock button from my side.

He climbed in, shut the door, and buckled his seat belt.

"Can I ask you why you put your seat belt on?" I asked.

He looked straight ahead. "I just wanted you to know I'm responsible," he said.

I cracked up.

"You have a great laugh," he said. "You should use it more often."

"Thank you," I said. "You know, you're a pretty funny guy."

"Thank you," he said. "Okay, we're compatible. Now can we go play miniature golf?"

I looked at my power watch. "It's twelve-fifty-seven. Our small-group coaching class starts in three minutes."

He shrugged. "So, let's skip."

I leaned back against the window on my side. "I thought you said you were responsible."

Rick wrinkled up his forehead. "I thought you said you wanted more fun in your life."

I smiled. "Sorry, but you're going to have to work a little harder than that."

We were both quiet walking into Fresh Horizons South. I chose a chair with empty seats on both sides of it.

Rick walked across the room and sat directly across from me. I pushed away a flicker of be-careful-what-you-wish-for disappointment.

My jet lag came in for a landing, and I drifted in and out of a fog. Brock videotaped two newbies, who seemed as dazed and confused as I'd been not so long ago. I was vaguely aware of Michael sitting across the room, trying to catch my eye. I ignored him.

Across from me, Rick put his hand up. Brock called on him, started the video camera, clapped his imaginary clapper. Rick looked right at the camera and introduced himself.

"I've made some good progress this past week," he said. "I've done some real soul searching about what I want my life to be. How I want to spend my days, how I can make a real contribution to the world . . ."

Brock was nodding proudly, and none of the Wii guys even made a crack.

". . . and I think I've finally figured out what I need to make my life complete."

Everybody leaned forward in their chairs.

Rick smiled. "I know now, beyond a shadow of a doubt, that if I can find the right person to play miniature golf with, everything else in my life will fall into place. Why, you might ask?" He cleared his throat. "Well, the little known truth is that you can figure out everything you need to know about a person in the first nine holes of a miniature golf game."

"Balls," one of the scruffy guys said, "you can never have enough of them."

Rick ignored him and looked right at me. "It might seem like just an insignificant game, but when your partner gets stuck in a sand trap, does she handle it with grace and tenacity? Do you? If your ball drops through the wrong hole or lands in the waterfall, does your partner just laugh at you, or does she laugh and then say, hey, tough break, but hang in there and you'll make it. When you find yourselves trapped in an old fortress with only a cannon to protect you, and pirates are attacking, do you have each other's back, or is it every man and woman for him-or herself? And, maybe most important of all, when you're tilting at windmills, it's not everyone who has the guts to give you the dose of reality you need. The little known fact is that you can recognize that person in an ordinary game of miniature golf, and when you do, you'll know the two of you have a shot together."

We took off as soon as the small-group class was over, while people were still milling around. Michael looked like he was about to say something to me as I walked by, but then he got pulled onto a Wii tennis team just in the nick of time.

"Nice job," I said.

"Thanks," Rick said. "I gave it everything I had."

He held the door open, and I climbed into his Honda. We found a miniature golf place right down the street. I'd driven past it a thousand times and never even noticed it.

"I can't believe we're doing this," I said.

He wrinkled his forehead. "Afraid you won't measure up?"

I walked ahead of him to pick out my club. "And I thought you were supposed to have my back."

"The better to kick your butt," he said.

"Be afraid," I said. "Be very afraid. I come from a long line of gifted professional mini golfers."

Fortunately, things were slow at Putt Putt Paradise, since my first shot went over Noah's Ark and hit the wooden pirate at the next hole right between the eyes.

"Oops," I said.

Rick leaned over his club. "You didn't do that on purpose?"

He executed a perfect shot past a couple of horses and through the opening in the ark. His ball rolled out the other side and came to a stop inches in front of the first hole.

I walked over to the next hole, retrieved my ball from the pirate, and went back to the beginning.

This time I managed to hit one of the horses in the shin. "Actually," I said, "I haven't played miniature golf since I was a kid."

"You'd never guess it," Rick said. "You're a natural."

"Right," I said.

"Can I give you a few pointers?" Rick asked when my next turn came.

"Please do," I said.

He put his arms around me and his hands over mine on the club. If I could have frozen a moment in time, this would have been it. I loved the smell of his hair, the warmth of his chest, the weight of his forearms. Maybe we could spend the rest of our lives as adjoining statues in Putt Putt Paradise.

We swung my club. My ball went high, then landed and rolled back down the hill and caught up to Jack and Jill, who were sprawled in a heap along with their empty pail of water.

I wriggled out from under Rick's arms. "That was helpful."

"Sorry," he said. "I got distracted."

Nine holes were over before we knew it. "Want to make it eighteen?" Rick asked.

"I'd love to," I said, "but I'm pretty tired. How about a rain check?"

"Absolutely."

Rick pulled his car up next to mine in the Fresh Horizons parking lot. "Thanks," I said. I leaned over and gave him a kiss on the cheek. "That was really fun."

"Thank *you*. You're the perfect miniature golf date, and I don't say that lightly."

We smiled into each other's eyes.

I floated over to my own car. I turned and waved, then unlocked the doors and climbed inside.

A minute later Rick was sitting in my passenger seat. "You sure you don't want to have a late lunch? Or an early dinner? You must need some kind of meal."

I shook my head. "Thanks. I appreciate the offer, but I'm on borrowed time already. I think I'll just go home and make myself a sandwich and go to bed."

"I don't suppose you want any company," Rick said.

I laughed. "It's our first date," I said.

"It's our second date," he said. He counted them off on his fingers. "Date number one, Wii bowling date. Date number two, miniature golf date." He looked up at the roof of my car. "If you'd let me buy you a sandwich, we could count it as date number three, and then I could kiss you. I make it a rule never to kiss until the third date."

He looked at me. I smiled. "I'm a second-date kind of kisser," I said.

"You hussy," Rick said. And then he kissed me.

It was a great kiss, but I didn't have much time to bask in it. When I opened my eyes, Michael was standing next to my car.

I couldn't think of another option, so I lowered my window.

"Listen," Michael said, "I really need to talk to you, Nora."

"Not now," I said.

"Listen," Michael said again. "We have a lot of time invested in our relationship, and I'm not going to let you go without a fight."

I heard my passenger door open with a click.

"Wait," I said.

Rick walked across the parking lot without looking back.

"Thanks, pal," Michael yelled.

"Tell me you didn't just say that in front of him," I said. I couldn't take my eyes off Rick. I watched him climb into his Honda and pull away.

Michael leaned over my window and blocked my view. "It's true," he said.

I opened my car door right into Michael.

He jumped back. "Hey," he said. "Watch the suit."

I climbed out. "I can't believe you even have the nerve to talk to me. You made me all sorts of half promises, talked me into taking a buyout, and then you dumped me. You wouldn't even take my phone calls." I crossed my arms over my chest. "And let's not forget about you and Sherry."

Michael ran one hand through his perfect brown hair. "Sherry who?" he said.

I opened my car door again. "I don't have time for this kind of conversation," I said. I climbed in and slammed the car door.

"Nora," Michael said. He reached for the car door.

I hit the lever and locked it, even though the window was still down. "Get out of my way," I said. "Or I'll drive right over you *and* your suit."

I pulled into the beach parking lot, so I could take a quick walk on the way home. I still had the rest of today's ten thousand steps to get in, and the good news about my confrontation with Michael was that now I was wide awake and I'd lost my appetite.

I didn't have my sneakers with me, so when I reached the sand, I just kicked off my sandals and carried them. As I walked, I wove my way among families with young kids, who were starting to pack up and head home to think about dinner. I watched a man rub sunscreen on a woman's shoulders.

After Michael and I started sneaking around, I used to sit in my office and wait for him to walk by, so I could see what he was wearing. I'd time my trips down the hallway to coincide with his, just so I could stand close enough to smell him. When we were in a meeting together, I'd look around the table and wonder what everyone would think if they *knew.*

The worst part of it was that, looking back, the sneaking around part might have been a big part of the draw. It was hard to imagine I'd ever been that bored or needy.

I walked down to the edge of the ocean and splashed through the cold, salty water. The tide had turned and was on its way out, leaving a fresh, ever-expanding beach that felt new and clean and ready to be discovered.

After I finished walking, I drove home barefoot, windows down, radio blasting, singing along with David Ogden's "No Better Place."

When I turned on to Wildwater Way, I could see Michael's red vintage Mustang convertible sitting in my driveway with the top down. My first impulse was to circle the cul-de-sac and drive right out again, but I figured I might as well get it over with.

As soon as I turned off my radio, I heard chickens clucking like crazy.

"Nora," Michael yelled. "Call nine-one-one!"

The Supremes had him backed up against my front door, and they were pecking at his shoes.

He gave his foot a little kick. "Come on, knock it off," he said. "That's Italian leather."

I got out of my car so I could get a better view. "How's it going?" I asked.

"Hurry up," Michael said. "Do something."

"Here's the thing about hens," I said. "They don't take disloyalty lightly. These three ganged up on a rooster once and killed him, just because he didn't really give a shit about them."

"Ouch," Michael said. "Hey, come on, what did I ever do to them?"

"It might be time to reassess your life," I said, "when even the chickens have got your number." Then I went in through my back door to get some cereal.

"So, that's it?" Michael said after I'd

finished walking the Supremes halfway down the path back to Rosie's house. "They just wanted a snack?" He was leaning up against his car, trying to be cool, but I could tell he was ready to jump in and make a quick getaway if he had to.

"Why are you here?" I asked.

"I wanted to talk to you," he said.

I reached in for a handful of Kashi Good Friends, then held the box out to Michael. He shook his head.

I popped some cereal into my mouth. "So," I said. "Talk."

"I think I might have a lead on a job," Michael said. "A start-up shoe company on the Left Coast. I'm over the whole EBAC thing."

It was like he was speaking a language I no longer understood. I vaguely remembered VRIF was the Voluntary Reductions in Force phase, and IRIF the Involuntary Reductions in Force phase. CAD was Computer Aided Disaster and GIGO meant Garbage In Gospel Out. All this corporate speak seemed like such a long, long time ago.

"EBAC?" I said.

Michael flashed his perfect teeth. "Extremely Big-Ass Corporation. This one is small enough that I'm hoping I can talk them into letting me consult under the table at a reduced rate until my benefits run out. I mean, what's not to like? It's a total WW."

I raised an eyebrow.

"Win-win," he said. "Anyway, I was thinking you should come with me, Nora. You know, fresh start and all that. I mean, what's holding either of us back?"

"I'm sorry," I said.

"That's okay," Michael said. "Stuff happens. I think we both have to turn the page and move forward."

I popped some more cereal into my mouth and chewed while I let Michael's profound cluelessness sink in. I hoped it was a measure of my recent growth that I could no longer imagine being even remotely attracted to him. He looked like a pair of my mother's penguin earrings in that stupid suit.

"No," I said, "that's not what I meant. I'm trying to say that I'm sorry any of it happened. I mean, all that sneaking around . . ."

He raised an eyebrow. "Well, you have to admit, it was pretty hot."

I didn't bother to say that I thought the idea of it had been hotter than the actuality.

"I was kidding," Michael said. "Come on."

I shrugged.

"It's about Sherry, isn't it?"

"No," I said, "it really isn't."

"That guy who was in your car?"

I knew that even with a hundred guesses, Michael would never get it, so I told him.

"It's me," I said. "I know what I want now. Or at least I know what I don't want."

Michael reached for a handful of cereal. "Listen, it doesn't matter how things started. What matters is that we both want it to work. Come on, we have so much commonality, so many shared memories. . . ."

I started closing up the cereal box. "I'm going inside now. It's over. And I really need a glass of milk."

I turned and started walking toward my house.

"Okay," he yelled, just as I was opening my front door. "But don't think you can call me a few months from now when things don't work out with that guy you were kissing. This is a take-it-or-leave-it one-time offer, Nora."

I turned around.

"Oh, Michael," I said. "Grow up."

Day 30:
10,349 STEPS

"You are not going to believe this," Tess yelled from her front steps, even though it was 8 A.M.

"What?" Rosie and I stage-whispered.

"I am so incredibly pissed off," Tess said as we all walked out to Wildwater Way. "There are two women going around town claiming to be the ones who put bubbles in the fountain. I mean, you leave Marshbury for one lousy weekend, and suddenly people are impersonating you."

"Wait," I said. Rosie moved up in front of us so Tess and I could walk side by side. "Isn't this a good thing? Call me crazy, but if anybody gets arrested for putting bubbles in the fountain, I'd actually prefer it to be someone other than me."

"That's ridiculous," Tess said. "I hate that they're taking credit. Okay, we have to step things up a notch before anybody else thinks of it. As soon as we finish walking, we make

338

up some flyers. We deliver them house to house, and anywhere we see a clothesline and/or a sign, we knock and extend a personal invitation."

Rosie turned around. "To what?"

We caught up with her and crossed the street. Then we spread out across our shortcut road. "To a secret meeting of the Marshbury Ban the Ban Alliance. We'll plan our strategy at the first meeting. I was thinking we should get the group to storm a selectmen's meeting, but we might want to just cut to the chase and ask them to put us on the agenda."

"Can we have the meeting in my lavender shed?" Rosie asked. "It's almost all cleaned up, thanks to Noreen's mother and my father. It looks so great, and I really should be thinking about drumming up some business. Unless you think that's too self-serving?"

"Nah," Tess said. "It's just good multitasking. Your shed would be perfect. And we can set up chairs on the lawn if we get an overflow crowd."

"Great," Rosie said. "I've got some tiki torches I can burn citronella and lavender oil in to keep the mosquitoes away."

"You might want to lock up Rod and the Supremes, too," I said. "So your dad doesn't have to rescue my mom again."

Rosie gave me a little smile as we walked across the beach parking lot. "I think that's half the fun," she said.

We walked single file through the opening in the seawall and spread out across the hard-packed sand closest to the water. The tide was almost dead low again, and we had to jump over ribbons of seaweed as we walked. I wondered if the next tide, or the one after that, would bring Rick back into my life. I liked him. I hoped he'd call, but I was okay if he didn't.

The wheels that had been turning in some mysterious part of my brain suddenly clicked into alignment. I raced to the hardware store and bought all ten retractable clotheslines they had left.

"Wow," the woman behind the counter said as she rang them up. "You must have some serious dirty laundry. You know, there's been a real run on clothespins lately, too. Time to reorder, I guess."

I pulled a flyer out of my purse. BAN THE BAN, it said. THE MARSHBURY CLOTHES-LINE ALLIANCE CORDIALLY INVITES YOU TO LEARN MORE ABOUT HOW GREEN IS THE NEW BLACK AND CLOTHESLINES ARE THE NEW COOL. 7 P.M. AT THE LAVENDER

FARM ON HIGH STREET.

The woman finished reading and looked up again. She pointed. "You can hang it up right there," she said.

"No pun intended," I said.

She laughed. "I'll spread the word," she said. "And you just might see me there, too."

Next, I stopped at the drugstore and bought ten little clear plastic travel-size spray bottles. I was hoping for purple, but I had to settle for sage green.

I left my car in the driveway and covered the nonexercise half of my garage floor with newspapers the minute I got home. Then I started making some sample painted retractable clotheslines. I got the one I'd painted for my mother out of my closet, unwrapped it, and painted another one just like it. Then I painted one that looked like a tiger-striped cat all curled up in a ball.

I covered another in green paint and added darker green stripes, and painted pink polka dots over an orange base on another. Then I painted one sea green, and spattered blues and greens and whites all over it until it looked like the ocean on a wild day. I didn't think I'd been this happy since my childhood finger painting days. I stayed relaxed and didn't worry about them coming out perfectly. I just wanted them to be fun.

I'd stayed up late last night scrolling through photos and drawings of lavender on the Internet, and I'd finally come up with my trademark design: a single bloom of lavender blowing in the wind. I painted my last five retractable clotheslines a pale lavender color, then painted my original lavender design in sage green and dark purple on top of that.

I went back to the nonlavender clotheslines and painted a tiny, logo-size lavender plant down near the bracket end on each one. Finally, I hand-lettered my company name on each of the ten clothesline reels: LAVENDER LINES.

I stood back and took a good look. I sat down on the floor with the spray bottles and carefully painted a tiny lavender bloom on each one. Then I called Rosie.

I had just enough time to take a water break and touch up a few spots I'd missed before Rosie came over.

She ducked under the half-opened garage door and started circling the patchwork of newspaper on the floor. "These are amazing, Noreen. I love them."

"Really?" I said. "Enough to sell them at the lavender shed? I was thinking I could fill the little bottles with lavender water and include one with each clothesline."

Rosie fluffed up her red curls with both hands. "Of course we can sell them in the shed. Maybe it'll actually bring in some business." She put her hands on her hips. "Not in a million years would I have come up with an idea like this. Maybe I should hire you to take over the lavender farm."

"Actually," I said, "I'm not sure I'd want to take over the farm. But I think between your lavender and the clotheslines and some other ideas I have, we could have a great online business. You can sell my things in the shed, and I'll promote any lavender products you want to sell on my Lavender Lines Web site."

"Are you sure you don't want to at least take over the lavender shed?" Rosie said. "Maybe you can make it your office."

I shook my head. "Sorry. I definitely don't want to be tied down to a brick-and-mortar office, even one that smells like lavender. Ever again, if I can help it."

Day 31:
10,444 STEPS

The smell of freshly brewed coffee woke me up. I kicked off the covers and headed for the kitchen.

"Hey, Mom," I said. "How was Nantucket? Still wet?"

"Lovely," my mother said. "Just lovely."

My mother looked lovely, too. The silver dolphin earrings with blue glass inserts she was wearing weren't even half bad. "Nice earrings," I said.

She reached both hands to her ears and stroked the dolphins. "Thanks, honey. Kent bought them for me to remember our first trip together. Here, let me pour you a cup of coffee."

"Sit," I said. "I'll get it. You're really crazy about him, aren't you?"

My mother smiled. "We have fun together. Sometimes I think that might be the most important thing. When I remember your father, you'd suppose it would be the romance I'd remember, or all the firsts with you kids, but it's really the laughter I think about the most."

"Gee, thanks," I said.

My mother and I both laughed. I put a couple of pieces of whole wheat bread in the toaster and sat down at the table with my coffee.

"Aren't you going to fill me in on everybody?" I asked. I figured I might as well get it over with, so I gritted my teeth and got ready to hear how much better my sister and brothers were doing than I was.

"They're fine," my mother said. "Everybody's fine. How was your trip?"

"Really fun," I said. My toast popped up, and I jumped up to get it before my mother could.

"One thing, Noreen," my mother said.

I finished spreading on the peanut butter and turned around. "What?"

"Do you have any idea how my leopard bra got into the garage?"

When I pulled into my driveway after grocery shopping, Hannah was sitting cross-legged at the edge of her lawn. I stopped my car down by the road and got out.

"Hi," I said. "How's it going?"

"Ha," she said.

I sat down next to her and crossed my legs, too. "Your mother just wants you to be safe, you know."

Hannah shrugged and twirled a lock of hair around her finger.

"So do I. And if I ever see you doing anything you shouldn't be doing, I want you to know I'm going to tell her right away."

"Don't worry," she said in a sad little voice. "I'm never going anywhere again. My supposed friends totally sold me out."

"What happened?"

A tear rolled down one cheek, and she brushed it away. "Well, we all got caught equally, but then everybody else decided to say it was my fault. Like I kept them out all night without them having anything to do with it. So now nobody's allowed to hang out with me. As if I'd hang out with them anyway." She took a ragged breath. "I can't wait to get out of this stupid town. It's so annoying."

"Your life will get better," I said. "Next time you'll be smarter, and you'll pick better friends, too." I hesitated. "And a better boyfriend."

Hannah looked me right in the eyes. "Did my mother tell you?"

I nodded. "Here's my best advice: pick a guy who deserves you. And the smartest thing you can do is to make sure you don't get pregnant in the first place."

"No shit," Hannah said. She looked exactly like Tess when she said it.

We got a fabulous turnout at the first meeting of the Marshbury Clothesline Alliance. About thirty women and exactly three men, not counting Rosie's dad, Tess and Rosie's husbands, and Rosie's two sons, milled around in the lavender shed and sat on the lawn in folding chairs Tess had borrowed from her school. The citronella and lavender oil in the tiki torches Rosie had lit kept the mosquitoes at bay and also smelled great.

Rod Stewart *cock-a-doodle-do*ed a few times, and the Supremes took turns working the lock on their pen, but I could see that somebody, possibly my mother, had wrapped some extra wire around to hold the gate secure, so I knew they were out of luck, at least for tonight.

My mother and Rosie's dad were handling the cash box, while I took orders for custom clotheslines. Lots of them. Apparently clotheslines really were the new cool.

"Oh, that's a great idea, Lo," a woman was saying. "That lavender wreath would be perfect on my front door. And thanks, I didn't even see those lavender bath salts."

As soon as the woman walked away, my mother said, "I only wish we had my Florida friend up here selling her lingerie. It would be the hit of the party. Maybe you and Rosie should look into it as a sideline."

"That's a fine-looking plant," Rosie's dad was saying to another woman. "Here, let me get the wheelbarrow for you, and I'll wheel it out to your car."

"I got it, Mr. Stockton," Hannah said. She grabbed the wheelbarrow and started maneuvering it through the crowd.

Tess looked at me. "Scary," she said. "You don't think she has a body double, do you?"

"She's a great kid," I said. "She's going to be just fine."

Before we started the meeting, Rosie and Tess's husbands made sure everyone had either a glass of seltzer or some lavender black currant champagne, made the real way, without cutting any muddling corners.

Tess stood in front of the chairs and clapped her hands. I could suddenly picture her as a teacher. I bet the kids quieted down right away for her.

"Welcome to the first meeting of the Marshbury Clothesline Alliance," Tess said. "It all started with a few posters on a clothesline and a vast quantity of bubbles in the fountain, but on the advice of counsel, we're not allowed to discuss that."

Everybody cheered.

"Most days," Tess continued, "I am proud to live in this beautiful little town, but every so often I am outraged by the elitist, small-minded, judgmental, bourgeois. . . ."

I made a cutting motion across my neck.

"But I digress," Tess said. "Anyway, we're here tonight to strategize so we can right a simple wrong. Energy costs are crazy, and there's nothing like the smell of your sheets fresh off the line. Green is the new black, and clotheslines are as green as you can get. The Marshbury Clothesline Ban has seen its day, and it's up to intelligent people like us to make sure the ban is banned. I'd like to see a clothesline in every yard in Marshbury by the end of the year. Whether they want one or not!"

Everybody cheered again.

I stepped up beside Tess. "We'd like each of you to take a copy of the Ban the Marshbury Clothesline Ban petition. If you can circulate it for signatures, and drop it off back here at the lavender farm by August fifteenth, that would be great. We're hoping to go before the board of selectmen to present our case at the end of August. If we get enough signatures, they'll put a question on the ballot at the town election in November. And, of course, we'll win."

The cheering grew even louder, then tapered off. I waved to Sherry, who was sitting between two other women from work. It was nice to see them again.

Everybody started surging toward either the petitions or the lavender black currant champagne.

Something made me turn to look down Rosie's long driveway. A man was emerging from the path that ran through the pine grove from my house to Rosie's.

I threaded my way through the cars that lined both sides of the driveway and met him halfway.

"Hey," Rick said. "Some party."

"It is now," I said.

"Isn't it lovely you boys have so much in common?" my mother said. She lowered her voice and whispered, "I have a good feeling about this one, honey."

Rosie's dad had borrowed his grandsons' Wii, and he and Rick were getting it plugged into my television.

"So, what will it be, bowling or tennis?" Rick asked.

"Ladies' choice," Rosie's dad said.

"How about bowling?" I said. "I have fond

memories of Wii bowling."

Rick was squatting in front of the TV. He turned around, and his eyes met mine. My heart leaped, and we both smiled like we were kids again.

"Bowling's fine with me," my mother said.

"You'll love it," I said. "And don't worry, you'll pick it up right away."

"Oh, please," my mother said. "I'm on a Wii bowling league at my condo club house. I even have my own designer Mii."

After we finished playing, I walked Rick out to his Honda.

"Sorry about that," I said.

"What?" he said. "I had a great time. Plus, we kicked their butts."

I smiled. I'd had a great time, too, a grand time, as my mother would say. A grand time with a man who might or might not be able to dance, but he was definitely quite the nice guy.

We both looked up at the sky. The moon was almost full, and about a gazillion stars twinkled around it.

Rick put his arm around me.

"So what made you just show up tonight?" I asked.

"Well," he said. "I was going to wait and talk to you tomorrow at Fresh Horizons. You know, give you some time to figure out whatever you needed to with the guy in the suit."

I leaned into Rick. "Nothing to figure out. Old news."

"Good to know. But then I was afraid you might misinterpret it as a lack of interest on my part and take my head off in front of our small-group cohorts again."

I laughed. "I didn't take your head off. I was just drawing a line in the sand."

"Perfectly executed," he said. "That small-group stuff is really rubbing off on you, isn't it?"

And then he kissed me.

DAY 32:
10,001 STEPS

"So," Tess said. "What a great turnout last night."

"I was hoping a lawyer would show up," Rosie said. "It always helps to have a lawyer present your case at those selectmen's meetings. Otherwise, they try to trip you up."

"Just let 'em try it," Tess said. "A part of me is hoping they don't simply cave and ban the clothesline ban right away. Then we can get some picketing in."

"Just no bubbles," I said. "That's all I ask. And remind me to keep my ski mask on this time, okay?"

We took a right at the end of Wildwater Way. Tess moved up ahead, and Rosie stepped back beside me.

"So," Rosie said. "Those clotheslines of yours certainly were a big hit."

"I know," I said. "Do you believe it? And I heard you sold practically every lavender item in the shed."

"Yeah, it was great. Your mother promised she'd help me make lavender wands and more lavender wreaths. And she and my father are fine with keeping an eye on the shed through the season. After that they're talking about heading to Florida so your mom can show off my dad at her condo complex."

Tess turned around. "Hel-lo. I'm starting to feel left out up here."

We crossed the road to our side street shortcut, and Rosie and I arranged ourselves on either side of Tess. "I was thinking," I said. "Maybe you could put together an outreach program for schools and other groups. You know, tours and mini-workshops at the lavender farm on weekends and school vacations. . . ."

"Not that left out," Tess said.

We all laughed. It was hot and muggy already, but it felt good to sweat, to move. I couldn't get over how much stronger and fitter I was now than I'd been just over a month ago. I was eating better and even liking myself a lot more, too. This morning I'd dared to step on the scale in my bathroom again. I was seven pounds lighter. I'd tiptoed into my bedroom, stood in front of the full-length mirror on my closet door, and dropped my towel. Not bad. I mean, not perfect by any stretch, but the fitter I got, the more I was okay with looking like the best version of myself, instead of trying to mea sure up to some airbrushed Holly- wood fantasy.

We walked through the opening in the seawall. "Oh, I can't believe I almost forgot," Tess said. She pulled a folded note card out of her pocket.

Dear Tess, Noreen, and Rosie,
I will be taking over Ms. Grady's class until a permanent teacher is hired. The school year starts early down here in the South, and we'll be back at it in just over two weeks' time. Where does the sum- mer go?

I want to thank you for sending those precious lined journals and fancy pens for the students, which will help us out tremendously. That sweet clothesline will sure come in handy for drying our artwork in the classroom, too. The school custodian promises to hang it up for me any day now, but he's slower'n a bread wagon with biscuit wheels, so I'm not holding my breath. We'll get it up there eventually though, and please know that Ms. Grady the Great will shine on forever in our hearts.

Sincerely,
Laurel Cobb

Tess pulled out a photo of Annalisa with last year's class. "Be careful," she said. "Don't either of you dare get any tears on it."

Rosie sniffed loudly. "Oh," she said. "Look how happy they all are. And Annalisa is so beautiful. Well, maybe not beautiful, but she looks like one of us, doesn't she?"

I wiped my eyes with the sleeve of my T-shirt. "I think we should donate a portion of our profits to the Ms. Grady the Great Memorial Fund," I said.

"Absolutely," Tess said. "And don't forget about the Marshbury Clothesline Alliance. Activism doesn't come cheap, you know."

Rick picked me up in his blue Honda, and we drove to our Fresh Horizons South small-group meeting together. We were early, so we used the extra time to sit in the parking lot and kiss.

"I like this retro parking thing," I whispered into his ear.

"That's because you don't have the steering wheel wedged into your rib cage," he said.

Eventually, we made our way to the meeting. We found two vacant chairs next to each other and sat down. I'd forgotten all about Michael until I saw him sitting at the other end of a row of chairs. As soon as he saw me looking, he leaned over to the woman next to him and whispered something. She laughed.

Brock walked into the room and set up his video camera. He shut his eyes and let out three quick puffs of air. He opened his eyes again, tilted his chin up, and threw his shoulders back. "Welcome," he said. "Welcome to all of you."

"And make that welcome back if you've been here before," the rest of us said.

"My name is Brock," he said.

"And I'll be your Fresh Horizons certified small-group career coach for the next ninety minutes," we yelled.

Brock grinned. "Sounds like some of you are just about ready to graduate. Okay, who's first?"

Rick and I both put our hands up.

"Ladies first," Rick said.

"No, after you," I said.

"Really, I insist," Rick said.

"As do I," I said.

We both cracked up.

"Methinks I detect a hint of romance in

the air," one of the disheveled guys said.

Brock clapped his hands three times. Then he looked at me. "Ready?" he asked.

I licked my lips and nodded.

He pushed a button on the video camera. He lifted one hand over his head and brought it down like the clapper on a movie set. "Go," he said.

I looked right past the camera and smiled at Brock. "First of all, I want to thank you for that thing you said about making a fully conscious decision to invest in myself. I'd never thought of it that way before, and it really resonated for me."

"Kiss up," somebody said.

"Okay," I said. I looked at the camera. "My name is Noreen Kelly. It's not my favorite name in the world, but it's starting to grow on me. I want to do something creative, and I never want to be tied to a desk again. I've started designing custom clotheslines, and placing them at local shops, and I'm going to begin marketing them online as soon as possible. Energy costs are skyrocketing, and green is the new black, so I think there's real opportunity there.

"I've also been walking every day, eating healthy, and just taking better care of myself. I took a fun trip recently, and I'd like to do more traveling. And I even think I know what I want in my personal life now, but that's, well, personal." I took a deep breath. "And I also think I'm ready to graduate."

"Nice job," Brock said when everybody finished clapping.

He turned to Rick. "Okay, now you."

Rick stood up. "What she said," he said.

He sat down again.

He got a great laugh, and I watched him while he savored it. He was such a nice guy, I couldn't believe I hadn't picked him out of the group on my first day here. Maybe the simple fact was that I couldn't see him until I could see myself.

Rick stood up again. Brock lowered his imaginary movie clapper.

"My name is Rick Walker. I'm not as far along as the dazzling woman I'm following here. I've made a lot of mistakes in my life, but what I'm starting to figure out is that we can all give ourselves a second chance if we want to. And that I can use this free time to try some new things. I don't have to figure it all out at once. I'm thinking about taking a metal sculpture class, and I've always wanted to learn more about Web design. Oh, and I'm coming up on my ninth date with an amazing woman, so, hey, wish me luck."

As soon as small-group counseling was over, we made our Wii tennis excuses to the scruffy guys and headed out to the parking lot together. "We really wowed 'em, didn't we?" Rick said.

"We sure did," I said. "By the way, how'd you come up with that ninth date thing?"

He stopped, leaned back against a locker, and counted them off on his fingers. "Date number one, Wii bowling date. Date number two, miniature golf date. Date number three, kiss after miniature golf date. Date number four, clothesline activism date. Date number —"

I put my hand on top of his. He pulled me to him and we kissed, right there, leaning up against an old school locker.

"I believe you," I said when we came up for air. "Ninth date it is. You know what happens on the ninth date, don't you?"

He raised an eyebrow.

I raised an eyebrow to match his. Then I leaned over to check my pedometer. I still had a ways to go to reach my ten thousand steps today.

I looked up again and into his cat green eyes. "The ninth date always starts with a walk on the beach."

"Sounds great to me," Rick said. He

draped an arm over my shoulders, and I reached one around his waist. We started walking out to the parking lot. "Am I allowed to ask how the ninth date ends?"

"Trust me," I said. "You'll totally love the ending."

ABOUT THE AUTHOR

Claire Cook is the bestselling author of *Summer Blowout, Life's a Beach, Must Love Dogs, Multiple Choice,* and *Ready to Fall.* She teaches workshops for aspiring writers and women coming into their own at midlife, and has had previous stints as a fitness teacher and dance and aerobics choreographer. She lives in Scituate, Massachusetts, with her husband, where she walked 10,000 steps a day while writing this novel.